Praise for Fi

"Thoroughly engrossing journey down the rabbit hole with Corky, Smoke, and the Winnebago County Sheriff's Department. Revenge is a dish best served . . . flambéed!" ~Timya Owen, President, Twin Cities Sisters in Crime

"With dogged determination Sgt. Corky Aleckson, a tough female cop, ignores the dangers to her own life and searches for clues that will eventually lead her to the person responsible for barn burnings in her community in this latest Winnebago County Mystery series. A great story. Couldn't put it down. Loved the interaction of Ms. Husom's characters." ~Marlene Chabot, author of *Death of the Naked Lady* and *Death at the Bar X Ranch*

"Strange and weird things are happening all over Winnebago County. Sergeant Corky Aleckson and her team struggle to make sense of the crimes . . . how blobs of blood, dead rabbits, a charred corpse, and burning barns are all connected. Christine Husom kept my attention from beginning to end. I felt like I was searching the crime scenes and investigating with the characters who are now my friends. I will definitely read more of Husom's books." ~Barbara Schlichting, author of the First Ladies mystery series, *Body on the Tracks,* 1943 historical fiction, and *Whispers From the Wind,* poetry

"Christine Husom's *Firesetter in Blackwood Township* hooks the reader from the start. With great hanging questions that keep pages turning, compelling characters including Sergeant Corky and a wonderful Irish Setter named Queenie along with the gorgeous Minnesota setting, Husom's book only leaves one question—when will the next book come out?" ~Kathleen Donnelly, Lisa Jackson scholarship recipient, Top 20 Claymore Finalist

"An authentic, small town vibe with great plot twists and excellent intrigue! A fine addition to Christine Husom's successful Winnebago series that will give mystery fans an exciting ride." ~Lisa Towles, author *of Choke, Blackwater Tango,* and other books

"Welcome to Winnebago County, where family loyalty runs deep. Sergeant Corky Aleckson and Detective 'Smoke' Dawes risk their lives to catch a serial arsonist in this page-turning sheriff's department procedural, uncovering a carefully buried secret that will rock one family to its core. Fans of the series will enjoy the overlapping twists and turns as the action steadily builds to a shocking climax in *Firesetter in Blackwood Township.*" ~Patti Phillips, *Nightstand Book Reviews*

"Sherlock Holmes once said to his partner that, "It is my belief, Watson, founded upon my experience, that the lowest and vilest alleys in London do not present a more dreadful record of sin than does the smiling and beautiful countryside." For cops who work rural or small town beats, this is not just a theoretical belief, but a hard fact they live with every working day, a fact well-known to one-time Wright County, MN, Deputy Sheriff Christine Husom and to her superb character, Sgt. Corky Aleckson of fictional Winnebago County. In *Firesetter in Blackwood Township,* Corky's juggling multiple problems: a serial arsonist burning down barns in a particular township of her county, a female stalker who has a "fatal attraction" to one of the deputies, and her mom's romantic problems with Corky's boss, the County Sheriff. The seventh book in this excellent series features a character who is tough when she has to be, but who allows herself to be compassionate, and even sweet, when she doesn't have to be." ~Jim Doherty, full-time cop, part-time writer, long-time mystery fan, and award-winning author of *Just the Facts - True Tales of Cops & Criminals*

Also by Christine Husom

To Avar
Barns are
burning too close
to Corky's home.
Blessings!

FIRESETTER IN BLACKWOOD TOWNSHIP

Seventh in the Winnebago County Mystery Series

Christine Husom

The wRight Press

The wRight Press first edition published November, 2017.

Cover design by Precision Prints, Buffalo, Minnesota

The wRight Press
804 Circle Drive
Buffalo, Minnesota, 55313

Printed in the United States of America

ISBN 978-1-948068-00-0

This story is dedicated to the firefighters who risk life and limb, putting themselves in danger to save people, other living beings, and structures of all kinds. You are true servants, and I thank you very kindly.

Acknowledgements

It's a team effort to turn an idea into a published book, and get it into the hands of readers. My humble thanks to my faithful team of beta/proofreaders who gave me their time, careful reading, and sound advice: Arlene Asfeld, Judy Bergquist, Ken Hausladen, Elizabeth Husom, Chad Mead, and Edie Peterson. I greatly appreciate your willingness to lend a helping hand. To my editor, DJ Schuette, at Critical Eye Editing for the superb job, questioning, challenging, guiding me in the final process, and aiding me with publication. And to my husband and the rest of my family for their patience and understanding when I was stowed away for hours on end, researching and writing. Thank you all from the bottom of my heart.

1

"Sergeant Corky, I think I'm in trouble." Deputy Vince Weber's raspy voice came across the phone line with hushed intensity. It put me on alert.

"What do you mean, what's going on?"

"It's kind of personal, and with you being female and all, I thought you'd be a good one to talk to."

"Okay."

"Would it be all right if I swung by your place sometime? Like now, maybe?" Weber's appeal piqued my curiosity. Had he ever discussed any personal problems with me in our years together at the Winnebago County Sheriff's Department? Not that I could think of. He kept his gentle-heart side private and was more comfortable with his wise-guy side instead.

"Sure. I'm home all morning." It was the last of my three scheduled days off, with nothing major planned.

"Thanks, I'm almost at your house."

We disconnected, and I shook my head back and forth wondering what kind of personal trouble he was in. Queenie, my English Setter, pushed her nose against my hip and whimpered. I reached down and gave her head a little scratch. "I'm not shaking my head at you, girl. It's Weber. He's got me going, that's for sure."

I heard a vehicle rumble down the driveway, and Queenie was at my heels when I opened the front door. Weber's truck came to a quick stop then the door flew open and he slid to the ground. He had the body of a defensive tackle, and it had served him well in his college football days. He could outsprint me any day of the week, even though I ran on a regular basis. Weber was skilled at shorter distances. I paced myself for longer runs.

Sunlight reflected off his shaved head, but did nothing to brighten the strained look on his face. He lifted his hand and waved me over, not wasting time on greetings. "You gotta come out and see this."

I jogged down the sidewalk with Queenie close behind and joined him at his truck. She busied herself sniffing the wheels and the driver's door. Weber pointed at the windshield where there was an almost round deposit of what looked like blood on it. Its diameter was about one and a half inches and partially blocked the driver's view. "What is that? What's this about?" I asked.

"I've been wracking my brain over this whole deal since I saw it. So much that it hurts. Okay. Something similar, and equally weird, happened last week. It kind of gnawed at me, but I sort of let it slide 'til this morning when this stupid blob on my windshield brought it up again." He clenched his jaw.

I turned so we were face to face and studied him a moment. "Tell me what's going on, Vince. On the phone you said it was personal."

"Yeah well, I think it is, but I'm not a hundred percent sure of that." He made a fist and rubbed his cheek with his knuckles, maybe to help loosen his muscles.

"Has someone got a vendetta against you and you've been keeping it on the down low until you get it all figured out?"

He did a loud "ahem" throat clearing. "Something like that. If it's personal, I'm in trouble. If it's not, I'm in bigger trouble."

Not good. "Hey, if we're talking about something criminal going on here, we need to open a case. Involve the sheriff's office."

"Sergeant, you and me, we're both sworn deputies in the sheriff's office. And I'm already involved."

"And now that you're here with your show and tell, I am too. Tell me about the incident that happened last week and how it ties in with that." I pointed to the red droplet.

"It's like this, and it's kind of embarrassing." He paused so long I thought I'd have to pry it out of him. "I let myself get involved with someone I shouldn't have."

"You're not talking about Mandy?" Amanda Zubinski was a fellow deputy Vince had been hanging out with. I didn't know if they were officially dating, or what their status was.

The lines in his forehead deepened when he raised his eyebrows. "Mandy? Nah. We're more pals than anything else. So far, anyhow. Geez, I hate to even say this out loud. It's my sister-in-law, my wife's sister."

Weber had married his high school sweetheart and was left widowed when she was killed in a car crash a year later. He'd been cut to the core and kept it secret from his co-workers for a long time. When he spilled it out during a work-training exercise, I was taken aback and had felt closer to him ever since.

"Vince, you've been pretty private about your personal life, and I respect that. What happened to your wife is very painful for you—I can't even imagine. But you haven't told us much about her. Like that she even had a sister."

"Yeah well, she has two sisters. One's normal, one's not so normal. A little off would be a polite way to put it." He stuck his finger into the side of his head a few times.

"And I take it you got involved with the not-so-normal one?"

"Correctamundo. A big, big mistake and I've been paying for it ever since. Stacie, my wife, has been on my mind a lot lately, even more than usual. I just want to hold her in my arms again. I sort of let that slip to Darcie, and she came on to me, big time. Things got out of hand, and I stupidly let myself get persuaded to ah, you know what."

I knew what. "And now she's giving you a hard time about it?"

"Let's say a harder time of it. Darcie's liked this mug of mine since my high school football days. I took her out a few times back then. And then I met her sister, and it was all about Stacie from then on out."

I nodded. "When did it happen, with Darcie?"

"A little over three weeks ago now. She was living out of state and moved back maybe two months ago. She's staying with her folks up by St. Cloud." He paused and shook his head. "And this is what made the three little hairs I got on the back of my neck stand up. After we were together, and I was still trying to believe it actually happened, she says to me, 'I always knew we were destined to be together. That's why God told me to move back to Minnesota. To be with you.'"

That made the little hairs on the back of my neck stand up, too. "Oh boy."

"I know, right?"

"What about her parents, her other sister?"

"Her folks never really cozied up to me. They thought Stacie could do much better. Which she probably could have, if you're talking about marrying up."

"I don't know about that. You're as true blue as they come, Vince." I bopped his bicep with my fist.

He shrugged. "Thanks. And the folks thought we were too young. Yeah, we were kids, but it was the real deal so why wait?" He thought for a moment. "Enough about that and back to Darcie. After Stacie died, maybe three months after, not much more, Darcie very strongly hinted that she was waiting in the wings for me whenever I was ready. I managed to put her off long enough so she finally took a job offer in Kansas. I thought she'd given up on me. At least I was off the hook for some years."

"But now she's back. Would you say she's harassing you?" I said.

"Sort of, yeah. She's bugging me to no end. It's obvious she needs help, but she won't listen to anything I got to say about that."

"Have you thought about getting a restraining order?"

He shook his head. "You and I both know if someone's made up their mind to make your life miserable, those orders are only as good as the paper they're written on. And easy enough to burn."

"True, but at least it gives you reason to report her if she doesn't let up. And if so, she'll get arrested, and you won't be the one dealing with her."

"That sounds good in theory." He shrugged.

"And if she keeps harassing you, she'll get arrested again."

"Yeah well, it'll be bad enough when the guys find out I got a girl pestering me that I got no control of. But to get a restraining order on top of it, that would really frost the cake."

"Vince, I've been through things similar to this a few times myself, as you know. The difference is, I didn't have a personal relationship with any of them. I was just the unlucky one who got in their way."

"And that's the difference, all right. That's what the guys would razz me about to no end. How I got myself so jammed up."

"You can't worry about that, and you might be surprised. It's not like any of us have perfect lives. We've all made bad choices here and there. From what you've told me, it sounds like Darcie might be delusional, thinking you have a future together when you've told her you're not interested."

He leaned in closer. "Are you ready for the capper?"

There was more? "Um, okay."

"She told me she's sure she got pregnant during our one time together."

"*No*. Why does she think that? Do you think she's telling the truth?"

Weber's shoulder hitched up and down. "I don't think so. But it's the reason I think it's gotta be her doing this crap. Last week there was a dead rabbit, a little cottontail, laying by my back door at the bottom of the steps."

"A dead rabbit? I don't get it."

"You know that old saying about if the rabbit died it meant you were pregnant? It was some sort of test they did in the old days. I remember my mom using that expression."

"Sure, some people still say that. You think that was Darcie's way of telling you she got a positive pregnancy test?"

"I don't know what to think. I think her craziness must be rubbing off on me. And the other thing is she wouldn't even know for sure. I mean we'd only been together about two weeks before that."

"They do pregnancy tests pretty early nowadays. But leaving a dead rabbit on your steps as the way to deliver the news seems pretty far out there, Vince."

"I'm with you on that one, but we're talking about a not totally rational person here."

"Did you mention finding the rabbit to Darcie?"

"Nah, I haven't initiated a single conversation with her since she moved back. Or for umpteen years, as far as that goes. And I wouldn't have given the dead rabbit a second thought if I hadn't found this big blood drop on my windshield. If that's what it is. All I know is there is some crazy shit goin' on," he said.

I considered his dilemma for a moment. "Getting back to the rabbit, any idea how it died?"

"Nothin' apparent. No outward sign of it being anything other than natural. It wasn't bloody, like it'd been run over, or shot, or anything like that. I didn't exactly examine it, though. One odd thing I thought of when I saw it: I'd never had any kind of little critter laying dead in my backyard before. Not that it hasn't happened, but none that I ever seen. A predator would find it in no time."

I thought about that. "Now that you mention it, I guess I haven't either. Like a squirrel or chipmunk. Or a rabbit. So what'd you do with it?"

"Buried it behind my garage where the grass never grows."

"Where the grass never grows? That sounds like another mystery altogether, Vince."

He shrugged.

"We need to get some pictures of this red drop then we'll scrape it off and put it in an evidence bag before it gets compromised. With the sun beating down, it's getting hotter by the minute," I said.

"Yeah well, I guess we gotta try to figure this out. I took a few shots with my phone when I saw it, right before I headed over here."

I kept a supply bag in my squad car the days I was on duty then stored it on a garage shelf on my days off from work. I punched in the code on the keypad of my garage door opener and scooted in as the door lifted. I grabbed the bag then retrieved my camera, latex gloves, a scraper, and a small paper evidence bag from it.

When I was back outside, Weber nodded at the motion-detection camera mounted unobtrusively near a light on my garage. "So, no more exciting action captured on that thing after we finally caught and nailed gorilla man, huh?"

"Not that I know of, but I don't look at footage unless there's reason to. At least it's there in case something suspicious happens. And I have to admit it makes me feel more secure."

"I guess it wouldn't hurt for any of us to have one. Like you said, in case," he said.

Weber and I busied ourselves collecting evidence over the next minutes. Queenie had been exploring the yard until we started working on the car, and then returned to resume her sniffing. I studied the vehicle's windshield and hood from a few angles. "I'm not finding any fingerprints to lift—none that I can see anyway—that we can add to the probable blood evidence. You have one clean truck."

He squinted and had a close look himself. "Yeah, I washed it yesterday, so they'd be fresh prints too, if there are any. From what it looks like, whoever left this little dandy didn't touch the vehicle."

"Or they were wearing gloves."

"Right. Came prepared. And musta done it when I was sawin' zees sometime in the night. Too bad your pooch can't tell us what she's smelling."

"No kidding. Well, I'll get this into an evidence locker. Our guys will be able to determine whether or not it's blood, and will get it to the regional lab for DNA if it is." Weber looked down, like he was considering his options. "And Vince, nobody has to know about Darcie unless you decide to tell them," I assured him.

"I s'pose."

"You take off, and I'll take care of this."

He nodded. "Sarge, I didn't mean for you to have to work on your day off, and I appreciate it."

"Not to worry. And don't beat yourself up over this. We have a team that's got your back no matter how this turns out."

Weber gave a single nod. "Thanks."

I waved as he backed out then reached down and gave the fur on Queenie's head a little scratch. "Vince has me curious, that's for sure." She followed me into the living room and sat at attention as I opened the blinds and let the sun shine in. The beams danced across the floor, and I stood by the window for a moment, admiring my backyard acres. The property edge ran down to a small, very fine fishing lake. In the heat of summer, Queenie loved swimming there. And we'd had some hot days the past week, not atypical weather for July in Minnesota.

I thought of the evidence in my car. "I better get cracking," I told Queenie.

On my way to the Winnebago County Government Center I pondered the predicament Weber was in. If it turned out his sister-in-law was stalking him, would her parents comprehend how serious that was and side with Darcie anyway? They hadn't wanted Vincent Weber as their son-in-law all those years ago, and if Darcie was pregnant, he would be in a world of hurt all the way around.

The courthouse government center stood on the rise of a hill overlooking Bison Lake. I sat in my 1967 red, classic GTO for a minute, watching the rippling waves on the water's surface stirred by a gentle breeze. Then I gathered the evidence from the passenger seat and headed into the south side of the building, the outside entrance to the sheriff's office.

Detective Elton "Smoke" Dawes was walking down the corridor in my direction. Long and lean and sexy as all get out in a light gray suit, white shirt, and black and gray tie.

"Good morning, Detective. Special occasion?" I lifted my hand, indicating his fine outfit.

Smoke smiled enough to deepen his long dimples. "Yep, I got court." He glanced down at the paper evidence bag. "What have you got there? If memory serves, you have one more day off." He gave me a once over. "Not to mention, you're wearing jeans."

I lifted a shoulder. "Weber had a big drop, or drops, of what looked like dried blood on his windshield, so I wanted to get it checked out."

His eyebrows squeezed together. "Blood on his squad car?"

"No, his F-one fifty. We'll get it processed and see where that leads us. I got a case number started on it."

"Sounds to me like he thinks somebody purposely left a gift of blood for him." Smoke lowered his voice. "Is he being threatened in some way?"

"Not specifically." I lifted the bag to change the subject. "I'll get this in a locker and catch you later. Have fun in court."

"You know it."

I turned the evidence over to the technicians and was heading for the door when a call came over Channel 4, the fire channel, on the sheriff's radio. "Paging Oak Lea Fire Department. Barn on fire in Blackwood Township at 2463 Collins Avenue. Paging Oak Lea Fire."

My heart dropped into the pit of my stomach as the image of that Collins Avenue barn came to mind. It was about the same age as my mother's, built in the early 1900s. It wasn't six-sided like Mother's, but it was historic and well-built and I admired it almost as much as I did hers.

I was running full bore and almost lost my balance when I stopped abruptly by my car. I grabbed a quick breath, hopped in, and fired up the engine. Being off-duty, I wasn't required to report in, but it was good practice to tell Communications I was heading to the scene. I plucked the portable police radio from the passenger seat then set it back down, deciding a phone call was better.

"Nine-one-one—"

I cut her off. "Robin, it's Corky. I'm heading to the barn fire scene to see what's up."

"Sure thing, and thanks for letting us know."

Communications was busy dispatching deputies to a variety of calls. I switched to the channel reserved for fire calls and heard Oak Lea Fire Department requesting mutual aid from Emerald Lake, a town seven miles west, and about the same distance from the burning barn as Oak Lea was. I shifted into gear and drove west on the county road past the township road I lived on, and took the next left on Collins Avenue. Smoke was billowing above the trees and dissipating into the atmosphere.

Sounds of sirens from emergency vehicles were bouncing around the countryside, and it was difficult to tell where they were all coming from. I was the second one on the scene behind Deputy Todd Mason. He was standing outside his squad car close to the home's detached garage watching the blaze. I considered leaving my GTO on the township road, but with all the emergency vehicles en route, decided to pull onto the property instead. I headed to the opposite end of the farmstead, as far away from the barn and incoming traffic as possible.

I got out and jogged toward Mason. He glanced my way then shifted his eyes back to the flames shooting out from a partially open door and the roof. "Damn, what is taking them so long?" he said over the roar of the blaze.

We were standing a safe distance from the fire, but the heat was marked and increasing by the second. "The call went out five or so minutes ago, and by the sound of it, it'll be less than a minute." The county fire departments were staffed with volunteer firefighters. Men and women were off-site and reported to the station as fast as possible when they were paged. It amazed me how quickly they got the rigs out, considering. Some reported directly to the scene, if it was closer for them than the station was.

Mason shook his head. "It seems like forever."

"Always does when you're waiting." I looked around the property. "Homeowners are gone?"

"Appears so. I knocked on both the front and back doors of the house. No one answered. I took a look inside the barn— as much as I could see through the flames from a couple of the windows, that is. Did a quick search around the place, looked in the windows of the other buildings."

"What a thing to come home to. I think the owners that I knew of, an older couple, must have sold this place a while ago. I don't know who lives here now."

"No, me either." Todd shook his head. "The owner's name is listed as Harding."

"I was wrong then. That's the name of the folks I remember. Who called it in?"

He frowned. "An unidentified passerby, according to Communications. Sounded like a teenage boy, but he didn't leave a name. He was gone when I got here, not sixty seconds later. Most people that see something like this hang around to watch, at least until help arrives."

"Either on his way somewhere, or didn't want to get involved, probably."

We quit talking as two rigs pulled into the driveway. They'd killed their sirens, but the weight of the vehicles crunching on the gravel driveway was nearly as deafening. They came to a stop, and Mason and I stayed back as two guys jumped out of each rig, dragging gear bags with them. They wasted no time as they pulled on suits, boots, helmets, and gloves.

Oak Lea Fire Chief Corey Evans waved to Mason, and I tagged along as they met halfway. "The owners home?" Evans said.

"No."

"Any sign of animals in there, did you hear any noises?" Evans dipped his head to the right, toward the barn.

"No, and I didn't see any when I looked in the windows. Or in the other outbuildings, either." Besides the barn, there was as a detached garage, a chicken coop, and a small shed.

Chief Evans nodded. "Time to get to work."

When the rig from Emerald Lake Fire Department arrived a few minutes later, Evans put them on stand-by in case they needed more water or additional assistance.

I watched from a distance as they aimed the hoses at the base of the blaze. A warm summer gust carried a cool spray to my cheeks as the first timbers from the beautiful, old barn collapsed into the inferno.

2

Belle and Birdie

Belle climbed from board to board up the side of the tree. They'd nailed the steps in place some years before. With athletic ease she stepped onto the sturdy lowest branch that extended horizontally from the massive trunk and sat down next to her sister. Birdie had scooted up ahead of her. Belle watched in awe as flames shot out from the narrow open slats where the old wood planks of the barn had shrunk over time and pulled apart. The dry July weather and increasingly brisk air current speeded the fire's progress.

They saw the Oak Lea and Emerald Lake Fire Departments arrive. The firefighters raced against time trying to get the inferno under control. But their efforts were in vain, and there was no way they would be able to save the barn.

Belle turned to her sister to catch her reaction, but it was the same as usual. Birdie didn't display a particular expression, or emotional response. Belle's heart ached with disappointment. She hoped her sister would feel free at last from the burdens she had carried most of her life. That they would dissipate like the rising smoke as it lifted higher and higher toward the clouds.

Birdie turned to Belle and nodded. It was like looking at her own reflection, but there was no sparkle in Birdie's eyes. Would she ever see Birdie smile again?

3

Detective Elton Dawes was the go-to guy in the sheriff's office for fire investigations. All five of the detectives had been through the Minnesota State Fire Marshal's training, but Smoke was the most qualified overall. He was adept at determining whether a fire necessitated calling in the State Fire Marshal for a deeper probe. Some people thought that's how he'd earned his nickname, but it actually went back to his teen years following an unfortunate fire incident. Besides picking up the moniker, the experience had left Smoke with a keen awareness of how quickly a spark could roar into a full blaze, especially when helped along by an accelerant. In his case, it was kerosene in an oil lamp that he had accidentally knocked over.

Despite all the activity at the scene, my eyes were drawn to Collins Avenue and Smoke's department-issued Chevrolet as he pulled to a stop a half block from the driveway. A number of passersby had parked a safe distance away on Collins and were sitting in their vehicles watching the action.

The heat from the blaze felt hotter, more brutal, than the rays beating down from the late morning sun. Sweat beaded on my forehead and temples, and streams of it trickled down my spine. Smoke joined Mason and me by the house, perhaps two hundred feet from the barn.

"What happened with court?" I said.

He loosened his tie and undid the top two buttons of his shirt. "It settled. Shafer copped a plea, and that's just as well. For him, as well as for our tax-paying citizens, anyway. I doubt his defense would have been strong enough to convince a jury."

"Probably right about that."

Smoke shook his head and concentrated on the firefighters' battle. "What a gigantic bonfire, the likes of which I've seen only a time or two before this."

"There's a ton of kindling in that big old barn," Mason said.

"That's the sad truth, all right." Smoke waved his hand toward the house. "We were here one other time, maybe seven, eight years ago. Remember that? It was a strange one," he said.

"Sure, the call from the young girl," I said.

"That's the one. She called nine-one-one and reported her sister was dead, that she'd been killed. The girl wouldn't give her name or any other information, so we had no idea what we'd be faced with when the four of us responded. And it turned out to be more of a mystery than anything else."

Mason nodded. "I was with you. It was quiet when we got here, no indication that anyone was home. We pounded on the doors and looked in the windows before we went in the house and searched. Saw no signs of a struggle or anything that looked out of place."

"Puzzling, for sure," I said.

"I left a note on their door asking them to call me. A few hours later the owner, an older guy, a Mr. Harding, finally did. I told him a nine-one-one call had come from their residence—not saying what it was about—and he was pretty mystified. Harding said he and his wife had been out all morning and didn't know who would have been in their house. Said they should probably start locking their doors if kids are sneaking in when they're gone. I did some follow-up, checked with neighbors, asked if they had kids, what they'd been up to, that sort of thing. But nothing panned out," Smoke said.

"No one wants to believe their kids would be messing around like that, falsely reporting a crime," Mason said.

"And a most serious one at that," Smoke said.

"How true. I had another call here last summer. Somebody reported a scrawny-looking dog wandering around in the yard, hanging around the house. Said it looked like it had rabies. When I got here I grabbed my shotgun afraid I'd have to shoot the poor thing, but never found it. There was an awful stench near the house, and I figured there was a rotting critter nearby," I said.

"I remember you talking about that at the time," Mason said.

"Nobody home then either," I said.

"Seems to be a pattern," Mason said.

"Same deal. I left the Hardings a note saying I'd been there and to call if they spotted the dog. They didn't call, but when I was driving by the next day I stopped in and saw the note was gone, so I know they got it," I said.

"According to Communications, the Hardings are still the property owners. Robin tried to call them when the report came in, but they'd apparently dropped their landline," Mason said.

"Hmm. I never got to know them." I took a step back from the heat. "They kept to themselves, but I'd notice one of them out in the yard once in a while. I was surprised when Todd said they still lived here. They're getting up in years. Their lawn is mowed, but there hasn't been much activity around here for a while."

"There's a whole lot of it here right now," Smoke said.

"I'll say."

The curiosity-driven crowd continued to grow, drawn like moths to flames. The firefighters worked to prevent the fire from spreading to the other buildings, knowing the barn itself was lost. By the time a fire was fully involved, it was too late. The structure had withstood the extremes of Minnesota elements for over a hundred years, yet had no defense against the spark that led to its consuming blaze. It was reduced to a smoldering heap of old blackened barn wood in short order.

"Ever notice how a fire like that has a life of its own and assumes complete control when it gets a hold of something?" Smoke said.

I let out a loud breath. "Good way to put it. It's a futile effort, and the guys fighting it know there's nothing they can do to stop it."

Smoke reached over, gave my shoulder a squeeze, and then made his way closer to the barn for a better look. The firefighters started gathering their equipment together, and I watched for a while feeling a bit dazed. Corey Evans was standing by a rig, so I went over to talk to him. He pulled off his gloves first, then his helmet and eye protectors. Particles of soot clung to his damp skin. He looked like he'd been in a sauna far too long, and then someone had thrown dirt at him when he got out. One of the other firefighters tossed him a quart-size bottle of water, and Evans poured some of it over his head before downing the rest in impressive gulps.

He looked glum, downhearted. "I was afraid our tanks would run dry before we could stop her from spreading to the rest of the farm." He waved his hand in the direction of the acres behind where the barn had stood. "Or to that dry hayfield back there. Turns out we didn't need Emerald Lake's supply after all, but it was nice having them on site."

"Mutual aid is a good thing, knowing they're at the ready. Corey, your crew would've had to be here the minute the fire started for any chance of saving the barn."

"Yeah, I know that. And even then it'd be no guarantee. We knew she was a goner from the get-go, not what us firefighters like at all."

I was watching the happenings when a young woman came jogging down the driveway into the yard and caught my attention. The fire trucks were still there, and it was not the place for citizen gawkers. I hurried over and stepped in front of her, cutting her off at the pass.

We were about the same height, with petite builds. But that's where the similarity ended. Her dark brown hair was cut short, and she studied me with piercing, almond-shaped hazel eyes. Her intelligence and astuteness came across clearly, even in those first moments. She gave me the impression she had sized me up in a split second, faster than the average bear. A reporter? If so, she was missing the tools of her trade. Unless there was a notepad and pen tucked in the back pockets of her jeans.

"Excuse me, I'm Sergeant Corky Aleckson. Who are you, and where do you think you're going?"

"This is my grandparents' farm." She waved her hand at the barn. "What happened?"

"Oh, my apologies. We don't know what caused the fire. Your grandparents aren't home, and we haven't been able to reach them. Do you know where they are?"

"Yes, um, they're in Canada. With my uncle."

"So sorry this happened, especially when they're away. We'll need to get in touch with them, let them know. And they'll want to talk to their insurance provider, check on coverage."

"I'll take care of that," she said.

"You have their insurance information?"

"Yes, in the house."

"Okay, good. I didn't get your name," I said.

"Sybil Harding." Same last name as the property owners.

I nodded. "The detective in charge here will want to talk to you." I pointed in Smoke's direction. "His name is Elton Dawes."

Her shoulders visibly tightened. "Why?"

"It's part of the investigation. And he'll have a permission-to-search form for you to sign."

"I suppose. I don't know much about how that works." Sybil's head lifted slightly, and her eyes moved across the scene like she didn't comprehend what she was seeing. Not unexpected, given the circumstances.

Smoke noticed us and walked over. He narrowed his eyes on Sybil. "Miss?"

"Sybil Harding. I'm the owners' granddaughter."

His frown deepened. "This is a real shame, and it's gotta be a huge shock for you." He pulled a business card out of his breast pocket and handed it to her.

Sybil lifted her shoulders in a slight shrug then looked down and fingered the card.

"Where are your grandparents at?" Smoke continued.

"Canada, um, British Columbia. With my uncle," she said.

Smoke pulled a memo pad from his back pocket and a pen and reading glasses from his breast pocket. He slipped on the glasses, resting the bridge halfway down his nose. "British Columbia. That's quite a trek from here."

"My grandmother was born there and loved it."

"What's your uncle's name?"

"Um, Melvin Harding."

"And a phone number we can reach your grandparents at?"

She shook her head. "I communicate with them through emails instead. The cell phone service isn't good where they are. I have power of attorney and can handle any details that need to be taken care of. My grandparents aren't in the best of health, but I'll keep them in the loop."

Smoke looked at her over the top of his glasses. "Sybil, do you have your driver's license with you?"

"Um, no, I forgot my wallet," she said.

"Then how about giving me your full name and date of birth?"

Sybil's response prompted me to take a closer look at her. Her birth date put her age at twenty-six, but she didn't look a day over seventeen. Then again, most people guessed my age as younger than my thirty-one years.

"And your address?"

She gave one in Golden Valley, about thirty miles away, then said, "I try to come out to check on things pretty often."

"So your grandparents have been in Canada a while?" Smoke said.

"A couple of months."

"And you're the one who's looking after things. Where are your parents?"

"Um, they live in New Mexico now. We don't talk all that often, and I don't have their address memorized," she said.

"Not much communication with them?"

"No. They've got a busy life down there, I guess."

Smoke snuck a glance at her. "Do you have the name of your grandparents' insurance provider?"

Sybil frowned and tipped her head slightly like she was trying to understand the question. When she hadn't answered after a long moment, Smoke said, "So we know where to send the report when we wrap up our investigation."

"Oh. Well I don't know if the barn was insured, but I'll check on that." She gave him the company's name then stared at the charred remains of the barn for a few seconds. "What do you think started the fire?"

"At this point, we don't have a clue. I've got a form for you to sign, giving us your permission to search, and hopefully we'll get to the bottom of it very soon, get some answers for you."

Sybil nodded, and her eyes were drawn back to the barn.

"You can get us started by answering a few more questions," Smoke said.

She turned back to him with the same quizzical expression. "Like what?"

"Has the barn been in use recently?"

"No, not for quite a few years."

"So it's sat empty?"

"My grandfather used to milk cows, but it's been a long time. I'm not sure what was in there now. Not much. Maybe some straw left over from when they had animals."

"Some critters have likely made themselves at home in there by now. Mice. Birds. Bats," Smoke said.

"Maybe."

"From what I was able to observe, there wasn't a lock on the main door. Was there one that someone may have removed?"

"No, I guess there wasn't," she said.

Smoke gave a nod. "So just about anybody would have access."

Sybil lifted a shoulder. "I never really thought about that. I mean, I don't think there was anything in there worth stealing."

One person's trash was another one's treasure, as they say. And people had other reasons to trespass. Like if they were into barn burning and the owners weren't there to protect their property. It was likely Sybil hadn't considered that possibility. She came across as keenly bright, yet with a naiveté about her. And something else I couldn't put my finger on, something that didn't mesh with my brain-smart, but not street-smart observation.

"Sybil, this isn't the first time your grandparents had an unwanted guest. Some years ago, someone used their home phone when they were away and made what turned out to be a prank nine-one-one call," Smoke said.

Sybil's eyebrows shot up, and she pulled her chin in slightly. "What was that about?"

"You can ask them about it. Meantime, are you the only one who's keeping an eye on their place while they're out of the country?"

"I am." Her nostrils flared slightly, and her nose twitched, likely due to the tentacles of smoke that had shifted in our direction.

Smoke reached out, put a hand on each of our elbows, and steered us north, out of its path. We stood side by side a moment, watching a blackened plank fall over onto the floor of the barn.

"I'll grab that form from my car," Smoke said.

Sybil nodded and was silent until Smoke returned with it attached to a clipboard and handed it to her. She barely glanced at it when she accepted the pen Smoke offered and scribbled her signature on the bottom line.

4

Belle and Birdie

Belle stared with awe as hundreds of elongated fiery fingers reached out from inside the barn, separating, darkening, and reducing the planks to charred remains that became drifting ashes in no time. A series of feelings rolled through her like waves, moving in, cresting, and then crashing. How to describe what she felt? Mournful for all that had happened there, wishing a tornado or the strike of a match had taken it down years ago.

And now satisfied it no longer stood, holding the dark secrets that had both crippled and taken lives. She also felt conflicted because the people who should have seen it go down weren't there. On the one hand, she was glad they weren't. On the other hand, she wished they were.

The barn had been a chamber of horrors for her sister. Watching it succumb to the fire's power, with no ability to wage any kind of defense, gave her more pleasure than she could have imagined. The firefighters and cops were unable to save it. No surprises there. It was downright laughable how they kept spraying water at something they would never have control over.

And in this case, that was a good thing for her and her sister. The times they'd needed the authorities to help them, they hadn't been there. They'd failed them. It was about time the tables were turned, and they were the ones who felt helpless. She and Birdie would keep one step ahead of them until they'd finished all they needed to do.

She turned to her sister and wrapped an arm around her shoulders. "We're turning the tides, Birdie. Vengeance is finally ours."

Birdie stared at the fire and nodded.

5

It was some time later before the last trails of smoke lifted from the rubble, lazily drifted upward, and disappeared into the atmosphere.

Sybil Harding excused herself and wandered off. Aimlessly, it seemed to me, and I felt compelled to follow her. "Sybil?" When she didn't stop, I speeded up so I was walking next to her, but she didn't appear to notice me until I touched her forearm. "Sybil?"

She stopped and cocked her head with a puzzled look on her face. "Sergeant?"

"I wanted to make sure you're okay, that you have someone to help you deal with all this."

She paused a moment then nodded. "I do, um, thanks. If I didn't hear you, it was because I was thinking. Sorry."

"I understand. You have a lot to think through, that's for sure. We didn't ask if you have brothers or sisters, or other relatives close by."

"No, no I don't. Only child."

I nodded. "Detective Dawes gave you his card, but here's mine, too." I pulled the thin case out of the wallet in my back pocket, withdrew a business card, and handed it to her.

She gave it a quick glance then stuck it in the multi-colored cloth shoulder bag that was strapped across her chest, clinging close to her ribs. "Thanks."

"Call me any time. Will you do that?"

Sybil nodded, looked away for a second then back at me.

"Good deal," I said.

I watched as she walked toward the house, looking over her shoulder at the barn every few steps. She was like a lost lamb that had gotten separated from the flock. I'd make it a point to check in with her until I was convinced she was truly okay. Her grandparents were out of the country, and their barn was in a collapsed, burned heap. They knew their granddaughter as well as anyone and entrusted the care of their property and estate to her. I hoped she had good legal counsel because my gut told me Sybil Harding needed guidance more than a lot of others did.

If I'd known the scope of what that all entailed, I would have kept much closer tabs on her.

I joined Smoke and Corey Evans midway through their conversation.

"We'll put barricades with some Keep Out signs at the end of the driveway, and on the four sides of the rubble. Not that it will keep everyone out, but it will be a deterrent, and serve as a warning anyway," Smoke said.

"Good idea. It should be safe to start poking around in the rubbish later on today," Evans said.

"If we can locate the source of the fire, that'll be a good thing. Carlson will be rolling with the Major Crimes van any minute. Mason over there is the other half of the team today. The two of them will help me process this," Smoke said.

Vince Weber came walking down the driveway with his eyes on the barn, shaking his head.

"What are you doing in this neck of the woods?" Smoke asked him.

"On my way to Fairhaven County Park to do some fishing and, lo and behold, I come across a whole bunch of official vehicles belonging to you guys. Which explains all the sirens I heard an hour ago."

Evans drew his eyebrows together. "You didn't turn on your radio to find out?"

"Nah. You can't be on duty all the time." He nodded at me. "Of course our sergeant here basically ignores that rule."

I shrugged. "I have a thing for old barns."

"Yeah well, I can see why. Your mother has about the coolest barn in the county, maybe the whole state," he said.

I smiled. My great-grandfather, with some help from his brother, had designed and constructed the barn my mother now owned. They'd had a traditional barn raising, and that gave me pause every time I thought of how difficult construction must have been before the days of power tools. The main part of the barn was shaped like a hexagon and rose twenty-four feet to the roof. The six sides tapered and met in the apex. It also had two wings jutting out from the back sides. On the high point of the roof sat a cupola, a miniature model of the barn with a copper weathervane. Cut and hammered letters N, S, E, and W were attached to dowels, pointing the four directions. And there was a Belgian workhorse at the top.

"I'm partial of course, but I agree. The Harding barn wasn't as unique as hers is, still it was picturesque. When I heard the call I hoped the crews could get here in time," I said.

Weber nodded. "I drive by here often enough on duty and gotta admit it's going to be kind of sad the old barn is gone."

"Hey, send me on another guilt trip," Evans said.

Smoke gave him a pat on the back. "Your crew got here fast, and you kept it from spreading."

Evans grinned a little. "I know that, I just like giving Vince here some grief. Like Corky told me earlier, we would have had to be on site the minute it started for any hope of stopping it. It was dry kindling and made for a giant bonfire."

"No doubt. Well, I'm going to take a closer look-see, snap some photos," Smoke said.

Smoke headed to the barn and Evans went to his rig.

Weber leaned in closer to me. "Say Sergeant, thanks for helping me out and all, with my . . . ah, situation."

"Vince, you know I want to. We need to put a stop to the harassment."

"Yeah well, I don't know about harassment, but it is some weird shit, all right."

"If it's intentional, it's more than just weird," I said.

"Yeah well, my sister-in-law is more than just plain old weird."

I nudged him with my elbow. "Get out there and catch some fish. Forget about Darcie for a while. When we get the results back from the lab, we'll know if there's any meat to that theory of yours."

He folded his hands. "I'm prayin' there isn't."

"Me too."

Vince hitched up his shoulders then took off.

The fire crews loaded the last of the equipment onto their rigs. I looked around the scene, watched Smoke snap photos for a minute then headed to the Hardings' house for a final check on Sybil. I tried the doorbell, and when there was no answer, I knocked on the door. I waited some seconds then gave a final series of three hard raps.

If Sybil was inside, she wasn't answering and likely needed time alone to process losing the old barn. Not to mention breaking the news to her grandparents, possibly filing an insurance claim, and arranging to have the rubble removed. And whatever else might come up along the way.

Smoke was standing by the front southeast corner of the barn's base, and when he saw me he pointed. "The rocks are cooling down, now the fire's doused." The barn was built on a three-foot-high base of fieldstones. "They sure provided a sturdy foundation for the wood structure on top of 'em. It's no wonder it stood all these years, even given the weather and temperature swings in our fair state," Smoke said.

"How right you are. And with some maintenance, it could've been here another hundred years. I don't suppose they'll want to rebuild it." I studied the variety of sizes and colors of the rocks in the base and admired how the builder had fit them together like an intricate puzzle.

Smoke shook his head. "In another era, on a working farm, a new barn could be resurrected on that foundation. But with the Hardings, I have a strong hunch, given their advancing years—and the fact they haven't used it for years—the chances of that happening are slim to none."

My eyes scanned the ruins inside the stone wall. "Are you going to be able to find the needle in that haystack?"

Smoke looked at me over the top of his readers. "You mean figuring out what started the fire?"

"Yes."

Smoke's shoulder raised up a titch. "If we discover an accelerant was used, that will give us the evidence it was intentionally set. And it makes my job a whole lot easier when the party responsible leaves the fuel container at the scene to boot." He studied the scene a while. "I'm not spotting any irregular burn patterns on the dirt floor that would indicate an accelerant. But when we do our investigation, check out what's left of the animal stanchions and the rest of it, we'll see if it tells us something different."

I watched some remaining puffs of smoke rise from the burned mess. "Evidence of an accelerant is one thing, but you still have to figure out who used it. And why."

"That we do. That's when the fun begins." He tapped the screen of his phone to disengage the camera then dropped it into his pocket. "Change of subject. Speaking of evidence, I'm curious why you brought that blood in for testing earlier. What's going on in Weber's life that he needs somebody's blood identified?"

Smoke's question shifted my thoughts from the barn to Vince Weber and his problem with his not-very-stable relative. "We don't know for certain that it is blood, but the big drop on his windshield naturally got his attention."

"It's not duck hunting season so it probably wasn't an injured bird flying over that dropped some blood."

"Hmm. I wouldn't have thought of that."

"You might have. Go on."

"First he found a dead rabbit on his steps last week, which struck him as a little strange, like where do wild critters usually go to die—"

"Yeah, I had a dead squirrel by one of my trees some time back, and it made me realize that had never happened before. I figured the little guy must have just died, and I spotted it before the vultures swept in for him. I was in a rush and left him where he was. He was gone when I got home from work." He narrowed his eyes. "Sorry for the digression, and back to Weber's deal."

"He buried the rabbit, not thinking much more about it. But when the blood drop appeared this morning, days later, it got him wondering if someone was leaving him messages."

"Does he have any idea who that someone is and why they'd do that?" Smoke said.

"Weber doesn't know for sure, but he thinks it might be his sister-in-law."

"Say again?"

"Turns out his sister-in-law's had the hots for him for years, and she's convinced they should be together. He does not feel the same way. Her reality and his reality are worlds apart, and he figures if anyone's capable of doing crazy things, it's her."

Smoke frowned. "Is she stalking him?"

"It doesn't sound like it's gotten to that point yet. It's more like she's annoying him."

"I'm a little lost at how he connected the dead rabbit and blood on the windshield to his sister-in-law."

"I was too. According to Vince, they had sex, and afterwards she said something like, 'we'll have to see if the rabbit dies,'" I said.

"She sounds a little wacky, all right."

"Poor Vince. He's beating himself up over sleeping with her in the first place."

"And that begs the question, why did he? I thought he and Mandy Zubinski were an item."

"I got the impression from Vince they're just hanging out together, not officially a couple. Still, I have a strong feeling Mandy would not be happy if she found out Vince slept with his crazy sister-in-law. Vince said he let himself get seduced against his better judgment."

"And that is something that's been going on since the beginning of time."

"I guess. Keep it under your hat for now. Vince doesn't want the other deputies to know about it. Not yet anyway."

"And if his luck holds out, they may never have to."

"I'm hoping that's how it shakes out. And that his sister-in-law rides off into the sunset, or finds another man to love."

Smoke's face broke into a grin. "Yep, I'd say dream on, but what do I know? So, little lady, what are your plans for the rest of your day off work?"

"The first thing on my list, before the fire detoured me, was to stop by Mother's shop and see if I could help calm her down."

His long dimples deepened. "Kristen needs calming? Do tell."

"Where to start? My Grandma and Grandpa Aleckson will be back from their northern resort at the end of the month, and need to get ready for their move into town. You know, so John Carl can move in."

Smoke nodded. "That arrangement is a good thing all the way around. It gives your grandparents a reason to downsize, and Kristen has been wanting John Carl to move back ever since he left for Colorado all those years ago. So what's making her nervous?"

"I think it's all the moving parts and how they'll fit together when all is said and done. My grandparents still have a *lot* of stuff in that big house, not to mention all that's stored in an outbuilding. I think they're hoping John Carl will keep what they leave behind."

"I'm starting to feel sorry for John Carl," Smoke said.

"I've already told Mother I'll find a place for whatever he doesn't want."

"What are you going to do with it?"

"Swap out my newer furniture for some of their old pieces. Plus, I'm going to suggest we offer some things to Taylor." Taylor was our father's daughter. The one no one in our family—not even our father, before his death—knew about until recently.

"Taylor, huh? And how do you think your mom will react to that idea?" Mother was still struggling with the concept that Carl had conceived a child with another woman. John Carl, our grandparents, and I were all related to Taylor. But my mother was not, and she felt like the outsider the few times we'd all been together.

I shrugged. "It depends on the day, and how Denny is doing." My mother was engaged to Sheriff Dennis Twardy who was still recovering from a stroke he'd suffered. Mother was conflicted about how that, and some other things, had impacted their relationship. "I feel a little guilty saying this, but I think if they really wanted to get married, they would have done so a long time ago."

"That's crossed my mind a time or two. I'm sure dealing with the reality that Denny neglected to tell her he owned a house in Iowa hasn't helped, by any stretch of the imagination. And that she found out about it from someone other than Denny, under the worst of circumstances, besides."

"Mother lost a good measure of trust over that, no question. You know, she finally talked to him about it the other day. Asked him why he'd kept that from her."

"What'd Denny say to that?"

"He didn't give much in the way of an explanation. Just said he wasn't keeping it secret to be deceitful, something like that."

"Ah, that's a cop out if I ever heard one."

"So Mother interpreted that as he doesn't love her. Not deeply enough, anyway. Not if he's keeping the house his dead wife inherited hidden from her."

"I can't say I blame her."

"Me either. If Mother didn't feel Denny needed her right now, I think she'd be tempted to break their engagement."

Smoke raised his eyebrows and sucked in a big breath.

I drove home, and after attending to Queenie, stripped off my smoky-smelling clothes in the laundry room. A three-quarter bathroom with a walk-in shower was adjacent to it, via a connecting door. I headed in then shampooed, soaped, and rinsed twice. As I towel dried, I still imagined the odor of smoke clinging to my body, my hair. Some smells were like that. They lingered in the memory long after they had dissipated in reality.

I turned on the hair dryer and bent over to dry my long, blonde hair from the inside out. It was still damp when I brushed it and secured it behind my ears with barrettes. I dressed in a sleeveless top and shorts, slipped on sandals, and then Queenie and I headed over to Gramps' house. We spent a couple of hours enjoying each other's company, playing Scrabble, eating a bowl of ice cream, and talking about John Carl's upcoming move and Denny's recovery.

"Gramps, I'm heading into town to see Mom. Is it all right if Queenie stays here a while?"

"Of course she can. As long as you want."

"Can I pick up anything for you at the store?"

Gramps patted my hand. "I can't think of a thing I need from town."

I stood up and kissed his cheek. "I love you, Gramps."

I was at Kristen's Corner minutes later, expecting Mother to be there. But her helper, Candy, told me she'd left to meet a friend for a cup of coffee.

My mother wasn't the "meet a friend for coffee" type. Unless there was a specific reason to do so, usually relating to business or volunteer work. "Oh, okay. Who's she with?"

Candy shook her head. "She didn't say, and I didn't ask. She said she'd be back in a half hour or so. I'm sure she has her phone with her if you need to get hold of her."

"No biggie, I'll catch her later."

"All right then, Ms. Corky. I'll tell her you stopped by."

"Thanks." I walked to my car wondering why in the heck my mother's meeting a friend had piqued my interest like it did. Then I realized the simple truth—I was worried about her. Mother's mission in life was protecting her children to the best of her ability, and that often meant not telling John Carl and me things that might cause upset. Knowing how much stress she'd been under the last months made me wonder if she'd found someone outside the family to confide in, to lessen the burden for us.

I got in my car and swung around to the back parking lot, checking to see if Mother's car was there. It wasn't. It was easy enough to drive by the few coffee spots in town. When I saw her SUV parked in the side lot of The Coffee Shop—they were the first one in town to claim that not-so-original name—my curiosity got the best of me.

Plus, an iced latte seemed like a refreshing choice right about then. I wasn't six feet into the shop when I stopped dead in my tracks. My mother was sitting at a table with a man I knew from a previous case. They were holding hands and their heads were bent in close, like they were having a private conversation.

My mother was holding hands and talking intimately with a man who wasn't her fiancé. In public.

I bolted out of the shop and turned right, instead of left, taking the long way back to my car. I jogged around the block, slowed down somewhat by my flip-flop sandals. Then I took a few laps in the parking lot, trying to rein in my confused thoughts. Why was my mother cozying up to David Fryor, of all people? I had no doubts he was a good guy, and she'd known him since high school. Add to that they both had elderly fathers that needed their attention more and more as time went on. So they had that in common.

Maybe they were offering each other mutual support.

The problem I personally had was I'd killed David's brother in the line of duty, and that put me in a troubling position. Whether or not David and his father blamed me was not the point. It was that seeing him again brought me back to that awful day.

I climbed into my GTO thinking there were plenty of other people in the world my mother could commiserate with besides David Fryor. Like her fiancé, as the prime example. And that's when it hit me—when I'd looked at their interlocked hands, something was missing. Her custom-made engagement ring. Mother had a lot of explaining to do.

6

Belle and Birdie

The fire had done a fine job indeed. There was nothing left but a pile of blackened shards of what had been the barn's roof and walls. The barn had served as both a sanctuary for animals and a prison for her sister. For her gentle sister.

Belle wanted to cheer, to laugh, to celebrate, but when she looked at the sad, small smile on her sister's face, all she could manage was a dismal one of her own. "Birdie, we talked about this. A lot. I thought it would make you happy, that it would free you."

Birdie stared at her, making Belle understand there was more to do. Getting rid of the barn and the other things Belle was doing were all good, and they helped Birdie in her healing process. But it wasn't over yet. Birdie's imploring look confirmed what Belle knew too well.

"So where to next?" Belle asked.

Birdie lifted her eyebrows.

"Of course, that's exactly what I was thinking. But we should wait a while until things calm down a bit. Don't you think?"

Birdie shrugged.

"We've got plenty to keep us busy."

7

I sat in my car for a few minutes, watching the front of the coffee shop for Mother and David then fished the phone out of my shorts pocket and called Smoke. It was nearing five o'clock. "Are you at the office?"

"Nah, I couldn't stand the way I smelled any longer. I'm home, about to step in the shower. We wrapped up at the Hardings, and I'll finish the reports in the morning. I'm calling it quits for the day."

"What'd you find?" I said.

"No trace of any accelerants. We identified where the fire started, but not what sparked it."

"That's something, anyway. I can pick up something to eat, if you're hungry."

"Now that you mention it, I haven't eaten since breakfast. But I have to ask what this is really about, Corinne? I get the feeling it's more than a sudden compulsion to feed me."

"I need to run some things by you."

"About Weber?" he said.

"No, it's about all the moving parts I mentioned earlier."

"Ah. Okay then, how about this—I've got burgers in the freezer we can throw on the grill. You want to pick up buns and a side dish?"

"Do you have pickles?" I said.

I heard him rattling around, probably in his refrigerator. "That'd be negative. But I do have catsup and mustard."

"Baked beans?"

"Ah, let me look." I heard him moving cans in his cupboard. "Nope."

"I'll do a little shopping and be there in a half hour, maybe forty minutes."

"Don't go all crazy shopping, buying out the store," he said.

"Yeah right, you know how much I cook. I basically shop in the deli section and around the outside edges of the grocery store. The endcaps."

"From what I know about it, you don't need to do a whole lot of shopping. But then not everyone has a mother like Kristen who supplies her daughter with tasty dishes on a regular basis."

"I am spoiled having a mother who's an amazing cook, all right." Thinking of my mother and what was going on in her world made my shoulders tighten up. *And she's a keeper of secrets.* "See you in a bit."

Neither my mother nor David had left the coffee shop when I pulled out of the parking spot and drove to my favorite grocery store. One that had good deals on the ends of shelf rows, and saved me trips down the aisles on a quick stop. I picked up a jar of dill pickles sliced lengthwise for sandwiches, a can of baked beans, deli coleslaw, and a rotini pasta salad with tomatoes, cucumbers, and black olives dressed with Greek feta vinaigrette. I was in line at the checkout counter when I remembered the hamburger buns and headed to the bakery section. I spotted Sybil Harding picking out a package of the bakery's best chocolate-chocolate chip cookies.

"Hello, Sybil."

She lifted her head and looked at me from the other side of the cookie display table with the same quizzical expression she'd worn earlier.

I was casually dressed, but didn't look that different with my hair down, sans the badge and side arm. "Sergeant Aleckson," I said.

"Oh. Sure. I guess I wasn't expecting to see you. It threw me off for a minute." Noting our exchanges earlier in the day, I had a feeling things like that happened to her fairly often. "I better get going," she said.

"Take care, and like we told you earlier, call with any questions or concerns that may come up."

"I remember." She held the cookies to her chest and scooted away down the aisle. Places to go and things to do, it seemed.

I shifted the groceries in my arms and used my thumb and pinkie to secure a bag of buns. By the time I got back to the checkout, Sybil had paid and was hurrying out the exit door. It was probably best to give her a few days before contacting her again, after she'd had time to talk to her grandparents and got things figured out.

I took a side trip to the Hardings' farm so Smoke had enough time to get ready. I parked on the gravel road and sat in my car studying the scene. A puff of smoke surprised me when it escaped from the barn's debris then disappeared. It added to the sad and lonely feeling that hovered over the whole farmstead. Sybil said she checked on the place in her grandparents' absence, but I wondered if she spent any time there at all. It gave off strong vibes of being abandoned, especially now that the stately old barn was gone. There were no vehicles sitting in the yard. If Sybil was there, she could have parked in the garage and gotten into the house posthaste before my arrival.

I pulled into Smoke's driveway, knocked on the door that led from inside his garage to the kitchen, and then let myself in. Rex shifted his attention from Smoke to me and ran over and gave the back of my free hand a lick. "Hey boy, it's good to see you, too."

Smoke was pulling premade hamburger patties out of a box and setting them on a plate. We were both dressed in shorts and t-shirts, and when I saw he was barefoot, I kicked off my sandals. "You need help with the groceries?" he said.

"Thanks, I got it. You told me not to go crazy so I managed to limit myself to a single bag."

"Good girl. The grill is fired up, burning off whatever was left on the grates the last time I used it."

I set the bag on the counter and pulled out the groceries. "I'll put the salads in the fridge until we're ready."

"Mind grabbing me a beer? And one for yourself, of course."

While I popped the tops off the bottles, Smoke sprinkled steak seasoning on the burgers. I took a sip of the cold brew. "Mmm. Now that hits the spot."

Smoke picked up his bottle and clicked its neck against the neck of mine.

"Cheers. Hot day, cold beer," I said.

He took a good swig then set it down and leaned back against the counter. "You are right on there. So tell me what's up."

"You think David Fryor is a good man?"

Smoke's eyebrows came together as he considered. "I thought we had that conversation a few months ago. Why David all of the sudden, did something happen?"

I took another sip, set the bottle down, and shrugged. "It's not about his brother's case, if that's what you mean. No, it's about David and my mother."

He stood up straighter. "You're not thinking of setting Kristen up with him, if things go further south with Denny? The guy commutes from Texas to spend time with his dad."

"I know that, and no, no, not at all. Here's the deal, I saw the two of them at The Coffee Shop holding hands, with their faces this close to each other. . ." I stepped in so our faces were inches apart and was momentarily distracted. I backed up before I was tempted to completely close the gap. "And my mother was not wearing her engagement ring."

He shook his head. "I don't get it. Kristen was faithful to your father for nearly thirty years after his death, and now she's stepping out on Denny a year after their engagement?"

I reached back with both hands and pinched the back of my neck to release some tension. "I have no idea. Remember last spring, when I walked in on them hugging in her shop?"

"Yeah."

"Mother said they were comforting each other."

"Yeah."

"I'm giving her the benefit of the doubt here. Like you said, she's faithful to a fault, so I don't understand her behavior and I needed to talk to someone—you in particular."

"She's the one to talk to," Smoke said.

"I know, but I like running things by you first. It keeps me grounded."

He pulled me in his arms, and he felt even better than he looked or smelled. I moved my smooth leg slowly against his hairy one. His hold gradually changed from comforting to sensuous as his fingers moved from my shoulders to my back.

When Rex barked we both jumped slightly, and that's when we heard a car door slam in the driveway. Smoke pulled away. "Now, who's that?" He took a peek out the window, let out a noisy breath, then turned to me. "With the fire, and everything else today, I totally forgot Marcella was coming over."

"What?" Dr. Marcella Fisher, a psychologist we'd met on a case some time back. She'd been interested in Smoke ever since.

I stepped back into my sandals, and hoped to escape out the front door before she saw me, but I wasn't fast enough. Smoke opened the kitchen door for her. When Marcella walked in holding a carrying case, we shared an uncomfortable moment of staring and mutually sizing up the situation. Then she said, "Hi, Sergeant, I thought that was your car in the driveway." *How many other 1967 red GTOs were there in town?*

It took me a nanosecond to fabricate an explanation. "I just dropped some things off, and I'm on my way home. Have a good evening." I bolted, with Smoke on my heels.

"Corinne, stop. Come back."

I didn't turn around as I quietly spit out, "Three's a crowd." I climbed into my car then gathered every ounce of self control I could, preventing myself from peeling out of there and creating a worse scene. I was upset with my mother for confiding in David about whatever it was, angry at Smoke for being forgetful and dense, and jealous of Marcella.

Instead of going straight home, I turned on Collins Avenue for another look at the Harding property, mostly to distract myself from dwelling on personal issues. I parked about a hundred feet from their driveway, got out, and stood there reliving the events of that morning. It seemed like they had happened yesterday, or the day before that. The gravel on both Collins and the Hardings' driveway was dry and compact, so there weren't deep depressions from the heavy vehicles as one would expect. The hot air closed in around me, and coaxed beads of sweat from my pores.

There were only three other homes on that stretch of Collins Avenue. Deputies had interviewed the neighbors, asked them if they had an idea of what might have caused the fire. I was curious if they'd learned anything of value, and would find out when I was back at work. It struck me for the second time that evening how lonely the farmstead seemed. Eerily so. I visually scanned the stones of the barn's base again, admiring the way the mason had fit them together so artfully. I wondered if my great-grandfather had helped with the raising of it all those years ago. My Gramps Brandt might know the answer.

A movement in the attic window of the house caught my eye. I squinted against the early evening sun and focused on the window for a moment before looking over the rest of the house. I saw nothing else move inside. The leaves on the branches of a tree in the side yard waved back and forth as a gentle breeze disturbed the otherwise still air. That may have caused a moving reflection on the window's glass. Or else I was imagining things.

My phone buzzed in my pocket, and when I pulled it out and looked at the caller, I dropped it back in my pocket. Whatever Smoke had to say could wait until I was in a better mood. After a last look at the property, I climbed back in the car and headed home. When my phone buzzed a minute later, it stayed right where it was.

I picked up Queenie from Gramps, and when we pulled into my driveway, as the garage door was opening, I spotted something furry on my front step. I came to a quick stop in the garage, told Queenie I'd be back to get her, and jogged over to get a closer look. It was a rabbit, lying on its side and obviously dead. An ominous feeling settled in me as I thought about what Vince Weber had told me that morning. He'd found a dead rabbit on his step a few days before.

Smoke drove into my yard seconds later. Queenie started barking with persistence from inside the GTO. I fetched her leash from a hook in the garage, opened the car door, slipped the hook on her collar, and then held the leash when she jumped out. "You need to go in your kennel for a while, but I'll get you out as soon as I can." Smoke stepped out of his SUV, and walked into the garage as I was shutting the door to the kennel.

"Going somewhere?"

I dismissed my stubborn pride. "No. Where's Marcella?"

"Suffice it to say she left shortly after you did."

I walked past him and over to the front steps. He followed close behind me. "What've you got here?" He bent over and studied the rabbit. "What in the hell? No blood or obvious injuries that I can see. But the chances are slim to none he laid down and died right there."

"I'd say none." I had been threatened and assaulted a number of times in my career, but looking at the little rabbit that had likely been sacrificed to send me some kind of bizarre message—or warning—saddened me. Add to that the barn fire and two letdowns I'd already had that day. The cumulative effect brought tears to my eyes. I pulled the top of my shirt up and dabbed my eyes with the inside of it.

Smoke straightened up and snaked his arm around my shoulders. I didn't shrug it off. "Weber had one, now you got one, too. And I know you didn't get anyone pregnant."

I drew in a long, calming breath then shook my head. If I'd felt a little better his quip would've coaxed a smile out of me. "Have you ever taken an animal to a medical examiner?"

"If you include veterinarians in that list, then yes. I imagine a vet will be able to figure out what caused the little guy's death."

I pulled out my phone, and dialed a number. "I'm going to check in with Vince, see if he can come over and tell me if this looks like the same deal he had."

"Did he say if the one he had was a common cottontail like this one, not a pet breed of some sort?" Smoke said.

"Correct. He said it was a cottontail, not a domestic."

Weber picked up. "Hey, Sergeant."

"Catch any fish, Vince?"

"Nah, they weren't biting. Too damn hot."

"Busy right now?"

"If you call sitting on my couch, staring at not much of anything on the boob tube busy, then yeah. What's up?" he said.

"Can you swing over to my house? I got a dead rabbit on my front step—"

That's as far as I got. "You're shittin' me."

"I wish."

"There in a jiff."

After we'd hung up, Smoke said, "If you need to attend to Queenie, I'll stand guard here." She was whining, no doubt wondering what was going on.

"Yeah, I'll give her some treats and ask her to hang tough for a while." I went into the garage and got a small handful of Milk Bones out of the sealed container. Queenie heard me and came through the doggie door from her outdoor kennel into the enclosed space. I pushed a milk bone through an opening in the chicken wire. She took it from my fingers and scarfed it up. "Here's the deal. We need to take care of some business, and you need to be good. Consider this bunch of bones your treat. You'll get one more when we're done. Are you cool with that?"

Queenie loved the word "treat" and being rewarded, but figuring out the why, in this case, was beyond her ken. She stuck her nose through the wire and gave a single yelp, begging for the rest of the bones. I dropped them into a bowl inside then returned to the front yard.

Smoke was staring at the rabbit and holding some protective gloves and a large plastic evidence bag. He kept a stash in his vehicle for times such as this. He laid them on the bench by the steps then pulled out his phone and snapped photos of the critter from three sides.

"Do you suppose Vince's crazy sister-in-law followed him over here this morning, and saw us scraping the blood off his windshield? Is this her way of warning me to back off?" I said.

"Actually, a similar thought crossed my mind. Your motion-detection camera should give you the answer."

"Hopefully. I'll snap shots of the rabbit from its front side." I went through the garage entrance to the kitchen, then into the living room, opened the front door, squatted down, took a few pictures with my phone then went out the same way.

Smoke pulled on the gloves and handed me a pair. "You know all too well we've dealt with a lot of people whose actions make no logical sense. If Weber's sister-in-law is responsible for this, I have to agree with Weber, she is not rational. And some delusional people are dangerous."

My shoulders rolled forward in a quick twitch, an involuntary reaction. "Definitely, depending on what they believe reality is." I wiggled my hands into the gloves.

"And if they're paranoid or schizophrenic besides, that adds another whole dimension."

Vince Weber's truck came flying down Brandt Avenue, and the tires kicked up the gravel when he slowed down and made the turn into my driveway.

"That guy drives like a cop," Smoke said.

When Weber joined us, he looked ill. His face was ruby red with sweat popping out of his pores and running down the sides of his head.

"You're not stroking out, are you, Vince?" I said.

"Nah, forgot to wear a hat fishing and got burned. And I'm stoked up by your weird discovery."

Smoke nudged me with his elbow. "Stoked, not stroked." Weber was staring at the rabbit and didn't hear him.

I rolled my eyes at Smoke then turned to Weber. "What do you think?"

"Geez, I didn't think I had a reason to take a picture of the one on my step, but it looks like it's about the same size. And now that I think about it, it was laying there like it was waiting for me to come out of my door and find it. Since it was turned with the front of its body toward the house, like yours is."

"It wasn't here when I came home earlier today. I'm pretty sure I would've noticed it."

"And you let Queenie out then?" Smoke said.

"I did."

"She would have found it."

"Right." Of course.

"It's like déjà vu," Weber said.

"All over again," Smoke added. He was on a roll. "I'll bag it up and take it to the vet's office."

"The vet?" Weber said.

"We're looking for a cause of death. Since you both got the same surprise delivery, and the rabbits were positioned the same way, it's obviously not a coincidence," Smoke said.

"Yeah," Weber said.

"Want me to look up the vet's after-hours number?" I said.

Smoke shook his head. "I'll do it. Here you go, Vince." He gave him a pair of gloves, and when he had them on, Smoke handed him a medium-size paper bag. "You hold it open and I'll drop the little guy into it." They accomplished the task then Smoke pulled off the gloves, inside out.

Smoke nodded at the bench. "Corky, grab me a bag to dispose of these. And a larger plastic one for outside protection of the rabbit."

"Sure." I got them, and opened one where he deposited his gloves. Next I held up the other bag for Weber, and he put the rabbit carefully inside. Then he pulled off his gloves and disposed of them as well.

Smoke reached for the evidence bag, but Weber shook his head. "I'll put it in your vehicle."

When everything was secured, Smoke climbed in his Expedition. "I'll catch you both later." Then he was off.

"So, you told the detective about Darcie?" Weber said.

"I did, after I swore him to secrecy. We both agree that if Darcie did this, she has got some major issues."

"Tell me about it. And if it is her, I'm gonna feel like a heel that I pulled you into this whole ball of wax."

"Don't worry about that. At all."

He nodded. "Thanks."

"I'm going to get a bucket of soapy water to pour on the step so Queenie doesn't pick up the scent and roll around in it."

He winced. "Yuck. Good idea. Then how about we go have a look at what your video camera picked up."

8

Belle joined Birdie on the branch of their favorite tree and reached for her hand. "What are you staring at?"

Birdie turned her head to Belle. She did not utter a word, but the pleading look in her eyes displayed the essence of what she thought and felt. Belle had gotten adept over the years at reading Birdie's mind. After the trauma she'd endured finally silenced Birdie, made her lose her voice.

"You're wondering about the woman with that old model red car? It's Sergeant Aleckson. She was the one in jeans on the property when we were watching the barn burn. We've seen her before, you know who she is."

Belle leaned closer to Birdie, hoping for the ten thousandth time that she could hear her sweet voice once more. She briefly rested her head on Birdie's shoulder before answering the next question Birdie had.

"I don't know why she was just standing there by the farm, looking around. If she was trying to get the answer to how it happened, she'll have to forget about it. She'll never figure it out." Belle listened to the silence for another minute. "Yes, Birdie, I took care of that, too."

9

Queenie was over the moon when I freed her from her kennel. She begged for attention from both Weber and me, and after we'd given her plenty, I told her to run off some energy in the yard. Queenie raced around the backyard acres like a chicken with its head cut off, only faster.

"Man, that dog has energy," Weber said as we headed inside.

"Energy galore, but she'll tire out eventually. Let's see what the camera captured for us, if you're ready?"

"Yeah well, I'll brace myself for the inevitable," he said.

Except it didn't happen that way. We went into my den office, and I logged on to the computer then remotely accessed the footage from the motion-detection camera that was mounted on the front of the house. There was one on the back of the house, also. We'd set the sensitivity level so birds and small creatures didn't activate them, but larger animals and people did. We'd also set the distance at fifty feet, so the camera in front didn't click on with every passing vehicle on Brandt Avenue.

When an image showed up, I felt Vince breathing on my neck as he bent in for a closer view. I willed myself not to shift away. We watched as a person in a white jumpsuit—it was difficult to tell if it was a male or female—appeared on screen approaching from the north side of the house in a crouched-over position.

"Creeping in from the corn field, of all things," I said.

"What kind of garb has she got on? It looks like a space suit."

I smiled then squinted for better focus. The creeper was wearing a long-sleeved white jumpsuit, a hooded helmet hat with a nylon veil that covered the face, and elbow-length leather gloves that cradled a furry creature. "It's a beekeeper's suit."

"Yeah, I guess it is. Head veil, sting-proof gloves."

"Is Darcie a beekeeper?"

"No, but she's wacky enough to have bought a suit, I guess. In case someone spotted her, it'd look like she was tending to bees."

"A pretty good disguise. Clever. But those suits aren't exactly cheap."

"Never priced 'em, but I wouldn't doubt it. I don't think money is an issue for her."

We watched as she continued in a crouched position with her face toward the ground. When she reached the step, she paused then slowly lowered the rabbit onto it. The camera captured a front, side, and back view of her throughout the process.

I shook my head. "That's gotta be hard on her back, bent over like that." She disappeared back into the cornfield, still hunched over, and out of the camera's range. The recording was just over a minute long. "Did you recognize anything about her?"

"Covered from head to toe, creeping along in a goofy way I've never seen before? Nah, can't say I do. Can you play it again?"

We watched it four more times, pausing to try to pick out any facial features, but it was impossible. "Maybe forensics can look for the best images and blow them up," I said.

"She never looks in the direction of the camera. She had to know it was there."

"And the camera's not at the best angle for views of the north side, anyway."

"Like I said, she must've known it was there," Weber said.

"I'm wondering why she'd drop this off in the middle of the day and risk being seen, even in that outfit."

"You got me. I told you this morning, my reality is here on earth. Hers is floating out there on some other planet. Here's hoping forensics can pull up an image that will help us out here."

"Do you have a photo of Darcie?" I said.

He lightly scratched his sunburned head. "Yeah, somewhere, not very recent. Wait a minute. She sent me a selfie a while back. I was going to delete it, but I'm thankin' my lucky stars right about now that I didn't." He pulled his phone from his pocket and clicked and swiped until he found the picture, then he held it up for me.

I took the phone for a closer view. "Gee, Vince, she's pretty darn cute." Darcie had dark brown hair and pleasing features that were complemented by sparkling blue eyes, and a bright smile.

"Yeah well, you think that because you don't know her. I used to think that, too, once upon a time. That's when I learned that sometimes beauty really is only skin deep."

I agreed with that. "What's her height and weight?"

"She's maybe five five, five six, on the slim side. I'd say one twenty."

"Forensics can give us an approximate height and weight of our delivery person, although the jumpsuit might make her look bulkier in the video than she really is," I said.

"I gotta wonder if she's actually been following me."

I gave him back the phone. "If that's the case, and it turns out she left you the crude gifts besides, that constitutes stalking. What does she drive?"

"Silver Honda Civic."

"There are a fair number of those around. You got her plate number?"

"Sure."

As Vince recited it, I jotted it on the notepad I kept by the computer. "I'll keep a watch out."

"Yeah well, after all this I'll be on higher alert myself."

I inserted a flash drive in my computer and made a copy of the video to turn into evidence in the morning. "What about Mandy?"

"What about her?"

"Seriously, are you two together?"

"Nah, I told you we just hang out. No romance. But she's still gonna freak out when I tell her. After what she went through with Devin Stauder and all." Mandy had gotten involved with another deputy, one she thought she could trust, and had nearly lost her life in the process.

"It might bring up bad memories, but she needs to know. If Darcie's been keeping an eye on you, she might have seen you together. Maybe that's what's caused her to act out this way, do weird things."

"Mandy's gonna freak all right."

"I'm going to see if I can track the route the beekeeper took. Where she parked her car."

"Yeah, let's do it."

We hiked over to the cornfield north of my house. Weber took a left and walked to Brandt Avenue while I looked for signs in the crops that might indicate where the beekeeper had entered my property. With the dry soil, there were no obvious footprints, making it difficult to spot how the person had traveled. Some of the corn stalks were pushed one way or the next, but that was likely from deer passing through, given some older tracks no doubt made shortly after the last rain.

"Not seeing much on the road. There are tire tracks where the gravel's thicker, but they're not distinct by any means," Weber called out.

"No, nothing helpful here, either. The person probably parked out there, followed along the edge of the field, and then cut over to my place."

Weber walked back to where I stood, still scanning the area. "Too bad your camera didn't catch a better view of her," he said.

"Like you said, she must've known the camera was there. This land belongs to my grandfather, but a farmer rents the land, and grows the crops. A guy named Leroy. I've known him forever. He's friendly, likes to talk, and stops by Gramps' house on a regular basis. If Leroy had seen a beekeeper tramping through his crops, we would have heard about it right away. But I'll check with him, anyway."

"That'd be good."

It was just after seven thirty when Vince left—still long before sunset—and I needed to rid my body of built-up nervous energy. Queenie was keeping tabs on the backyard through the sliding glass door, her favorite place to watch for animal action. I went upstairs and changed into running shorts and a t-shirt, then collected my Smith and Wesson from the safe, slipped it in its pancake holster, and clipped it on the waistband of my shorts. As I zipped my phone into a side pocket I called out to my dog, "Hey girl, how about a short run?"

Queenie left her guard-duty position, yelped, and then moved her head back and forth, over and over. Seconds later her whole body was wiggling. "All right, let's go." We walked to the end of the driveway, turned right on Brandt, broke into a gentle jog then gradually speeded up. Queenie was trained to run beside me without a leash, and I did my best to maintain a nice, steady pace so she didn't wear out.

We'd almost reached the main county road when Smoke's SUV turned onto Brandt then pulled over and stopped. On a personal level, I was still upset with him over Marcella. But that was personal, after all.

When we caught up to him, he rolled down the passenger window and leaned out. When he lowered his sunglasses and his sky-blue eyes found mine, my heart did a little pitter-pattering. "The bunny's body is with the veterinarian. He'll do the exam in the next day or two," he said.

"Good."

"Exercising or burning off stress?"

He knew me well. "Both. We got a video of the intruder."

"Do tell."

"Probably a woman, but she was decked out from head to toe in beekeeper's garb and Vince couldn't make any kind of ID."

He shook his head. "A beekeeper? How about I go have a look-see?"

"That'd be good."

"Want a ride?"

"Thanks, no. Let yourself in with the garage door code. I left the flash drive with the video on the computer cabinet ledge."

Smoke nodded and took off. Queenie and I ran as fast as I felt comfortable pushing her in the heat. When we got back I filled her water dish and set it on the kitchen floor then got a tall glass for me. Smoke came in as I was pouring it down. "You'd be a worthy adversary in a beer-chugging contest."

I caught the breath the cold drink had taken from me. "Water I can chug, beer not so much."

He chuckled. "Well, I have to say your bee-keeping invader was well disguised."

"No kidding. On my run I dubbed her the 'beekeeper creeper.'"

Smoke laughed again. "Good one."

"We're hoping the forensic folks at the crime lab can pull a clear enough shot for an ID."

Smoke squinted like he was trying to imagine it. "They do perform miracles from time to time." Then his face relaxed and his eyes softened. "Change of subject. Corinne, you were obviously hurt when Marcella showed at my place—"

"You really should get a good calendar app on your phone with reminder alerts to help keep your social life straight."

Smoke sucked in a deep breath and stepped in, up close and personal. "You're right. Marcella sent me a text yesterday asking if she could bring over dinner. She wanted to run something by me. Between the fire and your concern over your mother, I just blanked it out."

"Not that's it's really any of my business, but did Marcella tell you what it was?"

"No. She skedaddled right after you left."

"Sorry for acting like a baby. I'll apologize to her."

Smoke put his hands on my shoulders and gently pulled my body against his. The anger I'd felt and the stress of the day melted in the heat of our embrace. Maybe it was my imagination or hopeful thinking, but it seemed Smoke was letting his guard down with me more and more. Like there was a chink in the armor of protection he had built around his heart. In the past couple of years our relationship had changed and evolved. We'd been trusted friends and confidants for years, and then one day I admitted the truth: I wanted much, much more. In my heart of hearts I knew Smoke did too, but he'd put up one roadblock after the next, preventing that from happening.

He was too old for me, and he'd been friends with my parents in high school. It would make our working relationship awkward. Blah, blah, blah. A long-time love had broken his heart, and he didn't want to go through that again. Who did? Most of the people I knew had been cut to the core by someone at some time in their lives.

Smoke was at the top of his game professionally, and loyal to his family and friends. But the thought of giving his heart and soul, his essence, to another woman scared the bejeebers out of him. I clung to the hope that someday I'd convince him what we had together was the real deal.

I pressed my body closer against his.

Smoke slid his hands down my damp shirt, and his left one touched my holster. "You remembered. Good deal." I'd been fairly faithful to arm myself when I went on runs after surviving a terrifying incident a couple of years before.

"I do most of the time."

"Strive for all of the time. It even saved my life once."

I nodded as we tightened our embrace, but didn't utter another word about that day. It was still too raw, too vivid. I eased myself back a step. "I'm sweating on you, sorry."

Smoke gave my chin a light pinch, and my cell phone interrupted whatever he was about to say. It was the ringtone I'd set for my mother, and we nodded at each other like it was the call we'd both been waiting for. I pulled it out of my pocket. "Mom?"

"Corinne. Is it okay if I come in?"

"Where are you?"

"At the end of your driveway. I see Elton is there so I didn't know if you were working, or what." *Or what.*

"No, come on in." I hung up. "Mother's here, so hopefully we'll find out what's going on." Queenie heard her car pull up to the house and ran to the side door, wagging her tail and whimpering.

My mother gave a single knock then stepped into the kitchen. She looked from Smoke to me then her eyes filled with tears, and a few spilled down her cheeks. Smoke was at her side in a second, and guided her to a stool at the kitchen island. I slid onto a stool next to her, and Smoke moved to the opposite side. Either to give her space or to observe her better.

"Do you need some alone time with your daughter, Kristen?" he said.

She shook her head and sniffled. "No."

I grabbed a tissue from a box on the counter behind me and handed it to her. "What is it, Mom?"

She lifted her head and used the tissue to dab at her eyes and nose. "It's Denny."

My body tensed, and the seconds ticked by then Smoke said, "Did something happen to him?"

Mother's shoulders lifted. "He broke up with me, ended our engagement."

I put my arms around her. She leaned her head on my shoulder and sobbed. "I'm so sorry, Mom."

"He just hasn't been the same since his stroke."

"No, he hasn't," I said.

"I mean his rehab has gone well, but he's not the man I fell in love with. Sometimes I wonder if I ever really knew him. I mean he owned a house in Iowa that he kept secret from me, and couldn't even tell me why he did that. What else has he kept from me?"

"Why did he break up with you, what did he say?" I said.

"Just that things had changed between us, and he couldn't marry me. Then he asked for his ring back." The one he had custom made for her, with a diamond in the center, surrounded by emeralds. She wept some more, and my heart ached.

Smoke eased his way over, and I backed away when he leaned over to give Mother a hug. "Kristen, I know that Denny was a much happier man after you came into his life, and I know he loved you. Why he didn't tell you—or any of us—about his property is anyone's guess. I'm not saying this to hurt you more, but maybe when the house business came out he realized he hadn't really let his wife go, emotionally speaking."

Mother nodded. "I think you're right, Elton."

I didn't know what to say. I was angry with the sheriff for hurting my mother so deeply, first by keeping secrets, and now by ending their relationship. "Can I get you something, Mom? I have some white wine in the fridge."

Smoke released his hold on her and took a seat on a stool.

"No thanks. I'm going to Gramps' to tell him about it."

I nodded. "You want me along for moral support?"

She shook her head and stood up.

"Okay." I gave her a parting hug, and she headed out the door.

"Damn that Twardy," Smoke said.

I found the wine in the refrigerator and set it on the counter in front of Smoke. "If you'll open this, I'll be back in a few." I went into the den, unhooked my holster and gun, and locked them in my safe. Then I hurried upstairs, stripped, showered, and dressed, wondering when would be a good time to ask Mother about David. I was back in the kitchen in no time.

Smoke lifted his eyebrows a tad. "You showered that fast?"

"It was my second one today, so it only took a minute."

He had two glasses of wine poured, handed one to me then raised the one he was holding. "Here's to a better day tomorrow."

"Yes." The wine was cold and crisp and downright good.

Smoke cleared his throat. "Two things I need to get off my chest." *What, pray tell?* "First off, I am not in love with Marcella Fischer. I admit that I like her a lot, and I appreciate all the help she's given me."

That didn't exactly clarify the status of their personal relationship, like just *how* personal it was. But I was too worn out to ask for details, so I nodded and took another sip of wine.

"And the other is about Kristen and Denny."

"What about them?" I said.

"Denny did the right thing, calling off their engagement. If I was Kristen, I'd be wondering what other big secret he might be keeping from me."

"I'm struggling with that, too. Thank God the house secret came out before they got married."

"If they'd been hitched it would've been a whole lot worse."

I lifted my glass. "Here's to near misses."

Smoke nodded, drank the rest of his wine in a long swallow then set his glass on the counter. "I should go since you have an early morning, and you need your beauty rest."

"Thanks a lot."

Smoke chuckled. "I'm not even going to try to backpedal my way out of that one."

"I've got leftover pizza from Gregor's if you want some before you go."

"Thanks, but I overdosed on pizza this week. Now if you'd offered me a delicacy your mother had made, I might've been tempted."

I shook my head. "All out. Mom hasn't done a lot of cooking lately. Not much time with running her shop, helping Gramps, and being with Denny after work."

"No. Speaking of work, are you gonna have a problem with the boss because of all this?"

"If I hadn't worked for him for so many years, it'd be worse. I don't have the same respect for him, but that's more personal than professional."

"That about sums it up for me, too. He's only there half the time anyway, and word is either he won't run for reelection, or he'll step down before that. Time will tell."

10

I was on patrol two days later, an hour into my shift, when Ben from the regional crime lab phoned me. "Sergeant, that blood sample you submitted is human and from a female. Would you like us to run DNA on it?" Vincent Weber would not be happy to hear the blood results.

"Female. Yes, go ahead and run the DNA, and see if she's in the system. And can you tell if she was pregnant or not?"

There was a pause. "Oh. Well yes, we can check. Human Chorionic Gonadotropin, or hCG, is a pregnancy hormone present in your blood from the time of conception. It shows up in a blood test about a week later."

I pulled over to the side of the road. "Can you spell that hormone for me? I'm grabbing my memo pad and pen." When I was ready, he gave me the information. "Got it, thanks."

"I'll let you know what we find out on the tests."

"We appreciate that, Ben."

I drove to the office, headed into the small sergeant's office, and phoned Vince Weber. "Yo, Sergeant Corky, what's up?"

"I got a call about the blood drop."

"Oh, yeah? What'd they say?"

"Human and female," I said.

"That's just great. Does wacky or crazy show up in blood?"

"Wishful thinking. No, but pregnancy does."

"Don't even tell me," he said.

"We don't have an answer to that one yet. They'll be running the tests, both the pregnancy and the DNA to see if they find a match. Try not to stress yourself out too much. If it turns out the pregnancy test is positive, we'll take it from there. Okay?"

"You know how you're always going on runs to help burn off stress? I may have to take it up myself."

"You hate running," I said.

"Doesn't matter. I know I got a brick shithouse of a body, but that's what I got to work with."

I snickered quietly. "You and your descriptions. Hang tight until we hear back from the lab."

"Thanks, Sarge."

I phoned Smoke next. "Hey, Detective, I was wondering if you'd heard from the vet yet, if he'd found out what caused the little rabbit's death?"

"Funny you should call three minutes after I got off the phone with him. The doc couldn't find a specific cause. He said the rabbit appeared healthy with no recognizable abnormalities. No signs of parasitic or other diseases. No trauma. Possibly gassed or suffocated. He's testing the blood for poison, but at this point it's undetermined," he said.

"I don't think it was natural."

"I'd say that's a given."

Midway through my shift, an alert from Channel 4 sounded on my sheriff's radio. "Paging Oak Lea Fire Department. Barn on fire in Blackwood Township. 3516 Ames Avenue. Paging Oak Lea Fire. Person reporting is a neighbor and states there are no livestock inside."

A few seconds later I got the call, "Winnebago County to Six oh eight."

"Six oh eight."

"Did you copy the fire page?"

"Ten-four, and I'm en route." Ames Avenue was about five miles east of my location. I flipped on my lights and sirens, did a quick U-turn, and pressed down the accelerator.

"At fourteen thirty-nine," Robin in Communications said. I would not be going off duty at 3:00 after all.

The same feeling of dread returned. The one I had when the Harding fire call went out. Followed by serious suspicion that another barn, two miles from the Hardings'—as the crow flies—would randomly and spontaneously start on fire two days later. The weather had been hot and dry, but those factors alone didn't generate a fire. My gut told me even though there was no evidence of an accelerant used in the Hardings' barn, we had a firesetter on our hands.

"Three forty, Six oh eight, on two." Smoke was calling me.

I switched to that radio band. "Go ahead on two."

"I'm on my way to Ames."

"Copy that."

I heard Deputies Amanda Zubinski and Vince Weber tell Communications they were reporting to the scene also. Oak

Lea Fire was rolling by the time I turned south on Ames Avenue. Smoke was billowing dark and high into the sky, orange sparks were spitting in all directions. I pulled to a stop by a driveway across the road from the burning barn where a husky middle-aged man stood watching the blaze. I knew him casually. "Hey, Lonnie, you the one who called it in?"

"Yeah, but man, I can't believe what I'm seein' over there. I was workin' in the garden and happened to notice some smoke comin' out from around the door there." He pointed at the barn with the cell phone in his hand. "I called nine-one-one as soon as I could punch in the numbers, and look at it now, not five, six minutes later."

"The wood in these century-old barns is so dry they're engulfed in no time. It's awful."

"You're scarin' me." He glanced back at his old barn. "First it was the Hardings', now it's the Simmonds'."

"You told the dispatcher they don't have animals in there?"

"Not yet, anyways. They moved in not two months ago," he said.

"Where are the Simmonds, do you know?"

He nodded. "On a camping trip with their kids. It's a heck of a thing to happen when they're away and all," Lonnie said.

"Do you have their cell phone number by any chance?"

"Yep." He swiped and tapped his phone a few times. "Here you go. His name is Brandon, hers is Angela. I got his number."

I had my pad and pen ready when he recited the number. "Thanks, I'll give them a call." I walked a short distance away and dialed the number. After six rings, it went to voicemail. I left my name and number, requested a return call, and then went back to Lonnie. "I had to leave a message. Did the Simmonds say where they were staying?"

"Sorry Sergeant, no they didn't. They're camping near Alexandria but didn't mention the name of the place." Alexandria was about 100 miles northwest of us.

"Okay. How about other family members, any nearby?"

"That I don't know, but the farm had belonged to Angela's grandparents. They moved out here from the cities. You know, to get away from the hustle and bustle. Now they got all this to deal with. All I can say is at least it wasn't the house."

Sirens screamed louder and louder around us, then were silenced as squad cars and fire trucks arrived on the scene. Zubinski was first, closely followed by two fire rigs. Weber and Smoke each rolled in a couple of minutes later. The fire trucks pulled into the Simmonds' yard, and the others parked on the road in a line behind my car. Smoke, Weber, and Zubinski joined us and I filled them in about the owners as we watched the firemen's futile efforts.

Smoke moved closer to Lonnie. "We'll be back to talk to you. Are you going to be around for a while?"

"Yes sir, all afternoon," Lonnie said.

Our team of four walked across the road to the Simmonds' farmstead and waited in the shade under a large maple tree. A slight breeze moved the hot air and cooled us by a fraction. The Simmonds' barn was one of the smaller ones in the county. It was constructed primarily of wood, with a few courses of block at the base.

"This doesn't seem real. Those barns have been part of the landscape all my life. Built to last centuries," I said.

"Raise your hand if you're a believer in coincidences," Weber said.

"If you're talking about two old barns blazing in Blackwood Township, then not me," Zubinski said.

"There is a snowball's chance in hell it is." Smoke said. "I talked to Fire Chief Corey when the call went out and told him to do what he could to preserve the immediate area around the barn so we could search for footprints and other evidence. He figured they wouldn't be using much water, if any, on the barn itself. The biggest concern is keeping the fire contained. And since it's not too windy, that helps."

Paul Moore, the stocky, middle-aged star reporter for the local paper, *Oak Lea Daily News,* got out of one of the cars parked on the shoulder of the township road. I hadn't noticed him until then, and wondered if he'd captured some first-class shots of the fire. "Detective Dawes, or Sergeant Aleckson, can I ask you a couple of questions?" Moore called out.

"I'll go talk to him," I told Smoke.

The heat of the sun zapped me when I stepped out of the shade. I met Moore by the road. "Hey, Paul."

"Mornin', Sergeant. This is the second barn fire this week. Are you looking at them as arson fires?" he said.

"We don't have any evidence to support that at this point, but we'll continue to investigate." The standard answer, but it was also the truth.

He raised his eyebrows. "That's it?"

"That's all I got for now." Chief Deputy Kenner was the official spokesman for the sheriff's office and would prepare something for the media outlets.

"All right, well, I'll check in with your office later then."
Moore knew the drill.

I returned to the group under the maple tree, still
focusing on the firefighters. It wasn't long before the
blackened wood was reduced to ashes. The crew sprayed the
ground around it, starting from about twenty feet out.

Smoke took a glance at his watch. "Vince, Mandy, it's past
the end of your shift, so go ahead and take off. Corky will
interview the farmer, and keep trying to contact the owners.
I'll get Major Crimes out here after we've cleared it with the
owners and it's safe enough to process. See what we can come
up with," Smoke said.

After they were gone, Smoke asked me, "Has Vince told
Mandy about his problem yet?"

"I don't know, but I doubt it. We heard back from the lab
today. The blood came from a human female, and they'll be
running DNA and pregnancy tests on the sample."

"I'll hold good thoughts they get a hit on the first and a
negative on the second."

"Same here. Weber is shaking in his boots."

Smoke nodded. "And you must be roasting in your vest.
I'm cooking without one."

"The sweat pouring out of my pores says it all."

Smoke raised his eyebrows and turned his attention back
to the firefighters. "I keep going back to the question, is there
a connection between the two fires? Specifically, were they lit
by the same person, or persons, and why?"

"I've been thinking about two similarities, the
commonalities: neither barn housed livestock, at least not

currently. And the owners of both properties were out of town when their barns burned," I said.

"Right, and is that what the connection boils down to? If the Hardings' barn was intentionally set on fire, they didn't use an accelerant. It wasn't a working farm so there wouldn't have been any fresh hay bales combusting and igniting it."

"I don't know why that concept is hard for me to grasp."

"You mean the chemical reaction when wet hay gets baled and starts fermenting until it gets so hot it spontaneously combusts?" he said.

"Yeah, that chemical reaction. I've seen it, I know it's true, but it still seems strange to me."

"I took shop class back in the Stone Age, and when we used linseed oil on projects, Mr. Nelson made us put the used rags in a metal bin. There was hell to pay if someone left an oily rag lying on a table. He had a major fear of fires."

"And with very good reason. A school fire would be the worst."

"You got that right."

A number of people had stopped their vehicles on the road for a time, watching the fire do its consuming damage to the barn, and the firefighters directing the water hoses at the perimeter of dry ground around it. Some came and went while others stayed and waited for the anti-climatic grand finale. I surveyed who was still there and recognized many of them. Paul Moore had likely gotten some eyewitness accounts from the crowd and left at some point.

"I'll go get Lonnie's info," I told Smoke.

He nodded. "And I'll have a chat with the fire chief."

Lonnie had a crowd gathered around him. People were questioning him, and when I joined them they turned their attention to me. They asked questions that I, for the most part, didn't have the answers to.

"What in the world started that fire?" one said.

"What's going on around here anyway, two barns burning down in our township like this?" another said.

I couldn't pick out all the comments because several of them were talking at once. They had legitimate concerns, and I shared them.

"Well folks, at this point we don't know what caused either fire. Nothing obvious has showed up in the Hardings' investigation. And Detective Dawes will be doing a thorough investigation of this fire as well."

More mumblings and chatter among the people.

I pulled out my memo pad and pen. "Did any of you folks hear anything, or see anyone, who acted suspiciously in the neighborhood the last day, maybe last few days?"

No one had.

"Anyone have an idea, a clue, or a crumb to throw us?" It was often surprising what people came up with.

"A fire's gotta get started somehow," one said. That we knew.

"I remember some years back that gang of teenagers was setting old outhouses on fire over in Bison Township. Since we've got two fires here now, maybe it's something like that," an older gentleman offered.

"Have any of you seen a group of teens on foot in the neighborhood?" I said.

They all shook their heads.

The older man shrugged. "Probably not then."

"We'll talk with others in the area, but if you hear anything, be sure to let me know." I handed out business cards. "In the meantime, I'd like to talk to Lonnie for a minute." I pulled him aside, and he provided the information I needed for the report: full name, date of birth, address, phone numbers, and the details of what he noticed about the fire when it started.

The group was dispersing as I excused myself and walked back to the Simmonds' place. Smoke was talking to Fire Chief Corey Evans, and the rest of the crew was putting equipment back in the trucks.

They both turned their attention to me. "What did the madding crowd have to say?" Smoke said.

"One of the men wondered if it was a gang of teens that set both barns on fire," I said.

"Hmm. Well, let's hope not. If we're talking about kids under eighteen, then the sad truth is the majority of those arson cases involve more than one youth. The most recent data I have from the State Fire Marshal is two years old now, but in the annual report it said around five hundred kids were involved in the three hundred youth cases they had. The problem they struggle with is youth fire setting isn't always reported, so they don't know how many there really are," Smoke said.

"That is true," Evans said.

"Someone would notice a gang of teenagers in the middle of the day sneaking around, if they were up to something," Smoke said.

"We'll interview the other neighbors," I said.

Evans shook his head. "Two barns burning down in the same neck of the woods in the same week seems suspicious, all right. But hey, it's not proof positive that they were set by someone, let alone kids. Life is full of weird coincidences."

11

Belle and Birdie

The dark smoke had stopped rising in the afternoon sky. Belle put her hand on Birdie's and gave it a gentle squeeze. "It's over, Birdie. The barn is gone, and it was like they didn't even try to save it. What a joke. The authorities might be starting to realize how ineffective they are. They don't help people like you and me. Like when we needed it back then. The tables have turned, and we're the ones in control now."

Birdie looked at Belle with the same sad look that broke her heart and made her feel like she wasn't doing enough.

"You know I'm trying to make it better for you, Birdie. And for me. You know that, don't you?"

Birdie gave a small nod and leaned her head over on Belle's shoulder.

"We're doing the things we need to do, right?" Belle said.

Belle thought she felt Birdie's tears falling on her neck, and it made her sadder still. But when she realized it was sweat dripping from her own temple she breathed a sigh of relief. When Birdie cried, it made Belle cry, too. She couldn't stop herself.

12

My phone rang at 4:23. I pulled it from its holder and looked at the face. "It's the owners."

"Good," Smoke said.

I pushed the talk button. "Sergeant Aleckson."

"This is Brandon Simmonds. I got your message to call, and you have us kind of worried here." His voice was shaky and strained.

"Hi Brandon. Yes, Detective Elton Dawes and I are at your place and I'm sorry to have to tell you this, but there was a fire on your farm this afternoon. Your barn burned down."

"*What did you say?*"

I told him again, filling in some more details about the neighbor reporting it, the firefighters' efforts, and how we were still on site, maintaining the scene.

"How could our barn have started on fire?" he said.

"We don't know at this point, but I can assure you we'll do our best to find that out."

"This doesn't seem real."

"I understand. It'll take a while. Brandon, when will you be home?"

"Uh, well . . . just a minute." I heard him talking to someone, presumably his wife. "Sergeant? We'll hook up the camper and be on our way. So it'll be a couple of hours."

"About two hours? Okay, that's good. I'm going to hand the phone over to Detective Dawes so hang on a moment," I said.

Smoke took over the phone call. "Dawes speaking. . . . We can't tell you much of anything at this point. We'd like your permission to conduct a search of your barn, see if we can figure that out. . . . Good. . . . We may finish up before you get here. If that's the case, I'd like you to call me when you're home. Have a safe drive." Smoke gave him his number, said they'd be in touch, and then disconnected.

"I hate giving people bad news like that over the phone," I said.

"You got that right, and for two good reasons. It's kinder, more personal face to face. And you can watch their reactions when they hear what it is," he said.

"Yes, there is that component too."

While we were waiting for the Major Crimes team, Smoke and I did a sweep around the outside of the barn, looking for footprints, clues, and other possible evidence. Deputies Brian Carlson and Todd Mason pulled up in the Winnebago County Mobile Crime Unit then got out and donned coveralls and boots. Carlson's eyes crinkled at the corners. "We have to stop meeting like this."

"Tell me about it. Let's put some tape across the end of the driveway to keep folks from meandering in," Smoke said.

Mason grabbed the tape and some stakes, and he and Carlson completed the task. People driving by either slowed or stopped to look at the scene. The four of us went to work like a well-oiled machine, first doing another search of the ground for prints of any kind. "Nothing discernible, Detective," Mason said.

"Nope, the dirt's been disturbed somewhat by the door, but nothing we can get a cast from," Smoke said.

We photographed the outside then stepped inside the collapsed structure, moving cautiously amid the debris. From the barn door, we systematically worked our way around from left to right. Unlike a working barn where there was equipment, the Simmonds' barn was virtually empty. The blackened iron remnants of burned garden tools was about it.

"No sign of an accelerant. But I'd say it got its start here." Smoke pointed at a darkened area on some west wall blocks, about eight feet from the back door where the animals would have been let out to pasture in the days when they were sheltered there.

"I'd say you're right, Detective," Mason said.

Carlson nodded and pointed at the back door. "Wonder if it was locked? If not, it would give someone easy access."

We poked around, looking for a padlock in the debris. "Here's the metal door handle. We'll ask the owners if they had a padlock, 'cause we're not finding one," Smoke said.

"If they didn't, that makes three similarities," I said.

"What do you mean?" Mason said.

"Between the Hardings' fire and this one. Old barns no longer housing animals, owners are gone, and they're accessible. Either no locks or ones that are easy enough to cut."

"That adds up to three, all right," Carlson said.

"I believe both barns were intentionally lit. The Hardings' fire was generated right about in the middle, where I'm guessing there was still straw bedding left from when they had cattle and such. The burn marks on the wood floor indicate that. With this one, I gotta wonder if there was a reason it was started on the back wall," Smoke said.

"Like to make sure it was really roaring before it was noticed from the front by a passerby or the neighbor across the road?" I said.

Smoke nodded. "That's a reasonable explanation. But at this point we can only guess what the firesetter was thinking."

"Detective, you must know more than anyone else in the department about people who set fires and why they do it," Mason said.

"I've had a lot of training, that's a fact. There's a long list of the types of people who set fires and a longer list of why they do it. With serial arsonists, you got both the organized and the disorganized. Fortunately, they're rare animals.

"Could be an attention-seeker, or someone who likes excitement, or someone seeking revenge. Some firesetters are mentally ill, and the reasons they do it can get pretty complicated. Like with pyromania where a person doesn't have impulse control, or may get aroused, or feel pleasure, or a sense of relief setting a fire. They also might stick around to witness the whole show, see what happens. Contrary to what you'd think watching movies, there are only a handful of pyromaniacs out there," he said.

"Yeah, the training we went to got into a lot of the personality disorders an arsonist or firesetter might have," Carlson said.

"Sometimes with alcohol or substance abuse," Mason said.

"True, the under-the-influence component is not uncommon. Experts are good at creating basic profiles based on info they get from interviews, but there are about as many factors as there are individuals," Smoke said.

I'd been through two fire marshal training seminars myself, one on youth firesetters and one on adults. The subject of fire setting was complex with more variables than I could have imagined. Smoke was right about factors and individuals. My head was spinning by the end of each of the seminars.

We worked for a while longer then Smoke said, "Well, team, I think we're done here for now. I'll give the Minnesota State Fire Marshal's Office a call and tell them about our two suspicious fires. When we finish our reports, we'll send them in for their records."

It was 6:36 p.m. when I pulled into my garage. A measure of guilt nudged me at Queenie's excited barking. She had room to roam in her kennel, and shelter from the hot sun in the garage, but she got lonely. After John Carl had settled in as my nearby neighbor, he'd be able to help when I worked overtime.

I cared for Queenie then went into the laundry room and took off my service belt and laid it on a chair. I kicked off my boots then peeled my damp clothes off and dropped them on the floor. My Kevlar vest was sticking to my skin like it would never let go. When I pried it off, I unzipped it and removed the outer shell. It needed washing as much as I did. I'd take care of my brass and service weapon and the other tools of my trade later on.

I appreciated the convenience of the adjoining shower; it saved me from tracking though the house feeling grimy. I turned the water to a lukewarm temperature, and by the time I'd soaped and shampooed and rinsed, my body was cooling down. I slipped on a light linen robe then went to the kitchen sink, filled a glass with water, downed it, and then filled another. I drank twenty-four ounces in about sixty seconds. Close to it, anyway.

My stomach rumbled, and I opened cupboards and the refrigerator, exploring available food options. My non-cooking choices boiled down to a bowl of cereal with a sliced banana topper, or a peanut butter and banana sandwich. I decided on the latter and, after it was assembled, I carried it to the back deck with the hope of relaxing, enjoying the summer evening with my dog at my side.

I gobbled down my supper with junior high school speed, driven more by inner tension than hunger. The discord and disasters of the last few days made it difficult for me to unwind. I concentrated on one problem for a while then my thoughts zoomed in on the next. Mother's engagement had ended. Denny had deceived her, and others. Barns were burning to the ground in my township, and Vincent Weber had made a big boo-boo that got him into some deep doo-doo.

And I might have been thrown in there with him. Guilt by association, as they say. I needed to meet Darcie, or at least see her, to get my own read on what she looked like, how she moved. Vince had a personal relationship with her, and given the negative opinions he'd voiced, he was not in the least bit objective.

I was still ruminating when my cell phone jingled. Smoke.

"Hello, Detective."

"Sergeant. Well, I just finished up with the Simmonds family. One difference from the Hardings, the Simmonds did have a padlock on their back barn door. Must've been cut off, and the firesetter took it with him, because we found no trace of it."

"Locked, but easy enough to access if you have bolt cutters," I said.

"True. They are mighty upset about what they came home to. Especially the missus, Angela. Since it was her grandparents' place, she had some fond memories of being there as a kid. When her grandma, Bernice Backstrom, died this past spring, the property was offered to family members before it went on the market. The Simmonds were pumped when their offer was accepted. They'd been talking about moving out of the city for some time so they could get some animals, get the kids into 4-H."

"That makes losing the barn even worse," I said.

"No doubt. And here's the kicker. Are you ready for this? Angela's grandmother and Sybil Harding's grandmother were sisters."

"*What*? They were sisters who both had barns burn down within days of each other? A weird coincidence, as Fire Chief Corey said? A little too weird if you ask me."

"I agree. But if there is a particular connection between the two, it'll take evidence, or witnesses, or confessions to prove that. Or that either fire was purposely set, for that matter," he said.

"Man. So if the grandmothers are sisters then Angela Simmonds and Sybil Harding have parents that are first cousins, and that makes the two of them second cousins. Wow. What did Angela say about the Hardings' barn burning down, too?"

"She didn't know about it until I told her."

"Seriously?" I said.

"Yep. The family was gone when it happened, for one thing. And according to Angela their families had a major falling out when they were young. Angela would be—let's see—two years older than Sybil, and Angela thinks she was eight at the time. Her father told her and her older brother that the two families had broken up, and that was that. It caused a rift between their grandparents, too. As far as she knows, no one in either family ever spoke to the other one again," Smoke said.

"That's beyond strange. It must have been something awfully serious."

"You'd think. Then again, we've seen how disagreements that don't seem like big deals to the rest of us have escalated into major feuds."

"True. I suppose it's better to stay clear of each than to fight," I said.

Smoke cleared his throat. "Angela's family had lived here in Winnebago County at the time then moved to Wisconsin not long after the break-up. Now that she's here again, she said she's been torn about what to do. She'd like to visit her great aunt, find out about other family members, but she doesn't want to go against her father's wishes."

"That'd be a tough one."

"Angela asked about the Hardings, and I told her they were visiting their son in Canada. And their granddaughter Sybil was watching their place. She didn't remember her cousin's name was Sybil. She thought it was something else," Smoke said.

"That's kind of odd, and what a shame. I especially wish for Sybil's sake that they'd connect. I think she could use some family support about now. She seems a little lost."

"Yeah, I noticed that too. She's gotta be feeling overwhelmed dealing with the property loss, with her grandparents being away besides."

"I think that's part of it, but not all," I said.

I heard his car door slam. "I'm home now, and Rex is begging for my attention."

"All right. Bye for now, and thanks for the update."

"Sure thing."

After we disconnected, my sense of unease grew so I went inside and started walking. If there was carpet instead of hardwood floors on the main level of my house, with all my years of pacing-thinking time, I would have worn a pathway through it by now. Was there a connection between the fires of the barns owned by the sisters? Mrs. Harding and Mrs. Backstrom were estranged. Mrs. Backstrom had died recently and her property was now in the hands of her granddaughter, but still.

Queenie whimpered then lay down as I wandered around the house convinced we had a firesetter—maybe more than one—on the loose. What was their motive? It was possible the Hardings' barn had spontaneously ignited, and the excitement of watching it burn had sparked a desire in someone to start another one. A thrill-seeker who thought they were just old barns that weren't being used anymore, so what was the harm?

Smoke had noted what made some firesetters tick, but there were many, many more profiles and indicators of others. The list of reasons was a mile long, too. My friend Sara Speiss, a probation officer for Winnebago County, had an arsonist on her caseload some years back. I reached for my home phone on the kitchen counter and dialed her number.

"Corky, I was going to call you later. Oh my gosh, *another* barn in your neighborhood?"

"It's awful. We don't believe it's a coincidence, but we don't have any proof yet," I said.

"That's not good."

"Sara, remember that arson case you had about five years ago? That guy you did the pre-sentence investigation on?"

"Oh, yes, he'd be a hard one to forget. Mr. 'I'm smarter than everyone else, and no one will figure out I'm torching my buildings for the insurance money.'"

I chuckled. "Hey, give the guy some credit. He was right about that for a while."

"He was, in the first three states he lived in until he finally screwed up here and got caught by our fine sheriff's detectives. When the State Fire Marshal linked him to fires in other counties, and then other states, there were enough charges to keep him in prison for a long time to come. When Minnesota's done with him, he'll be remanded to the next state waiting in line."

"And may never live as a free man again," I said.

"Not so smart after all."

"I wonder if he's figured that out?"

"You'd think. He lit the fires himself. Others hire people to set fires they're too scared to start themselves."

"Not so smart, either. How about those two guys who did it to hide a murder they'd committed? They set out to rob that elderly man in his home. Something went wrong so they shot him, and then lit the house on fire to cover their crime. Happened in Stearns County."

"That was a tragic case for sure," Sara said.

"Yes, it was. I've done research on the mindset of different types of people who set fires, and it's all over the board. I'm trying to figure out where our firesetter fits in. There's no specific profile for a serial arsonist, but fortunately they're pretty rare. Could be male, female, from any social background, often have some sort of physical or mental disability. They tend to be passive, and setting fires is a way for them to have some power and control."

"I know they don't respond well to treatment. But they don't scare me as much as kids who set fires," Sara said.

"I agree. They're about as likely to die in the fire as not. They don't know how many incidents there really are because parents, or other adults, don't always report them."

"I get why they don't, but it's wrong. Fire setting is not a behavior you should hide from the authorities."

"So true. Then you've got firesetters who do it as an act of revenge against someone. And the attention seekers, the curious, the anti-social, the pyromaniac. Also very rare," I said.

"Thank God."

"The strange one for me is the firefighter arsonist. They set a fire and then respond to it."

"That is so wrong. Corky, you think any of our guys in Winnebago County would do something like that?"

"I know most of the guys in the different fire departments. Of course, I don't want to believe any of them would be involved in that, but it happens and it's not all that rare. There are even training courses for fire chiefs on how to spot 'em."

"You said the barns were torched?" Sara said.

"It seems obvious, but we don't have evidence to support that."

"And sometimes old structures burn down."

"With a little help from the spontaneous combustion of hay bales or manure piles, or a lightning strike—"

"Or a firesetter," she said.

"Exactly."

13

I had just cleared a call in Emerald Lake the next day when my cell phone buzzed. I pulled over to the side of the road and pushed the talk button. "Sergeant Aleckson."

"Sergeant, it's Stuart here at the lab, calling with an update." He was the DNA scientist at the regional crime lab.

"Good to hear from you, Stuart. What have you got?"

"Unfortunately, or fortunately, depending on how you look at it, we've had zero success finding a DNA match on the blood sample you sent us. Not one hit."

"She's not in the system," I said.

"Correct. And you're right about her gender; the subject is female. And I can confirm she is not pregnant. So we got one of your questions answered, anyway."

I mouthed a silent "thank you" then said, "And a big question at that. I really appreciate the quick turn around on the DNA test. We've had some incidents bordering on criminal activity we're trying to get to the bottom of. If we figure out who's behind them, hopefully we can stop her before something else happens." After the dead rabbit deliveries, what might be next?

Stuart cleared his throat. "Glad to do what I can on this end, because I couldn't do what you do out there, dealing with criminals and the things they do. No thank you. Give me the samples to run and the results to analyze, and then you guys can take it from there."

I thought of what it'd be like to trade places with Stuart, even for a day. Running scientific tests and looking through a microscope for hours on end would push me over the edge, no doubt about it. "That's why we have different positions on the team."

"And we work for the same victims and their loved ones," Stuart said.

When we hung up, I phoned Vince Weber.

"Hey, Sarge, what's the good word?"

"Actually, I have two of them. Not pregnant."

His exhaled sigh of relief came across the phone line loud and clear. "I will get down on my knees as soon as I get out of my car and say 'thank you,' to the man upstairs. And what about the DNA? Were they able to get any results on it yet, find a match?"

"They got it done, but no match showed up in their database."

"I guess that doesn't surprise me if it's Darcie we're talkin' about. I don't know a reason she'd be in the system," he said.

"We'll need her DNA to compare the sample to. You don't happen to have an unwashed glass she used at your house, or anything else with her DNA on it?"

"Huh. No eating or drinking utensils. No articles of clothing."

"Did she use your comb or hairbrush?"

As soon as he said, "Ha!" I laughed. Vince had kept his head shaved for as long as I'd known him. "Do you even own a brush?" I said.

"That'd be no. No comb, no shampoo, no hairspray, no special gels, no fancy barrettes, nothin'."

The thought of the burly Vincent Weber with a head full of gelled hair made me smile. "Maybe I should simplify my life and start shaving my head."

"Yeah, you could probably pull it off. And you're right, a hairless head makes the grooming part of my life a lot simpler." He chuckled. "Well, I'll look around for something she might've left at my place, see if I can come up with anything."

The day was busy with calls, and between one and the next, my thoughts took turns flitting between my mother's situation and wondering if anything new had turned up on the barn fires. When there was a lull in complaint calls I phoned Smoke to check on the progress of the investigations.

"On my way to the Harding place now to have another look-see."

"I can meet you there."

"Sure. Another set of eyes is always good. And your observations are better than a lot of 'em."

"I'm in Emerald Lake and should be there in eight or nine." But a couple of minutes later, I met a Jeep on County Road 9 that my radar clocked doing seventy-one miles an hour. In a fifty-five mph zone. "Wouldn't you know it?" I slowed down enough to execute a safe U-turn then speeded up to catch the Jeep. By the time I was on his tail he was doing fifty-two, and when I activated the lights, he pulled onto the shoulder.

I punched in the license number. The plate matched the vehicle description, and the registered owner was someone I knew. With a valid driver's license and no violations. "Six oh eight, Winnebago County."

"Go ahead, Six oh eight," Robin in Communications said.

"I'll be out with plate number Four-Harry-Robert-Two-Four-Five on County Nine by Emerick Avenue."

"Copy, at fourteen-eleven." 2:11 p.m.

Every time I approached a vehicle on a traffic stop, routine or not, with someone I knew or not, my senses heightened. Along with my sixth sense and need for caution. I'd learned to expect the unexpected. I bent over behind the driver's shoulder and was only mildly surprised to see it wasn't Woody Nevins. Instead, a man some years his junior was behind the wheel, wearing a soiled ball cap and clothes that needed to be run through a few washing machine cycles. Dirt was embedded under his fingernails and in the creases of his cracked hands. He was unshaven and unkempt. What was his story?

"Afternoon, sir. Do you know why I stopped you?"

The man lifted one hand off the steering wheel and turned it palm up. "I guess I was speeding. When I saw you was behind me, I looked at the speedometer."

"I clocked you doing seventy-one." I pointed at the fifty-five mph speed sign about sixty feet ahead.

"Oh."

"I'll need your driver's license and proof of insurance," I said.

"Oh." He momentarily froze then he shifted and pulled out a thin wallet from his back pocket. His hands were a little shaky as he retrieved a worn Minnesota license and handed it over. It was about as grimy as the rest of him.

When I looked at it I knew why he'd hesitated. "Mr. Warren, it appears your license is expired."

His shoulders hitched up slightly. "Ah, I kind of forgot about that. I'll take care of it."

I read the information on the license. Ross Franklin Warren, age thirty-eight. "Is this your current address?"

Another pause before he answered. "That address is right."

"You're a ways from home." His city of residence was about forty miles away.

"I've been helping a friend with some chores," he said.

"Okay. How about that proof of insurance?"

"Ah, let me get that for you." He reached over, pushed the button on the glove box, and let it drop open. He fumbled around until he located the small blue card then looked at it and handed it over.

"You're not the registered owner," I said.

"This is my friend's Jeep. He let me borrow it to run an errand."

"Your friend's name?"

"Woodrow Nevins."

"You call him Woodrow?"

"Ah . . . mostly I call him Woody."

"I'll do some checking and will be back in a bit." When I opened my car door, cool air rushed out to welcome me. I slid onto the front seat, turned the chiller fan off, and rolled my window partway down. If Warren decided to make a run for it I'd hear the Jeep's accelerator before I'd see it move.

I punched Warren's license number into the mobile data terminal that was bolted to the center console, and the results popped up almost immediately. Aside from two parking violations, he had no driving offenses and wasn't wanted by any agency in the state on unresolved criminal matters. I phoned Communications. "Robin, it's Corky. Can you track down a phone number for me, Woody Nevins, Oak Lea address?"

It took her about thirteen seconds. I thanked her, hung up, and dialed the number. It went to voicemail after eight rings. "Hello, Woody, it's Sergeant Corinne Aleckson. I'm on a traffic stop with a Ross Warren. He's driving your Jeep, and says he has your permission to do so. I'm calling to verify that. Give me a call if that's not the case. Thank you." I left my number and hung up.

I pulled a pair of scissors out of my glove box and snipped off the top right corner of Warren's license number then studied it again. Something felt off, but what was it? My warrant search on Ross Warren didn't uncover anything so there was nothing to hold him on. I wrote him a ticket for driving with an expired license.

His car window was still rolled down, and I noticed him watching me approach his vehicle in his side view mirror—like most people did—but for some reason it unnerved me. He was tapping the steering wheel, no doubt wondering what I was going to do. I gave him the altered license and the ticket. Were his hands shaking from nerves, or was it a medical condition?

"Are you feeling okay, Mr. Warren?"

"Ah, a little nervous I guess." An officer of the law had that affect on people sometimes.

"No need to be nervous. Your driving record is clean, and I'm not going to spoil it by giving you a citation for speeding. This time. But you need to slow down. As far as your expired license, you have ten days to renew it without penalty. If you don't, the fine will be added, and you could lose your license."

"Oh. Well, thanks. Can I go then?"

"Yes."

He nodded, and as I turned to leave, I saw him set both the ticket and license on the passenger seat. I got back in my car and sat there wondering what his story was, what was going on in his life.

"Six oh eight, Winnebago County."

"Six oh eight," Robin said.

"I'm clearing the traffic stop."

"At fourteen twenty-nine."

I phoned Smoke. "I heard you take that little detour," he said.

"Sometimes those little detours are unavoidable. And in this case, the man I stopped for speeding had an expired license besides."

"Happens. There's no one around at the Hardings', and I've been poking around some more in the rubble."

"All righty, see you in a few."

When I pulled into the Hardings' yard, the first thing that struck me was Detective Elton Dawes was one fine figure of a man. From the top of his head on down. My respect and absolute trust in him had grown into deeper personal feelings. I took a moment to drink in his looks, and it brightened my spirits.

Smoke's sunglasses were resting on top of his head, and his readers were resting on the end of his nose. He was covered in both departments. "You finding anything in there?" I asked as I slipped under the yellow tape that spanned across the area where the barn's wide front door had been then stepped gingerly around charred pieces of wood.

"Nothing new. I can confirm the source of the fire is right here." He pointed to an area on the dirt floor that was blackened and had an irregular circular pattern. "But what started it in the first place is a mystery. That brings me back to the likelihood it was deliberately set. But who did it and why is the big question."

"And that brings up the next big question. Was that the case with the Simmonds' barn, too? We don't have the time or the manpower to keep an eye on all the old barns in the county, twenty-four seven," I said.

"That we don't. I've been in touch with the State Fire Marshal, and going on the probability that we have a firesetter on our hands, I'd like to get a profile of who we should be looking for."

"A bold one, I'd say. Starting fires in broad daylight."

"Or an inexperienced one, maybe a pair of them, that don't have a clue how dangerous it is to play with fire, especially when structures are involved."

"I remember reading that most children who die in fires are in ones they've set themselves."

"That's a tragic fact. Children cannot be allowed to play with matches or lighters. Period, end of story."

As I looked around, a strange sensation zinged through me. "Smoke, I have the feeling we're being watched."

"You and your doo-doo-doo-doo stuff, again."

"I can't help it, doo-doo-doo-doo or not. Are you sure no one's in the house?"

He stood up from his squatting position and took a glance at it. "No one answered the door, but I can't swear to it, no."

I turned away from the house. "It wouldn't surprise me if Sybil was in there and decided she didn't want to talk to you. Or any law enforcement. The day of the fire I saw her walking toward the house and thought she must have gone inside. But when I checked later, she didn't answer the door, and I figured if she was in there she couldn't make herself open it and talk to me."

"You might be right on there." He brushed some ashes off the bottom of his pant legs. "Nothing new uncovered on this third go round."

Passing Gramps' house on the way home sent me on a little guilt trip for not stopping to see him the past couple of days. And it reminded me I hadn't checked in with Leroy about the beekeeper. After I got home and took care of Queenie's needs, I changed into running clothes then the two of us set out for a visit.

Queenie slowed her pace to match mine. With the sun's sweltering heat beating down on us, I didn't want to go too fast. When we got to Gramps' door, I opened it and called his name. He was sitting in his usual chair in the living room listening to music on the radio. "Well, well, if you two aren't a sight for sore eyes."

I gave him a kiss on his cheek, and Queenie gave him a lick on his hand. He patted my hand then tousled Queenie's fur. "That's a good girl."

"How are you doing with this heat wave, Gramps?" I plopped down on the nearby couch, and Queenie stayed at his side.

"Oh, not too bad. I get outside a little, early in the morning." That meant he walked the short distance with his cane from his living room chair to his deck chair. My mother and I both encouraged him to do more walking and assisted him as much as possible. But after my grandmother died a few years before, he wasn't motivated much anymore. He told us, "my legs are all played out," on a fairly regular basis.

I leaned in from where I was sitting. "Gramps, Mom talked to you about Denny, right?"

He looked up from Queenie, jutted out his lips then nodded. "She did, and I have to say I'm relieved. Don't get me wrong, I like the man, but I don't think he ever quite got over losing his wife. And it gave me some heartache thinking Kristen might've been playing second fiddle to her."

Gramps had never said a word about that before. He often kept his deeper feelings close to the vest. "When did you figure that out, Gramps?"

He scratched at the whiskers on his chin. "Oh well, I guess not long after they got engaged. Seemed to me that's when some of the spark went out of their romance. And it wasn't all Denny's fault. Your mother was taken with him, that's a fact, but not the way she was with your father."

"I'm with you on that one, Gramps. Carl died before I was born but sometimes it seemed like he was in the next room. I thought Mother was waiting until John Carl and I grew up to find someone new, and then someone found her instead. Denny swept her off her feet, all right. He was one lonely man after his wife died." I regretted the words the second they were out of my mouth. I could have been talking about Gramps since Gram died.

Gramps sniffed. "I'd never wish a stroke on anybody, but in Denny's case it brought out secrets that never shoulda been kept in the first place. Not between two people who planned to spend the rest of their lives together."

Secrets. And big ones at that. "Our family's had some major things to deal with this year." Like discovering John Carl and I had an older sister no one knew about. We were all still off-kilter about that life-changing revelation.

"That's a fact. And for an old guy like me you gotta wonder how much the old ticker can take before it stops ticking."

I stood up and laid my hand on his heart. "It's ticking a nice strong rhythm at the moment."

He gathered my hand in his and squeezed. "I'll do my best to keep 'er going for a while yet."

"Good. Gramps, besides Mom's sad news, there's a couple of other things I was wondering about."

"Oh?"

"Have you noticed a beekeeper working in the neighborhood? I saw someone in a suit over by my house, by Leroy's field. I intended to ask him about it."

"A beekeeper, huh? Why, no, I haven't. And Leroy would've mentioned if someone was keeping bees over at his place. He lets me know what's going on."

"Okay, just curious," I said.

"You got a nice bunch of clover on your lawn. Maybe a beekeeper stopped to check out some bees getting the nectar from it."

"That's a thought." *Or to deliver a little rabbit.* "And I wanted to ask you about the barns that burned, the Hardings' and the Simmonds'."

"Corky, you're the deputy in this family. I wouldn't know anything about that."

I snickered at his words. "I meant about the barns themselves, when they were built."

"As old as I am, that was even before my time."

I laughed some more. "I know how old you are. I thought your father might have told you barn-raising stories when you were young, like the one he built for his family. The one you owned before you gave your homestead to my mother."

"Well, I heard plenty about that one, that's a fact. Seems to me my father was handy at most everything he put his mind to do. And come to think about it, he talked about helping a few neighbors raise their barns. When we went for Sunday drives, he'd point them out. And the Hardings' was one of them I do believe. I kind of forgot about that."

"It was one of my favorites in the county. Did your father say anything about it, any fun facts?"

Gramps thought a moment. "No, not that I can recall. Just that it was a hard day's work, but it made a man feel good to help out his neighbor put up a barn like that. They'd have all the lumber cut and laid out ahead of time, and the men would show up with tools and muscles. The womenfolk brought baskets with enough food to feed the whole county."

"The good old days, huh Gramps?"

"Most of them were, but some of them weren't." He scratched his chin. "What other barns did my dad point out that he'd helped put up? Oh yes, one that belonged to a family named Grant. It's over there on Collins, down the road a piece from the Hardings. The Grants were getting up there in years and moved into town. Both of them passed on years ago. Nevins lives there now. Another one was over on Adler. It's long gone now."

He shook his fingers in one direction, and then another. "The bank took the farm from 'em in the thirties, toward the end of the Great Depression. It eventually got sold to some other folks. They wanted the land, but not the buildings. The house, barn, chicken coop, and the rest of the buildings all collapsed over time. They removed them somewhere along the line. I haven't thought about all that in a coon's age."

"I like it when you take a walk down memory lane," I said.

"I could keep on going until the cows came home, and then some."

14

I showered and slipped into my sleeping outfit of a tank top and pajama shorts then headed to the kitchen for more rehydrating water. Queenie was at my heels when I carried the glass outside to the back deck. The evening sun was on the other side of the house, and I sat in a lounge chair in the shade, watching the leaves of the trees on the back of my property gently wave and twist in the breeze. Then another movement captured my attention. Something—someone—was on the ground dashing from behind one tree to another, pausing briefly each time.

What in the heck? Bebee Lake was on the other side of the grove of trees. There was a little-used public access on its opposite shore, and it was not an easy trek from there to my property. I got the impression the person was on the average side, but at one hundred yards away and with an obstructed view besides, it was difficult to tell. I rushed into the house for a set of binoculars.

I found them on the end table in the living room then ran upstairs to my bedroom for a better vantage point. Queenie was excited at the action and gave a little bark on her way up the steps behind me. I dropped to my knees a few feet from the window, scooted up to it, and peered through the lenses, adjusting them so the back area came into focus. A squirrel scampering up a tree was the only live action I saw.

The tree line was too far away to activate my motion-detection camera, so that was no help. It was rare for anyone to be back there. Sometimes kids explored around the lake when their parents were fishing, but I'd only seen that happen a few times over the years. The person—I guessed was a woman—had darted from tree to tree like she was either playing hide and seek with someone or was trying to find cover. Since she appeared to be alone and was on my property, I wondered if she'd been spying on me.

That thought sent the sensation of little critters crawling from my spine to the back of my neck. I wasn't exactly frightened, but why would someone be watching me? I put down the binoculars and visually scanned the surrounding area with my naked eyes. The woman seemed to have vanished in the minute it took me to get from the deck to my bedroom.

What in the world had she been up to? I pulled my cell phone out of my pajama pocket and called Vince Weber. "Yo, Sergeant, what's up?"

"Hey Vince, can you talk?"

"Yeah, I'm alone, if that's what you mean. What?"

"I was wondering if you've had any contact with Darcie in the last hour or so?" I kept an eye on my back property while we talked.

"Uh, it's possible. She sends me text messages on a regular basis, which I ignore for the most part. Hold on and I'll look." There was a click and he was gone for some seconds. When he came back, he said, "The last one was at six forty-one. A little over an hour ago. Why do you want to know, if I can ask?"

"She lives in St. Cloud?"

"Yeah, this side of it, about twenty-five miles from here."

I headed down the stairs as I told him about the creeper on the back lot.

"If I'm the one that brought that loony lady into your life, I am really sorry."

"Vincent Weber, do not go there. We don't know that it's Darcie, but I think it'd be a good idea for me to get a look at her in person. Someone delivered that bunny, and now someone's been on my back property. If it's the same person, things are escalating."

"If it's fruitcake Darcie then they are definitely escalating."

"You said she's still contacting you several times a day, or trying to?"

"It's been a lot more lately, maybe because I'm pretty much ignoring her. Ten, twelve text messages a day. A bunch of phone calls."

"Saying anything threatening?"

"Nah, it's the same stuff. 'Vincent'—that's what she calls me. 'Vincent, just checking to see if you'd like to come over for dinner. Vincent, give me a call when you get off work. I've been looking at a dress, and I want to know if you like it.' Stuff like that."

"Does she drop by, or have you seen her car parked in your neighborhood?"

"She did stop at my house yesterday when I was at work and left me a note. If she hangs out when I'm gone, I dunno. I haven't seen her parked nearby, watching me, nothing like that, or I would have dealt with it."

"Vince, that's stalking. You don't think so?"

"Not exactly. It's more like she's pestering me, hopin' I'll give in."

"Okay, how about this? You meet her somewhere for a burger to tell her it's over. You're sorry, but you can't see her anymore."

"What if she deals me the pregnancy card?" he said.

"Tell her you'd like to go with to her doctor visit, see how she reacts."

"Huh."

"I'd like to be there so I can observe the way she walks, how she looks when she moves, see if she looks familiar, like one of the creepers."

"You gonna be in the restaurant or hanging out in the parking lot, what?"

"We'll figure that part out. After you set the place and date."

"Date. That's a word I don't wanna use for our meeting."

"Make it day and time then. Place, day, time."

"All right. I like that better. I know you're right about me needing to end it once and for all. I shouldn't have let it go on this long, but it makes it all the more awkward with her parents being my in-laws and all, whether they have much to do with me or not. But I gotta make a clean cut with Darcie. Especially if she's spying on you."

"It needs to happen with or without me in the equation."

"Right. But I'm starting to think I should just ask her about the shenanigans. If she'd tell me the truth."

"And that's just it. You haven't seen her doing what you suspect her of. At this point it'd be a case of he said/she said."

"I forgot to tell you, I talked to my neighbors, asked 'em if they seen anybody on my property, and they haven't. A reliable witness would be a godsend about now."

"For your deal, for my deal, and for the barn fires."

"You know it. Take care, huh?"

"You too." I dropped the phone back in my pocket, wondering about Darcie. Vince Weber and I had been together a number of times in the last few days. If Darcie was keeping close tabs on Vince, she might suspect we had something going on. She could have seen him at my house when he drove over with the blood drop. Or later that day when he'd stopped by the Hardings' after the fire. It was possible she'd been in one of the cars that came and went during those hours. If she had seen Vince and me having our private discussion, away from the others, that might've led her to draw false conclusions.

If Darcie was living in a fantasy world, she needed help, and that needed to happen sooner rather than later. Vince could get jammed up in a New York minute, and I did not want that to happen. He was a stand-up guy and a topnotch, rock-solid deputy.

I went back downstairs and wandered around the main level, from kitchen to living room to den, taking loop after loop. I thought about calling Smoke, but there was no real reason to tell him about the suspicious person on my back property right then.

Queenie plopped down on the big area rug by the patio door then divided her attention between her best human friend and the great outdoors. I stopped for a second here and there to gaze out the window and look for trespassers. As a kid, I had loved exploring and creating simple forts, places to retreat to when I needed some time alone. But I did that on my mother's or grandparents' land where I had permission, not on someone else's.

Was the person sneaking around on my back property still there, even though I couldn't see her? She may be sitting on the hill overlooking the lake. Or hiding and watching. I ran back upstairs and changed into shorts, a t-shirt, and my running shoes then found Queenie by the patio door as I clipped my cell phone case on my waistband. "Want to go for a little hike, girl?"

She jumped up and moved her head back and forth. "Front door," I said. She ran on ahead and waited for me to open it. Then she ran around in circles wondering which direction we were headed. Queenie was only two, but I seldom leashed her, unless we went running on a county road. She was friendly and curious and checked things out, but she was trained to obey, and did so for the most part. What had I done when I lived in my house all by my lonesome?

The sun was lower in the sky, but would not set for about a half hour.

"We're going down to Bebee Lake, and I need you to heel."

"Heel" was not a command I usually gave when we were out exploring the acres I owned, but she stayed with me as I jogged toward the wooded area. When we reached the tree line, I stopped and looked around but saw no one. The air had stilled, and I listened for the sounds of human movement but heard none. It was the time of evening when the daytime creatures had hunkered down until the sun rose again and the night creatures were starting to stir in their nests or other shelters.

Queenie sniffed the ground, playing with fern fronds and other taller weeds that tickled her nose. I poked around checking for anything my trespasser might have left behind. Much of the grassy underbrush had turned brown with the heat and lack of rain. I studied the ground and the intermittent flattened depressions on the vegetation, made by either an animal or a human. I squatted down for a closer look. The pattern told me they weren't made by a four-legged creature—it was either a heavier person with long strides, or a smaller one who'd jumped from point to point. What I'd observed from those few quick glimpses was an individual of average size, certainly not very large.

I followed the path of depressions for a ways south along the tree line until they turned east. Then I stopped at the top of the hill overlooking Beebe Lake and visually scanned the area. The person had likely accessed my property from the public boat landing on the other side of the lake. But why? The hike from there to here took some effort. Add to that the curious behavior of the jumping, or stepping, from one tree to the next. From what I noticed, there were no flattened areas to suggest that he, or she, had sat down to rest or spend time there.

I turned around to head home when something caught my eye. The sun's rays were reflecting off a small object in the weeds between two trees. I went down on one knee to see what it was: a vintage silver flint lighter, the kind Gramps used when he'd puff on a pipe in his younger years. It looked old and had shallow scratches and a raised symbol of an anchor with the initials USN on it. United States Navy.

Had my uninvited visitor left it behind? If so, was it forgotten or did it fall out of a pocket when the person was on the move? I worried about him or her smoking there. With the dry conditions and the recent barn fires, that posed a major hazard. I picked up a stick and separated weed stalks from other brush, but didn't find any discarded butts in the area. Thankfully.

Another possibility occurred to me. Was it deliberately left there as a message or a warning? I pulled my cell phone from its case and snapped shots of the disturbed earth from the footfalls, and then honed in on the lighter. Chills ran up my spine then down my arms, alerting me. Had the slight breeze stirred a reaction on my damp skin, or was it something more sinister? I didn't have gloves or an evidence bag or even a tissue with me. After I'd captured a couple of photos of the lighter, I called to Queenie. "Race you home."

But I was no threat to her ongoing first-place champion status. The farther we ran, the more distance she gained. She was waiting by the front door, her pants rivaling the wags of her tail in counts per second. I opened the front door and followed her inside. "You be good, and I'll be back in a bit." I grabbed my car keys from a drawer in the kitchen then went into the garage and popped open my squad car trunk. My case of goodies was tucked in on the right side. I grabbed a pair of latex gloves and a small evidence bag then closed the case and the trunk and went out via the service door in the back, pausing for a moment to listen for anything unusual and look for anything out of place. Like a person retracing his steps looking for a lost lighter, for instance.

Aside from faint sounds in the distance—a train whistle blowing, a dog barking, and some type of farm machinery motoring along—it was an otherwise fairly quiet evening. I broke into a run across the hayfield to my destination. My hands were damp, so I dried them on my shorts then pulled on the gloves and picked the lighter from its resting spot. I looked at the bottom. It was a Zippo.

I turned it to the other side and read the name Buzz engraved into the surface. My heart speeded its tempo. I didn't know anyone with the nickname Buzz, but it was something to hang onto, a clue to investigate. I dropped it into the evidence bag and jogged back to my house. The sun was about to set, and a large cloud drifted in front of it making the yellow, orange, and pink streaks look like they were shooting out from behind it.

Twilight. The hot sun of summer was dropping below the horizon, giving our parched earth a reprieve from its baking rays. I put the lighter-filled evidence bag in my squad car then joined Queenie inside. As I replenished her water bowl, I thought about the strange happenings of the last few days. Had stars and planets collided somewhere, causing extra chaos in our Winnebago County world? My mother and

Denny Twardy, Vince and his troubles, gifts of blood and dead rabbits, barn fires, a prowler on my property who had probably left an engraved lighter behind. Was a former United States Navy man who called himself Buzz involved in setting barns on fire in Blackwood Township?

15

Belle and Birdie

"**B**irdie, where is it?" Belle implored gently, hearing that impatience had inveigled itself into her words.

Birdie lifted her nose toward the night sky, avoiding both Belle's eyes and her question.

Belle laid her hand on Birdie's. "I'm sorry. I'm not accusing you of taking it. It's just that you always seem to know where things are, don't you? You have helped me find a long list of things I've misplaced over the years."

Belle secretly suspected Birdie had hid things from her at times so Belle would reward her when she told her where they were. Whatever. That wasn't the important thing to Belle. Finding her lost property was.

Belle's assurance brought Birdie out of her sulking withdrawal, and she turned to her with the pure expression that always had a calming effect on Belle, especially in the worst of circumstances. Belle thought the angels themselves must look just like that when they were helping someone in great need, or in times of trouble. Birdie's face was serene, like she was floating on a sea of perfect peace. Her frown line smoothed. Her lips turned up at the corners, and she beamed from the inside out. Her eyes were sparkling clear with a hint of moisture in them.

Belle had asked Birdie more times than she could remember how she did it. How she was able to exude ethereal beauty in times of distress. It was a secret she hadn't shared, and Belle finally decided it had been intrinsically knitted into her nature even before she was born. Belle was often the instigator and deserved the discipline, but it was Birdie who got the brunt of it. The 'why' was a huge puzzle Belle often pondered about. Until she was older, that is, and finally figured it out. Disciplining Birdie was much harder on Belle than if she had gotten it herself. Their caregivers hadn't given care, not by a long shot.

"Well, Birdie?" she implored softly. Birdie raised her eyebrows, and Belle knew in an instant where it must be.

16

I went on-duty at 6:53 the next morning and sent Smoke a text message asking him to call me when he was clear. My phone rang seconds later. "Morning."

"Morning. What's up?" he said.

I dove right into it. "Here's the skinny. Somebody I couldn't ID was back by the tree line on my property last night, acting strange—"

He interrupted, "Whoa, say what?"

"Sneaking around, hiding behind trees—"

"Teenager, adult, male, female?"

"I didn't get a good enough look to be able to say for sure. My impression was female, average size, and someone who moved easily, who was spry."

"Not dressed in beekeeper's garb, I take it?"

"Ha."

"Makes me wonder if this incident is related to the dead bunnies you and Weber had dropped off on your doorsteps. No doubt the beekeeper left both of them."

"Must've. It's really rare to see anyone on my back property. It was just days after I got the rabbit, so who knows. Are the two things related, or not? I found something curious back there."

"What was that?" Smoke's voice lowered.

"Queenie and I checked out the area—mostly to try to figure out what that person was doing there—and I found an old Zippo lighter, the kind with a flint, lying in the weeds."

"We got barns burning and someone gifts you with a Zippo on your back forty?"

"It had a U.S. Navy emblem on one side and the name Buzz on the other side."

"Damn."

"You know anyone named Buzz?"

"No one comes to mind at the moment. That confuses things, doesn't it? I'm having trouble connecting the dots of how that could be related to the bunnies on the steps," he said.

"Same here. The incidents might have nothing to do with each other, but given how strange they are it made me wonder if it is Darcie, Weber's sister-in-law, after all. She'd be the common denominator."

"Maybe. Let's look at this from another angle. Say the two incidents are not connected. We know we must have a firesetter or two out there, and they've been clever. Hiding in plain sight. They could have been traveling the tree lines to avoid detection. We got tree lines on about every farm in the county."

"That dawned on me, too. And the lighter could have accidentally fallen out of his or her pocket as they were jumping around back there."

"And we might've just caught a break and gotten a lead. Any idea how old the lighter is, what era?" he said.

"It's been around a while, but I have no idea."

"I'll take a look at it."

"I'm on my way to the office with it." My phoned beeped. "Smoke, I'm getting a call."

"Meet me at my desk."

I found Smoke in his cubicle reviewing the reports on the fires. He looked up when I set the bag-enclosed lighter on his desk. He nodded, picked up the bag, examined all four sides of it through the plastic then pulled a magnifying glass from his desk drawer. He partially turned the lighter to a different angle and smiled. "We got a print next to the name."

"Really?" I moved behind him and leaned in over his shoulder for the same view. "Wow."

Smoke handed me the bag of evidence. "Did you do a search on this model?"

"Not yet."

"I'd say it's either Korean War or Vietnam War era, but I'm not an expert on all the Zippos out there. They're collectibles; that much I do know. I'll check with Angela Simmonds, see if she knows anyone named Buzz."

"And I'll ask Sybil Harding."

Smoke nodded. "And it wouldn't hurt to check with the local Legion and VFW clubs. I'll make some calls."

"Good idea."

"Did you hear Twardy is in this morning?"

My heart pounded out a little boom-boom at the thought of facing the man who had wronged my mother. "No. Have you talked to him?"

"I said 'hi, good to see you' on the way by."

"Hmm. Well, I'll get a case number for this and get it into evidence," I said.

"A service branch, a nickname, and a fingerprint should lead you somewhere."

As it turned out, that somewhere was at the end of a long and winding road that was difficult to navigate.

I got a case number from Communications and wrote a short report detailing the incident on my back property and the resulting find. Then I filled in the information on the evidence bag, attached a copy of the report to it, and submitted it to the evidence technician. She glanced over the report and gave me a nod and a smile before shifting her focus back to her work at hand.

I was tempted to slip out of the building and get back on patrol but decided to stop by Denny's office first. I couldn't avoid my boss forever.

I knocked on his doorframe and stuck my head in his office. "Den . . . er . . . Sheriff?"

He was standing behind his desk putting a stack of papers into a cardboard box. It took him a few seconds to look up. "Come in, Corinne." Before he started dating my mother he'd always called me Corky, but now he used my given name. "I'm cleaning old stuff out of my file cabinets and drawers. I wonder why I kept most of it in the first place." My mind honed in on a clue we'd found in his massive file collection that helped us locate him after he'd gone missing some months before.

"A lot of history, I guess," I said.

"I guess. What brings you here?"

I joined him by his desk. "I don't like to get into personal things on the job, but it seems like the sooner we clear the air, the better."

"Your mother, our plans to get married?"

I was surprised when my eyes got misty. "Yes."

"There are too many unknowns with my health being what it is. Things changed after my stroke," he said.

No good response came to mind so I nodded. He picked up the framed picture of his wife. It had sat on the shelf behind his desk for years. He must have moved it after he'd gotten serious about my mother because I hadn't seen it for a while. Now it was back. "I'm not proud to admit this, but there were a lot of years I was married more to my job than my wife. I don't know how she put up with me." Denny was devastated when she'd died several years before.

He held the photo up in front of me. I touched the edge of the frame with one hand and Denny's shoulder with the other. "She was very lovely." And then I noticed it, the jeweled ring on her left hand. Damn. I needed to make a quick escape and Communications picked the perfect moment to page me on the radio. I released a breath then responded, "Go ahead, Winnebago County." I nodded at Sheriff Dennis Twardy and bolted out of his office and off to a theft complaint.

Smoke sent me a text mid-morning saying that he'd spoken with Angela Simmonds and she didn't know anyone named Buzz. Early afternoon, there was finally a break in the calls for service action so I phoned Sybil to ask her the same question. She didn't answer and hadn't returned the call by the end of my shift. I sat in my squad car debating whether to try her again then decided to wait for her to get back to me instead. She might have been at work or taking care of family business, and my question was not time-sensitive. Not yet, anyway.

When I got home, I changed into summer clothes and was playing with Queenie in the front yard wondering what to do with the new information I'd gotten about Denny's wife's ring. Vince Weber pulled into the driveway in his truck. "Sorry I didn't call first," he said as he slammed his door behind him. He looked relieved to be out of uniform, dressed in khaki shorts and a tan t-shirt.

"What's up?" I was holding a rubber ball and gave it another toss for Queenie to fetch.

"A couple of things. I scheduled a place, day, and time to meet Darcie." He said place, day, and time with special emphasis then cracked a little smile.

"Good going, when is it?" Queenie brought back the ball and dropped it at my feet. When I told her, "That's all for now, girl," she closed in on Vince and stuck her head in his hand.

"Hey, Queenie. River's Edge tomorrow night at six, before the place gets too crowded. They got a nice bar where we can talk. Cross your fingers I don't get tagged for overtime."

I nodded. "If Darcie knows who I am it'd seem awfully suspicious if I just happen to be there at the same place, day, and time."

Weber grinned again. "Right. I was thinking either you get there ahead of time—borrow somebody else's car—so you'll spot her when she gets there. Or bring a date for dinner."

There were a number of friends I could ask, but keeping it simple seemed the better choice. "I will drive something other than my GTO and sit as inconspicuously as possible in the parking lot until she shows up."

Weber ran the back of his hand under his chin to catch the sweat beads that had gathered before they fell. "This means a lot to me. Thanks."

"I'm the one who asked you to do it in the first place."

"Yeah well, it's a team effort. And the other thing I was wondering about is your trespasser from last night. Figure anything out?"

"Not exactly. I ended up hiking back there and found something that made me pretty curious."

"Yeah?"

I filled him in on the details then said, "Is there anyone in Darcie's family named Buzz who was in the Navy, possibly Korea or Vietnam?"

"Nah, can't think of anyone. Not my father-in-law or his brothers, for sure."

"And that lighter could have been there for a while. The good news is there was a fingerprint on it. Probably a thumbprint."

"Nice. Hey, here's hopin' you find a match. If you ask me, with all the weirdness that's been happening lately, my bet is that lighter belongs to the guy or gal that was back there last night." He raised his hand and used his thumb to point that direction. "That'd rule out Darcie on the one nutso activity, anyway."

"I have a feeling it belongs to the trespasser, too. Now the question is was it left there accidentally or on purpose?"

"Yeah well, depending on what that answer turns out to be, things could swing in the right direction."

I nodded and crossed my fingers. "I had a couple of thoughts on that. I only saw one person, but there could've been more. One of the Simmonds' neighbors mentioned those teens that were setting old outhouses on fire back when. It must have been five years ago now."

"I remember. Kids you wouldn't have pegged as criminals following that hooligan, Patterson."

"Whatever happened to Patterson after he got out of detention?" I said.

"I guess he musta got scared straight."

"You're probably right. We haven't had a call on him since."

Weber bobbed his head up and down a couple of times. "You were saying?"

"If a gang is casing the neighborhood looking for trouble, the barns they lit on fire would have been ones they considered easy pickings. Crimes of opportunity."

"Ya got a point there. They don't see the owners around, or maybe they saw one drive off in a vehicle packed with camping gear."

Like the Simmonds. "That's a possibility, all right. Smoke and I were talking about how they might be traveling by foot through the tree lines on farms. And one of them just happened to lose his lighter passing through mine."

Weber shrugged. "So that's your 'accidentally' theory. What's the 'on purpose' one?"

"Somebody was planting false evidence," I said.

"How do you figure that one?"

"This is a bit of a stretch, but say the firesetter is someone who knows me, knows I've been at both fires, and decides to do something to get my attention, send me chasing after a false lead that eventually comes to a dead end?"

"By pretending to hide by your trees? I don't get it."

"He or she could have been waiting for me to notice them and saw me when I went out to my deck. Then acted suspiciously so I'd have to check it out. And lo and behold, I find a lighter with Buzz engraved in it."

"No offense, that sounds kinda wacky. But some criminals are smart and like to play with us, throw us off track. They might think of something like that. It'd be nice and neat if we'd turn the tables on them, find a connection between that particular lighter and those particular barn fires."

"That would be nice and neat. But theories are one thing. What we need is the truth and the evidence to back that up," I said.

"Right you are."

After Weber left, Queenie and I went into the house to cool off. My friend Sara phoned a while later. "Hey, Corky, I've barely talked to you all week. What are you doing tonight?" Friday was our usual girl's get together night whenever we could make it work.

"You're not heading up to your parents' place for your monthly visit?"

"No, my dad's got his class reunion, and it's like a whole weekend deal. They're busier now that they've retired than ever before."

"I've heard that happens."

"And honestly, as much as I love seeing them every month, the way time flies, I've been thinking every other month would be enough. We talk and text and email when we need to. The bonus is it would cut down on the number of times they'd be able to ask me if I've met a nice young man yet," she said.

I laughed. "You've met lots of nice young men. But so far none of them have been the right young man for you."

She laughed in kind. "Someday my prince will come."

"Don't give your glass slippers away."

"I won't," she said.

"Getting back to what I'm doing tonight. No special plans at all. You want to come over, go grab a bite somewhere, what?"

"You tell me."

"All right then, come to my house. We can talk privately here without worrying about anybody overhearing us," I said.

"You have private things to talk about?"

"Boy, do I ever."

"Oh boy. I'll pick up something to eat. Chinese or Mexican?" she said.

"Mexican sounds good. Anything you want."

"Drinks?"

"I've got both beer and wine."

"Then we're set. Is six thirty good?"

"It's perfect. I work tomorrow, so I turn into a pumpkin at ten," I said.

"That's too early for the prince to show up," she said.

We were both chuckling when we disconnected.

"I should spruce the place up a bit," I told Queenie as I picked up a couple of throw rugs and carried them to the back deck. I was about to shake out one of them when I heard strange sounds from the back tree line. Like branches on the ground breaking from something stepping on them.

I was barefoot so I ran in to the front closet where I'd left my running shoes. Queenie gave a little yelp at my heightened state. "Sorry, you have to stay here," I said as I tied the laces on my shoes. I slipped out the back door and sprinted across the field to the small woods. I was panting and sweat had pushed its way out of most of my pores by the time I stopped to survey the area. The only living creature I saw was a sparrow sitting on a branch of a tree.

I walked a few yards looking for signs, and that's when I noticed some broken twigs. I picked one up, and the white interior indicated the break was fresh. I followed what appeared to be the path the trespasser had taken. It looked like he had gotten to the other side of the lake, but was nowhere in sight now. How fast was that guy, anyway?

I looked around and listened for another minute or two then jogged back to my house. Queenie was watching me from the sliding glass, barking and wagging her tail. I stopped to shake out the rugs then went back inside. "Who do you suppose was back there this time? The same person, looking for his lighter maybe?"

I cleaned through the house, not to my mother's standards by any means, but the bathrooms and kitchen were sanitized, and the rest of it looked good to me. Then I watered some of my outdoor plantings that were stressed from the tropical heat wave without the benefit of any saving rain showers.

By six thirty I'd showered and changed into a sleeveless, lightweight dress and laid out table settings, serving spoons, and bottles of water on the dining table. Queenie alerted me when Sara's car rolled down the driveway. She let herself in the front door. "Honey, I'm home!" And when she saw me she added, "And you put on a pretty dress and everything." It was white, with delicate peach and lime green flowers.

I gave her a warm hug and took the take-out bag from her hand. "You know what, if we're still doing this twenty years from now, that'd be okay by me. And you look very cute in that sundress."

"Thanks, and guess where I got it?" she said.

"At Kristen's Corner. Isn't it nice Mother has good taste and a sense of style? When I go in there she tells me what I should get, and she's right on. Saves me the stress of shopping."

"You're funny. Some of us love to shop."

"Yes, you do. That shade of lilac is great with your coloring," I said.

"Thanks." Sara had strawberry blonde hair and green eyes that changed shades depending on what she was wearing, what the lighting was, or how angry she was. The darkest I'd seen them was when she was raking one of her probationers over the coals for violating a condition of his release. She even had me shaking a little. Her tactic worked well in that instance, and the violator repented and toed the line after that. I would have too.

I put the bag on the table and pulled some containers out and set them down. "This smells so good. I don't think I ate lunch."

"Then you are in luck. Your favorite: shrimp fajitas. And your second favorite: margarita chicken. And all the good stuff to go with them."

"I'm in heaven. What do you want to drink?"

"You got a Corona?" she said.

"I do. Coronas and Modelos, both."

"I have to make a choice? I better have a Corona. Less alcohol."

"With our two-drink limit, it shouldn't make much difference," I said.

"I just don't want to fall asleep before you tell me all your private information."

We ate, and I filled her in on the happenings of the past three days. From my mother having coffee with David, Denny breaking their engagement, the shocker that the ring he'd given her belonged to his dead wife first, a deputy friend of mine—I couldn't say who without his permission—was having a personal problem with a relative, we'd both gotten gifts of dead rabbits, a beekeeper creeper was caught on video delivering mine, the trespasser who may or may not have left a lighter on my property, and finally that someone—maybe the same person—had been back there a couple of hours earlier.

Sara asked a ton of questions as I made my way through the stories of the different situations and then asked if there was anything she could do to help. "Corky, you make my life seem so boring. Thankfully so."

"I don't think that's altogether true. I know most of your probationers."

She raised her eyebrows and laughed. "Some of them keep me on my toes all right." She leaned back in her chair and patted her stomach. "I ate too much."

"Me too, and it really hit the spot. Thank you." I stood up and gathered the remains of our meal. "Let's go sit on the deck. It's cooling down a little."

"I'm fine with eighty degrees as long as the dew point doesn't rival that number," she said.

Sara helped me clear the table then washed and dried the few dishes—even when I told her not to—while I wiped the table and counter. "Would you like something to drink?" I said.

"I'm fine with water for now. Maybe a wine later, when I'm not so full."

We settled in Adirondack chairs on the deck, relaxing in each other's company. Sara was my best girlfriend, and there was little she didn't know about me, my family, my other friends, and my relationships. And vice versa. We'd helped each other through some rocky times and rejoiced in our good ones.

"Sara, getting back to what we talked about earlier, you know, seeing my mother's engagement ring on Denny's wife's finger. I was honestly freaked out. Should I tell Mother?"

"I'd let it ride for now. Would telling her serve any real purpose?"

"Probably not. It adds to the list of reasons in the 'it's a good thing they broke up' column, but I think she'll keep feeling more and more relieved about that as time goes on, anyway."

Sara nodded then cleared her throat as she leaned over the side of her chair and held my eyes with hers. "I have to tell you who invited me out for dinner tomorrow night. And I won't make you guess because you couldn't." She looked like the cat that swallowed the canary.

She hadn't talked about anyone in particular for a while. "Who?"

"John Carl."

"John Carl, my *brother*? That John Carl?"

Sara reached over and gave my cheek a tweak. "I offered to help him with his home project. It's more at the planning stage right now, as you know. Deciding what rooms to paint, whether to refinish the wood floors, things like that."

I was stunned. Every so often I felt like an outsider in my own family. Like when they forgot to tell me big news or to include me in big decisions. My brother had pined for his wife for a long time after she'd left him a couple of years before. "When did all this happen?"

"Today."

"Just today?" Okay, I didn't feel quite so left out.

"You know John and I have been emailing and texting back and forth for, I don't know, maybe two months now. With the things your mother's dealing with and how nervous she's been, he wanted to make this move as seamless as possible. John said when your grandparents get back from their resort at the end of the month, they're planning to pack up and move to their condo in town," she said.

"That's right. They've been going through things, getting rid of the stuff they've accumulated over the years that they don't need. I guess their plan is to take some of the furniture and leave the rest for John Carl. He wants me to take any heirlooms I'd like, and I think our sister, Taylor, should get something, too. If she's interested."

"I haven't gotten used to hearing you say 'our sister.'"

"We haven't gotten used to it either. Or having a sister in the first place, for that matter. And for the record, I think it's cool you'll be hanging out with my privacy-loving brother. You can be my spy."

Sara shook her head, and we shared a good laugh before saying our good nights. I pulled out my phone and sent my brother a text message, "I hear you have a date tomorrow night." A few seconds later my phone dinged, "You can call it what you want." I sent him a heart icon in return and then smiled.

John Carl and Sara were a study in opposites and would be good together. When she was the storm, he'd be the calming presence. When he withdrew into his shell, she'd find a way to pull him out. When he married the first time I didn't gain a sister, I lost a brother. If he married Sara I'd have both.

"Corky, you're putting the cart before the horse. You need to let nature take its course." I smiled at my rhymed words then ruffled the fur on Queenie's head. "Time for bed."

17

Belle and Birdie

Belle found Birdie sitting on their favorite branch of their special tree. Birdie seemed upset, and Belle had a strong indication of why. She sat down beside her and used her thumb and forefinger to gingerly turn Birdie's face toward her own. "I don't know how to tell you this, but it is gone. Maybe forever. I looked everywhere, retracing my steps three times, but I couldn't find it anywhere."

Birdie drew her eyebrows together slightly, but not enough to cause a crease. She looked intently at Belle.

"Birdie, are you telling me to find another one, a replacement?"

Birdie nodded then turned her head in the direction of their old house.

"All right. It might not be the same, but we'll make it work. I'll go see what I can come up with and meet you back here later."

18

Saturday dawned hazy and a little cooler, but still no rain in the forecast for at least two days. The water levels of the lakes and ponds were down, and it seemed all of nature was begging for the skies to open up and deliver a good downpour.

The five Winnebago County detectives rotated on-call duty on the weekends, and about as often as not, there were crimes that required them to report to the scenes. It was Smoke's weekend on, and his vehicle was there when I pulled into the sheriff's parking lot.

I swiped my access card to get into the office and was struck by the silence. Without the hustle and bustle of sheriff's command and clerical staff handling criminal and citizen complaints, stacks of never-ending paperwork, and all the other issues, it felt like a ghost town. Unless something major happened, the high-ranking officials had weekends off.

Smoke's cubicle was my first stop, and I found him leaning back in his chair reading a report. I sat down on a side chair. "Good morning. You're here early. Something happen during the night that I missed?" I said.

He pulled off his readers and rubbed his right eyelid. "Morning, Corky. Nope, nothing new. I got a stack of reports to review, and it's a whole lot faster to get through it on a Saturday or a Sunday."

"I hear ya."

He pinched the area between his eyes. "At the end of a busy week, I appreciate a change of pace."

Hear, hear. It was easier for me to concentrate when I wrote reports and reviewed those from the deputies I supervised if I wasn't interrupted every five minutes. "To let you know, there was another uninvited visitor on my back property last night."

Smoke tossed the paper on his desk and sat up straighter in his chair. "Same person?" He held a slight frown through my entire account then said, "We should think about installing a motion-detection camera on one of the trees back there. You found a lighter there Wednesday night after you spotted that trespasser, and my gut's telling me it's connected to the barn fires in Blackwood Township. I'm leaning more and more toward the theory they're using farmers' tree lines to get around covertly, and have been moving around virtually unnoticed."

"It seems like a good theory, Smoke. When that older gentleman made a similar suggestion after the Simmonds' fire, no one there had seen anyone suspicious in the area. And I know you detectives have talked to the neighbors out there."

"I got a press release going into tomorrow's paper." He slid a sheet of paper my way. It said if anyone had information on the barn fires in Blackwood Township they should call the sheriff's office.

"Good. And if it's kids doing it one of them may feel guilty enough to sing."

"If it's kids, there may be up to three of them. No more. A bigger gang would have caught someone's attention. It's likely people know them, or would at least recognize them. Our deputies are out there patrolling the roads on a regular basis. My training leads me to believe it's someone who lives in the area."

"I agree. Aside from the two incidents back by the lake—not including the beekeeper, that is—I haven't seen others sneaking around, and no group of any kind. But I'm gone a lot during the day, when the fires were set."

"We'll catch 'em."

I switched my train of thoughts. "Tell me more about the Simmonds. What were your observations of them, in general?"

"Good people with well-behaved kids. They had a lot of plans, getting into 4-H and whatnot. In a nutshell, after a couple of hours talking with them, let's just say they went from being excited about finding their dream place to wondering if they're being targeted for some reason."

"They did? Of course we're considering the same thing, given the family connection. And the fact they were estranged from each other adds another layer."

"No doubt. It'll take a while for the Simmonds to get over their state of shock. Angela wants to reach out to her cousin, but needs to talk to her father about it first. And she'll be able to do so very soon—she told me her parents are on their way from Wisconsin to visit."

"That's good. I hope they can resolve their differences with the rest of their family. Sybil told me she has support, but it seems to me she could use more. And she doesn't return my phone calls, which is driving me nuts."

"Could be she's retreating in her Golden Valley apartment, shutting herself off from the rest of the world while she takes care of everything she needs to."

"That's fine as long as she's doing okay. And returns my phone calls."

"Right."

"Smoke, I have something to run by you before I take off. I talked to Sara about it last night."

"What's that?"

"I found out the engagement ring Denny supposedly had custom made for my mother—"

"With the emeralds around the diamond—"

"Right. The emerald is her birthstone, and it must have been his wife's too."

"Why's that?" he said.

"I was in his office, and he had his wife's photo out again. I spotted that same ring on her finger."

His chin pulled back. "What?"

"He used to have the photo displayed, but hasn't since he and my mom got engaged. I guess I never paid attention to the ring she was wearing. It's so small in the picture," I said.

"I didn't catch that either. But what in the world?"

"I know, and the question is, should I tell Mother that Denny deceived her, letting her think it was specially made for her?"

"Damn." Smoke studied his hands a moment. "As much as I hold to being truthful, that's a tough one. I don't think you have to offer information that's hurtful if it serves no real purpose to do so. What'd Sara say?"

"Basically the same thing," I said.

"Sounds like we agree on that."

"And so do I. I guess we'll play it by ear." I reached over and laid my hand on his. "Oh, then Sara dropped a little bombshell and told me my brother asked her out for dinner tonight."

"John Carl and Sara on a date?" Smoke smiled. "I think that's a good thing. For both of them."

I'd pulled up to a service station on the north side of Oak Lea for a late morning cup of coffee when my phone rang. I smiled when I recognized the number on the display. "Sergeant Aleckson."

"Um, hello Sergeant, it's Sybil Harding. You left me a message."

"Yes, thank you for returning my call, Sybil. How's everything going?"

"Fine, okay."

Fine, okay? "Anything the sheriff's office can help you with?"

"No, thank you. Is that why you called me, to check?" she said.

"That was one reason. The other is I'm wondering if you know anyone who goes by the name of Buzz. He was in the U.S. Navy, probably either during the Korean War or the Vietnam War."

It took her a while to answer. "Why are you asking?"

"We're following up on a possible lead," I said.

"Oh. Um, no, I guess I don't."

"Sybil, are you going to be back in Oak Lea in the next day or so? I'd like to talk to you about a couple of things."

"Like what kind of things?"

"We've had another fire in Blackwood Township and we're trying to figure out if there's any connection to your grandparents' fire," I said.

"Oh. Um, well, I could be there today, I think. Maybe in the later afternoon."

"That will work for me. My shift is from seven to three. Give me a call when you get into town, and we can meet at your grandparents' house. Or at the sheriff's office, if that's better."

"Okay. I'll call you."

"Thanks." I turned off my vehicle and was about to get out when a fire call came over Channel 4 on the sheriff's radio. "Paging Oak Lea Fire Department. Barn on fire in Blackwood Township, 4663 Collins Avenue. Paging Oak Lea Fire."

What in the world? My heart jumped around in my chest as I re-buckled my seat belt, turned the ignition back on, and shifted into drive. "Six oh eight to Winnebago County. I copied the fire page, and I'm en route from the Oak Lea Holiday station."

"Ten-four, Six oh eight. At ten twenty-two."

I checked to be sure the coast was clear and then sped away from the service station toward the fire on Collins Avenue, five long miles away. A message from Smoke appeared on my mobile data terminal. "I'll beat you there."

Under other circumstances I might have sent him a smiley face, but there was no smiling when I saw smoke swirling into the atmosphere. Given the distance I was from the site, it was an ominous sign. The barn would suffer the same fate as the other two had. Three giant tinderboxes in a county filled with dozens upon dozens more. The all-too-familiar feeling of gloom seeped into my bones.

I pulled up in front of the farmstead expecting the worst, and that's what I got. The gathering crowd was watching a show that rivaled any high-buck fireworks display I'd ever seen. The Oak Lea Fire Department was just arriving on the scene, and Emerald Lake was close behind. I parked my squad car on the road at a safe distance from the fire. Smoke was standing near the house. Woody Nevins' home. And that's when I remembered he hadn't returned the call I'd made at the traffic stop involving his Jeep—the one driven by a man named Ross Warren.

Smoke glanced at me when I stepped in beside him. Neither of us had words. We both just shook our heads and watched the crew of firefighters battle the third barn fire of the week. If there was a question in anyone's mind that it was happenstance, a bizarre coincidence that two old barns had spontaneously combusted, seeing the third one go up in smoke squelched any doubts.

We were standing on the north side of the building, a good distance away, and the breeze was carrying the smoke in the opposite direction. If it stayed that way, I wouldn't need a face mask.

"I reminded Fire Chief Evans when the call went out to try not to blast water on the ground by the doors, if possible, so we can check for any footprints, especially on the backside. The point of entry is likely back there." He looked down and shook his head. "But nobody's leaving any tracks to speak of, just stirring the gravel up a bit. So unless we catch a big break, we might not find any."

The crews knew the barn was a lost cause by the time they got there, and it wasn't long before the fire had consumed it. The crew directed their water hoses at the charred remains to cool them down and put out sparks that could fly and ignite another fire. And then they drenched the surrounding area to prevent its spread to the house and outbuildings and across the dry fields.

"Winnebago County to Six oh eight and Seven fourteen," Communications Officer Robin's voice came over the radio.

"Six oh eight," I said.

"Seven fourteen," Weber responded.

"Domestic assault in progress at 3516 Ames Avenue, the Brandon Simmonds' residence. A child is the reporting party, and she's locked herself in her room. My partner is on the line with her. Unknown if there are any weapons involved."

"Copy and I'll be en route from Collins Avenue," I said.

"Seven fourteen and Seven twenty-eight copy and are en route," Weber said. He and Amanda Zubinski must have been on lunch break together.

Smoke turned to me with a mystified look on his face. "You think the fight was brought on by their fire? You got good backup, but be cautious." He lifted his hand in a wave as I turned away and jogged to my car. Smoke knew he didn't have to warn me, but reminders to stay vigilant never hurt any of us.

As I got behind the wheel, I sent up a prayer for the safety of everyone in the disputing household and for those of us responding. Domestics by their very nature carried a measure of danger for everyone involved. We were about two miles away, as the crow flies, and close to four via the county roads. There had been plenty of sirens thirty minutes before, but the Simmonds didn't need to hear us coming.

"Six oh eight to Seven fourteen and Seven twenty-eight, lights only," I instructed, and they both copied.

I hadn't met the Simmonds, but considering what Smoke had said, I wondered if the stress of losing their barn and dashing some of their hopes and dreams had triggered a fight that was bad enough to cause their daughter to hide in her room and dial 911. "Six oh eight, Winnebago County."

"Go ahead, Sergeant," Robin said.

"Any more from the PR on the domestic?"

"Negative, Six oh eight. She's crying and not saying much."

"Copy that. The three of us are ten-six at the residence."

"Ten-four at eleven sixteen."

I pulled to a stop north of the Simmonds' house with Weber and Zubinski right behind me. We moved quickly to the front door. A man's angry-sounding voice was booming with fury-filled force. No wonder the daughter had locked herself in her room. I climbed the three steps, pulled open the screen door, and rapped loudly on the door. "It's Sergeant Aleckson from the sheriff's office." Then I stepped aside, out of the line of fire.

Weber and Zubinski waited at the bottom of the steps on either side of the concrete sidewalk positioned behind tall arborvitae bushes, blocked from view of the front door and windows. When there was no response from inside, I gave the door a few good kicks with my boot and announced my presence again.

The man's voice quieted within. "Please open the door. *Now*," I called out. I heard shuffling around inside, heightening my sense of alert. My hand instinctively went to my Glock, and I knew my backup team was preparing for whatever happened next.

A younger-sounding woman called out, "I'm coming." She opened the door slowly and frowned when she saw me. Her eyes were red, and remnants of tears clung to her lashes. "Is this about our fire?"

"We had a report of a dispute, and we heard a man yelling when we arrived. We'll need to come in to make sure everyone is all right." I sensed Weber's and Zubinski's presence behind me.

"We're all right," she said.

"We need to check things out."

"Okay. Come in." She stepped back, and I stepped in followed by Weber on my back left, and Zubinski on my back right.

I took in the scene, noting no obvious signs of a physical altercation, at least not in the living room. It was tidy. There was a middle-aged woman sitting in a side chair, working her thumbs around on her folded hands. A middle-aged man was standing on the other side of the couch. His beet-red face carried a dour expression. No doubt he was one of the involved parties. After a long, cold stare at the three of us he turned to leave. "Sir, we'll need to talk to you," I said. He slowly pivoted back to the couch, dug his hands into it then dropped his head.

I introduced myself and the other two deputies then singled out the younger woman. "Are you Angela Simmonds?"

"Yes, I am."

"Where is your husband?"

She sniffled and wiped her hand across her eyes. "He went into town to get some groceries for supper."

"Okay." I took a couple of steps toward the woman in the chair and pulled out my memo pad. "And what's your name, ma'am?"

"Kaye Backstrom. I'm Angela's mother," she said.

That saved me a question. "All right." I looked at the man. "And you, sir?"

"Damon Backstrom."

I nodded and jotted that down. "Mrs. Simmonds, where are your children?"

"My son went with his dad, and my daughter is in her room," Angela said

A girl around ten years old peeked her head around the corner from the hallway. "I'm here, Mom."

"What's your name?" I asked her.

"Naomi."

I lifted my hand toward Amanda Zubinski. "Naomi, this is Deputy Mandy. She'd like you to show her your room while we talk to your mother and grandparents."

"Okay." Zubinski followed Naomi around the corner and would find out why she had called 911.

My brief assessment of Damon Backstrom led me to believe he'd prefer having Weber interview him over me. "Mr.

Backstrom, you and Deputy Weber can talk in the kitchen," I said.

Backstrom's expression was grimmer still when he left the room with Weber trailing behind him.

"All right, Mrs. Simmonds—Angela—are you comfortable having your mother here when I ask you a few questions?" She took a quick glance at Kaye and nodded. I asked each of them for their full name, date of birth, address, and phone number, and then directed Angela to give me an account of what had happened.

Tears welled in her pleading hazel eyes. "We were talking about the two barn fires, at our house and at the Hardings'. And then I said that Sybil Harding was looking after her grandparents' place while they were gone, and I was hoping to meet her, and maybe my great aunt and uncle when they got back. And that's when my dad blew up."

"Blew up, how?"

"First he gave the wall a punch." She pointed, and I noticed a picture some feet away was a little crooked, but with the old lathe and plaster construction it would take more than a single punch to damage it. "I'd never seen him do anything like that before."

Kaye shook her head.

"Mrs. Backstrom, do you concur with that?" I said.

"Yes, I do. And I've been married to Damon for over thirty years."

I turned back to Angela. "Go on with your story."

"And then Dad started yelling, telling me that I was not to have any contact whatsoever with any member of the Harding family. That they were bad news, every one of them. I asked why he thought that about Sybil. I mean, we don't even know her.

"And he said the Hardings poisoned our family relationship, it was their family against our family. I asked him how, and then he got even madder and started demanding how I even knew who Sybil was in the first place, had she said anything to me? And things like that. I can't even remember all that he said because it's hard to hear everything when someone's yelling at you. I was scared and didn't get why he was so angry."

"Do you feel threatened in any way? Are you afraid of your father?"

Angela shook her head. "No."

"Mrs. Backstrom, do you have anything to add?"

"No," she said.

I studied her a moment. "Are you afraid of your husband?"

"No, I'm not. Not at all."

"All right. I need to tell you that Naomi called nine-one-one, because she was afraid. She was crying. She'll need to be soothed and calmed down."

New tears formed in Angela's eyes, and she looked at her mother. Kaye Backstrom nodded. "I think we should get a hotel room in town for tonight and come back tomorrow when Naomi feels better. I'm so sorry her grandpa scared her. I just want to hold her and tell her it will never happen again."

"That'd be good, Mom. Brandon and I don't yell like that, so it's no wonder she was scared," Angela said.

I carried victim notification cards with me and pulled two out of my back pocket then handed one to each of them, along with my business card. "If you ever feel you're in danger, here's a list of resources of people and organizations to help you. And there's my name and contact information." I got up from the chair. "I'm going to check with the other deputies, see if we need anything more."

Weber and Damon Backstrom were sitting on bentwood chairs at an old oak pedestal table in the kitchen. Either Backstrom had a naturally hang-dog look or he was feeling badly. "Deputy Weber, I've finished my interview with Mrs. Simmonds, and I have a question or two for Mr. Backstrom when you're done," I said.

"Go ahead, Sergeant." Weber stood up, and I took his chair, across from Backstrom.

"Mr. Backstrom, did Deputy Weber tell you who called nine-one-one?"

He looked down at his hands. "Yes. And I'm very sorry. I don't know what got into me. My daughter asked about family things that happened years ago. I'm embarrassed that it made me lose it like I did."

"Something that was serious enough for your family to be estranged from the Harding family all these years?"

"Yes."

"What could be that bad?" I said.

"It's a private family matter."

"But when it causes you to lose control to the point your granddaughter needs to call nine-one-one, then it becomes a police matter."

When he looked up there were tears in his eyes. "I can assure you it won't happen again."

"Good. I'm holding you to your word." I excused myself and found Naomi's open bedroom door. Mandy Zubinski was sitting on a desk chair and Naomi was lying on her stomach on the bed, appearing much calmer. They both looked up when I joined them. "How are you doing, Naomi?" I said.

"Good. I felt better as soon as you got here." She had round brown eyes on a sweet face.

"I'm glad to hear that. The favorite part of our job is helping people, making them feel better. Did you tell Deputy Mandy everything you wanted to?"

"Yes. There wasn't much to tell. My grandpa scared me when he hit the wall and started yelling. I got the phone and called nine-one-one because I thought that's what I was supposed to do," she said.

"You're a smart girl. Thank you for doing that. Well, I guess we're all set then."

Zubinski thanked Naomi, and we left the room and found Weber in the living room waiting for us. "Call if you need anything," I told the women.

"Sergeant, I have a question, if I can ask," Angela said.

"Sure, what is it?"

"What were those sirens for about an hour ago? There were a lot of them."

"Unfortunately, it was another barn fire, down the road from the Hardings," I said.

Her mouth dropped open, and her eyes widened. "Another one? That just gives me a sick feeling in the pit of my stomach. Someone must be doing this on purpose."

"That's what we intend to find out. Take care of your family, all right?"

"We will," Angela said.

19

Belle and Birdie

"**W**e're making progress, Birdie."

Birdie stared straight ahead.

"I know you're upset with me, but I didn't lose it on purpose. And besides, I didn't need it after all. I made do without it, just like we knew I would."

Birdie turned to her, seeking an explanation.

Belle laid her hand on Birdie's. "I did some digging and found another one almost exactly like it. That makes you feel better, doesn't it?"

Birdie leaned over and kissed Belle on the cheek then laid her head on her shoulder.

"And it worked just fine. Every bit as good as the other one." Belle put her arm around Birdie and closed her eyes. "We're in this together, and we'll never be apart. Ever. You believe that, right?" Belle felt Birdie's gentle nod and smiled.

20

I told Communications I was clearing the scene then checked my mobile data terminal for any pending routine calls that hadn't gone out over the radio. There was one from someone requesting a phone call, but when I picked up my cell phone, it rang before I could dial the number.

"Hey Smoke, what's up?"

"I just heard you clear. You're gonna want to come back to the Nevins' farm. Our firesetter just upped the ante."

"How so?"

"We found a charred body in the barn, presumably a male's," he said.

Angela had cited a sinking feeling not three minutes before. Smoke's news sent the same sensation through me then goose bumps popped up all over my body. "Dear God. Is it Woody Nevins?"

"There's no way to ID him by appearance only. We notified the sheriff, the fire marshal, and I'm about to call the medical examiner."

"Is the sheriff on his way out there?"

"No, he isn't. It's not like the old days when he stopped whatever he was doing when we had an unusual death and was at the scene a-sap. I think he's lost his coping skills. When I told him what we had, he said he'd wait for the report."

As much as I believed the chief law enforcement officer should be there, I was relieved I wouldn't have to see Denny so soon after learning he'd deceived my mother. "Hmm. Okay, see you in a few." I phoned Communications to tell them I was returning to the barn fire scene.

Robin answered. "Thanks, Sergeant. Detective Dawes told us what they have out there. A real tragedy."

"The worst." The kind of thing that chipped away at your soul. I sent a message to Weber and Zubinski, asking them to head to the Nevins' farm as well. We'd need crowd control, especially if news of a body leaked out. I pulled over on Collins, in front of the Nevins' farm a few minutes later.

I'd only had one case with a couple that had burned to death, and it was something I hoped I'd never see again. I left my squad car on the road and hurried over to meet Smoke and Fire Chief Corey Evans. They were standing close together on the other side of the barn. Smoke handed me a clipboard with a sheet everyone at the scene would need to sign in and out on, per department policy. Each one of us would be required to write a report. I scribbled my signature and noted the time.

"Have you located Woody Nevins yet?"I said.

Smoke shook his head. "We got his listed number from Communications, but there's been no answer. And the trucking company he drives for is closed on Saturdays, so we can't verify whether he's on the road or not. One of the neighbors we talked to said he hasn't seen Woody for a few days, but that's not unusual. Sometimes he's gone a week at a time. The neighbor gave us Woody's sister's name, said she lives in Victoria, so we're trying to track her down. You'd think one of Woody's neighbors would have his cell number, seeing how he's gone so much."

"I'm sure one of them does and maybe they'll contact Woody when he hears about the fire. I knew his son from school. He was a few years behind me. The last I heard he was in Oregon, working for the State Game Warden," I said.

Smoke pulled out his memo pad and pen. "What's his name?"

"Hunter."

He jotted that down. "Fits right in with the job. Do you know where he lives, what city?"

"I don't."

"Okay, I'll have Communications do a search. He should be easy enough to find.

I moved closer to the stone base of the barn. It was similar to the Hardings' but not as high, a little over three feet. Looking in I had a clear view of the corpse, but it took my brain a moment to process what I was seeing. A blackened figure lay face down on the dirt floor. Why hadn't he escaped when the barn started burning? Had he confronted the firesetter—or firesetters—and been knocked out by him—them? Being unconscious and dying of smoke inhalation was preferable to being burned alive.

Smoke appeared at my side and brushed my arm with his. "A helluva deal, all the way around."

"I've been agonizing over what his last moments were like. What was he doing here? Did he have an altercation with the firesetter, or was he the firesetter? My hope is that he was overcome by smoke, fell unconscious, and died before he started on fire."

"I share that same hope. One thing rattling around in my brain—was this the end game after all?"

"Meaning?"

"The other two fires were dress rehearsals for the real deal. This was a planned homicide, and the others were to mislead us into thinking someone was burning down old barns for shits and giggles, something like that. Then he sets this one, and if he gets caught he plans to claim ignorance: 'I had no idea anyone was in there.' And then he'd take a plea on a lesser charge," he said.

"That's feasible. Or maybe it was to cover up a murder he'd already committed. That could explain why this is the third fire in six days. He had to act quickly, especially in this heat when the decaying process really accelerates." I braved another look at the corpse. "But if it's Woody, I wonder who would have a bone to pick with him?"

Smoke shook his head. "I don't know him or his habits well enough to comment."

"I left him a voicemail on his home phone when I made that traffic stop Thursday, and he hasn't gotten back to me yet."

"That's not a good sign," he said.

"I know. And that reminded me about the guy that I stopped driving Woody's vehicle. Where is he now, is that him?" I waved my hand toward the corpse.

"We'll find out. Meantime, we'll try to contact him. You got his address, phone number?" he said.

"I do. In my memo book and on my copy of the ticket I issued him."

"Sure."

"I'm going to take a look in the garage, see if the Jeep is in there," I said.

"I looked in the windows. I think it is. There's a vehicle in there anyway."

"I'll double check."

It was a relief to slip away from the death scene and focus on something else for a time. I spotted both Zubinski and Weber walking from the road to the farmstead, and we met between the house and the garage.

Weber waved his hand toward the barn. "Someone got caught in there, huh?"

"Yeah, and it's a pretty gruesome sight. Dawes has a sign-in sheet, and he'll let you know if he needs one or both of you to secure the scene when the State Fire Marshal and the ME get here."

They nodded then headed toward Smoke, and I checked out the garage. It was detached from the house, two stalls wide with small windows on three sides. It was decades newer than the house and barn, likely twenty or thirty years old. I peered in a window. The Jeep was parked inside, all right, and it looked like the keys were in the ignition. I moved to the next window for a better view and confirmed it was keys I was seeing. Did Ross Warren forget to take them out after driving Woody's Jeep? Not something you should forget.

I moved to the service door and tried the doorknob. I was a little surprised when it turned and the door opened. People didn't normally leave town for days at a time without locking their garage, especially with the keys in their vehicle. Easy pickings for a thief. But that should have been Ross Warren's responsibility, if he was the last one who drove the Jeep.

I didn't have an official reason to go into the garage, so I stayed in the doorway. From my vantage point I noticed evidence that another vehicle had been parked there. I pulled my cell phone from its holder and called Communications. "Hi Robin, it's Corky. Will you run a check on Woodrow Nevins, see what vehicles he owns? I have a plate number on his Jeep."

"Sure, go ahead." As I recited it, I heard her striking keys on her computer, and in seconds she had the answer. "Besides the Jeep, Woodrow Nevins also owns a Dodge Ram fifteen hundred."

"Okay, thanks." I hung up and looked at the deposited gravel tracks left behind by the wheels of a large vehicle. Most likely from Woody's truck. I hoped it was a good sign, that he had taken it somewhere and was not the deceased victim in the barn. Then I wondered about Ross Warren's personal vehicle, what he owned. So I phoned Robin back and asked. It took a while before she told me, "I'm not finding any vehicles registered to Ross Franklin Warren in Minnesota."

"Really? Huh."

"Any other state you want me to check?" she said.

"Not at the moment, but thanks."

I pulled the door shut and saw Weber and Zubinski cordoning off the east side of the barn with yellow crime scene tape. I stepped under it and walked to the west side where Smoke was taking photos of the scene. "Woody Nevins owns another vehicle besides the Jeep. It's not in his garage, so two things occurred to me: either he drove it somewhere, or the firesetter stole it after he started the fire. The garage door wasn't locked, and the keys to the Jeep are in the ignition."

"That's not good."

"And I checked on any vehicles Ross Warren might own. Are you ready for this? None. Not in Minnesota anyway."

"So a friend dropped him off here to help Woody, or Woody picked him up somewhere?"

"We'll have to ask Woody about that."

"Even though Woody's Jeep is the only vehicle on the property here, we can't rule out Ross Warren as the possible victim," Smoke said.

"Correct."

"We can't ID this body soon enough. Why can't we reach Woody, or someone in his family?"

"Very frustrating when it seems to take forever," I said.

"Tell me about the domestic at the Simmonds', what was that all about?" I filled him in then he said, "Family feuds can drive people to an early grave."

I was thinking about Smoke's words when the mobile crime unit drove into the yard and parked. Todd Mason and Brian Carlson got out wearing sunglasses, tan cargo pants, and black polo shirts with Major Crimes Unit embroidered across their backs and their last names above their right breast pockets.

When they joined us, Carlson pushed his glasses to the top of his head, and Mason stuck his in his pocket. They both squinted against the bright sunlight assaulting their eyes. "The ME and the investigator from the fire marshal's office should be here shortly. It's a toss-up who'll get here first," Mason said. He and Carlson glanced over the scene then focused all of their attention on the blackened body on the barn floor.

Smoke's phone jingled and he pushed the talk button without looking at the dial. "Detective Dawes." He sucked in a breath and caught my eyes when he responded, "Yes Hunter, I'm glad Communications was able to get a hold of you. We've got a situation at your father's place—there was a fire in his barn—and we haven't been able to reach him."

Smoke listened for a while then said, "Sorry to tell you the barn is a total loss. Does your dad have anyone looking after things while he's away? . . . No? Okay. What's his cell phone number? We're waiting on the fire marshal. There are release forms they like to have signed before they start poking around, but verbal consent works, too."

Smoke indicated I should get out my pad and pen. He repeated out loud what Hunter said, and I recorded it. "Thank you. Is the number you're calling from a good one to reach you at? . . . Good. We'll be in touch."

Smoke disconnected and shook his head. "I didn't want to tell Hunter about the fatality, since it's not his property, and it's probably not Woody Nevins' body in there. According to Hunter, he talked to his dad Thursday. Woody had gotten back to Minnesota from a four-day truck run and was heading to his girlfriend's place for the weekend. They had tickets for the Twins game this afternoon." Smoke looked at his watch.

"And they should be there about now. The game starts at one thirty if I'm not mistaken."

I nodded. "And I'm sure Gramps will be enjoying it from the comfort of his living room. So Woody didn't have anyone checking on the place, is that what Hunter said?"

"No one special, according to Hunter. He has neighbors, friends, what have you, keeping an eye on things when he's away." He pushed the talk button, asked me to repeat Woody's number, and as he punched it in, he said, "Sorry, Woody, but this trumps the Twins winning streak." After what seemed like forever, he left a voicemail and hung up. "He wouldn't know my number and probably thought I was a telemarketer trying to sell him a timeshare or something. Hope he listens to my message sooner rather than later."

The Midwest Medical Examiner's van got our attention when it rolled into the farmyard. I recognized both occupants. Dr. Calvin Helsing got out of the driver's seat and Dr. Bridey Patrick got out of the passenger's side. She had a clipboard tucked under one arm and held a phone to her ear with the opposite hand.

Helsing was of American Indian descent with striking good looks: a Roman nose, prominent cheekbones, and full lips. Patrick was the no-nonsense chief examiner at the office, a short, stocky woman with spiked gray hair and piercing brown eyes. She gave the impression that every step she took and every action she performed had a specific purpose.

Dr. Patrick ended the call then stuck her phone in her pants pocket and waited as Dr. Helsing rolled a gurney out of the back of the van. Patrick marched ahead of him and announced, "Bridey Patrick and Calvin Helsing," to the group.

Dr. Helsing singled me out with an eye blink then nodded at the others in general. Dr. Patrick directed her attention to Smoke. "Detective, this is your scene?"

"Until the investigator from the State Fire Marshal's Office gets here, it is," he said.

Patrick narrowed her eyes. "Any idea what happened?"

"We're leaning toward arson, but we'll see what the evidence tells us. This is the third barn fire of the week but the first body. From what we know, none of them had housed any animals for a long time. At this point we are completely in the dark. Especially so with this one, after finding the victim."

"Do you have a possible ID on the decedent?" Patrick said.

"Not yet. We've been trying to reach the property owner. He's supposedly at the Twins game but hasn't answered his cell, so we can't confirm that."

Both doctors shook their heads slightly as they did a visual inspection of the area inside the barn and then honed in on the body. "However this turns out, I pray to God he was dead before the fire started," Dr. Patrick said.

Despite the sun's early afternoon intensity, her words sent shivers up my arms, around my neck, and down my spine.

Dr. Patrick looked at the victim. "And none of your officers have been inside, is that correct?"

"That's correct. As you know, Minnesota statute gives us clear guidelines to follow on that. Aside from shooting some pictures, we're waiting for the fire investigator," Smoke said. The body couldn't be removed until he said so.

"Good. Got his ETA?" Dr. Patrick pulled the clipboard from under her arm and handed it to Dr. Helsing.

"Any time now," Mason said.

Dr. Patrick asked Smoke a number of questions, and Dr. Helsing noted the answers while aptly balancing the clipboard on his arm. The rest of us either listened in or milled around waiting for the next step. The old hurry up and wait routine.

21

Minnesota State Fire Marshal Investigator Emmet Chapman's area included six Minnesota counties, including Winnebago. He arrived at Woody's farm at 1:33 p.m. in his specially-equipped vehicle with the department's logo painted on the sides. He stepped out with a backpack and pulled the straps of it over his shoulders. The other responders stepped back, creating a natural pathway for Chapman to follow to the death scene. The backpack contained some of the tools of his trade, and I knew there were more in his vehicle. I'd seen Chapman work a few scenes over the years and his focused style was impressive indeed.

Chapman was around fifty, fit, and had likely spent much of his time in the great outdoors, given the deep creases in his face. The twinkle in his eyes and his unruffled demeanor made me think off-duty Emmet Chapman would be a fun guy to hang out with in a casual setting, sharing an after-work bottle of beer, or shooting a game of pool. But when he was on the job and went into professional investigative mode, he was all business. He didn't want chitchatting or joke-telling distractions, like many of the investigators I knew.

Smoke nodded as Chapman approached him. "Afternoon, Investigator."

"Detective." Then he greeted the rest of us and had a few words with Dr. Patrick before he turned back to Smoke. "Have you got an ID on the victim?"

"Not yet. We're waiting for a phone call from the property owner to confirm it's not him."

"Check. Has your team processed anything, collected any evidence so far?" Chapman said.

"We did a perimeter check, looking for signs of a person or a vehicle entering the farm from any area other than the driveway. No vehicle tracks of any kind. Or horse prints. If someone was here on foot they didn't leave any discernible tracks behind. But with the ground being as hard as rock that's not a surprise," Smoke said.

"No, it's not. What about on the driveway?"

"The two fire rigs were the only official vehicles that rolled in on the driveway this afternoon—before Major Crimes and the ME got here, that is. There was a set of tire impressions that must have been made shortly after the last rain, given the deeper impressions. So that was over a week ago, maybe ten days now. Aside from very faint ones from a vehicle that drove into the garage in the last day or so, there's no indication that other vehicles have been here," Smoke said.

"Check." Chapman walked over to the partial stone wall and stood for a moment. He moved his head slowly from left to right as he took in the scene. Then he pulled a large memo pad and pen from a leg pocket in his cargo pants and began sketching and writing. After some minutes, he turned and singled out Dr. Bridey Patrick. "I'll get my part done so we can get the body released to you."

The single nod she gave sent the clear message that every passing minute was one too many. They should have had the victim's body back at her office—preparing for the exam—by now.

Chapman stuck the writing materials back in one pocket and pulled out a pair of disposable shoe protectors from another. With practiced ease he lifted first one foot to his knee, and then the other, and slipped them on. Disposable gloves were next and they slid on fine, despite the heat of the day. He entered what remained of the structure through the door opening and took a left, moving slowly along the perimeter as he studied the stones of the base and the dirt floor a few feet out from it. He snapped photos along the way.

When Chapman completed his first circuit, he set out on a second one, about six feet out then stopped after walking after eight feet. He squatted down and took photos of an area on the ground. When he stood up again, he slid the backpack onto one arm, pulled out some small thin-staked marking flags, plastic evidence bags, and a stainless steel spoon. Then he moved the pack back into place.

Chapman stuck six flags in the dirt around the area then collected samples of the blackened dirt from several spots, sealed them in the bags, and marked them. He shifted the backpack down his arm again, put the bags inside, and slipped it back in place. Next he pulled two tape measures from a pants pocket, stretched them out, positioned them on the ground near the flags, and photographed them.

The third round brought Chapman close to the body that was lying about twelve feet from the west wall. He took photos from all angles then finished his round and returned to where the body lay. The doctors, Smoke, and I all slipped into coveralls and boot covers while Chapman was taking notes, marking the area, snapping more photos, and collecting samples of the dirt floor. He bent over, picked up a frosted white booze bottle, held it up for us to see then put it in an evidence bag. Then he pointed to a largely burned camper's pack. The side metal pieces were intact as were two small cooking pots and a metal cup. Any clothing or other personal items that might have been inside were toast. He photographed, marked, and bagged them.

After a time Chapman turned to us, his captive audience. "You can bring in the gurney, Doc."

"Right," Dr. Patrick said. She gave Helsing a "let's go" head signal then looked at Smoke and me. "Are you ready, Detective, Sergeant?"

Smoke nodded, snapped on a pair of gloves, and turned to me as I did the same. "Okay?"

"Yep," I said.

Mason and Carlson would be sitting out for this part of the investigation. I started to follow the doctors and Smoke into the barn when my phone rang. I pulled it out of its case to check. It was Sybil. The meeting we'd talked about had slipped my mind. "Sergeant Aleckson."

"Hello, it's Sybil Harding. You said to call."

"Sure."

"Um, well, I'm sorry, but I can't make it after all."

"Don't worry about it. As it turns out, I'm in the middle of something myself. Are you available tomorrow?"

"That might work better," she said.

"All right then, we'll be in touch. Bye, Sybil." I dropped the phone back in its case and joined the group gathered around leader Chapman. He pointed at the ground on the north side of the body. "I found no signs of a struggle, but you can see where he appears to have crawled a few feet."

We studied the area. "Yes. It looks like he was on the ground, made it a short distance, and stopped. Likely overcome by the smoke," Dr. Patrick said. "His arms are tucked in what looks like a protective act, but may be the result of muscle and tissue shrinkage, dehydration from the high heat. Pugilistic attitude. The main questions are, who is he and what was he doing here?"

"Yes they are. The victim was inside what used to be an animal stanchion. Not much left of it now, but that leads me to believe he was sleeping there. There may have been a bed of straw to lie on, but that would've all been consumed." Chapman waved his hand toward the flags jutting up from the ground some feet away. "That's the single ignition point. I didn't find another one anywhere else in the barn. And no sign of an accelerant used."

"Like with the other two barn fires. You think it was intentionally set?" Smoke said.

"Yes. Loose, dry straw doesn't spontaneously combust. And if it was spontaneous, say from a wet bale, it would produce a different ignition pattern. And a much larger one besides."

"I've seen that myself a time or two," Smoke said, and the rest of us nodded. We all had.

"It could be what's left of his wallet in his back pocket area," Chapman said, pointing at the slightly-raised rectangle shape there.

"The chances are slim, but it's possible forensics can capture his ID from his license," Smoke said.

Dr. Patrick did a visual examination of the body and took some measurements. Odors of burned wood and other objects were all around us but none of them impacted and assaulted my senses like the victim's body did. Burned human flesh was not something I could adequately describe because there was nothing else like it. Strangely sweet, nauseatingly so. And so thick it was as much a taste as a smell. Combined with the acrid stink of burned hair. Smells that held steadfast in your olfactory for days then were stored in the recesses of your mind and, from time to time, reared their ugly heads, triggered by any number of reasons.

"I don't detect a methane odor that would indicate he had started decaying prior to the fire," Patrick said.

"No," Helsing agreed.

That discounted the theory that he had died days ago and the fire was set to cover his homicide. Decomposing bodies produced a much worse stench due to the bacteria inside the organs that released gases.

The doctors had the bag on the gurney open, ready to receive the body. Patrick picked up a plastic sheet from the gurney, unfolded it partway, and handed two corners to Helsing. Together they opened it and laid it on the ground next to the body. "We'll roll the deceased over onto this and then we'll be able to lift him more easily, do less damage," she said.

Smoke's phone rang, and we all stopped when he looked at the dial and said, "It's the property owner."

Looking at the victim on the ground in front of us and learning it wasn't Woody Nevins filled me with a large measure of relief.

"Mr. Nevins, we're still at your place. . . . Has someone been staying here while you're gone? . . . No? We have a mystery on our hands then. There was a man in your barn when it started on fire. We found his body inside. . . ." Smoke mouthed the words, "Woody is flabbergasted, to say the least." Then he returned to the call. "No idea? . . . That'd be good. We have forms for you to sign for the investigation reports."

I raised my hand and softly asked, "Can I talk to him?"

"Woody, Sergeant Aleckson is here and needs to talk to you."

Smoke handed me the phone. "Hi, Woody, it's Corky."

Woody's voice was strained. "Well Corky, this is a helluva unbelievable deal. I don't know what to do."

"It's a big shock that's for sure, and we'll do what we can to help you. Woody, I wanted to talk to you about something else. I left a message on your home phone Thursday, and I'm wondering if you got it."

"No, I haven't been home since then. I got an answering machine, but never got set up with voicemail. I figure the people that need it have my cell number if they have to get a hold of me when I'm on the road. What was it about?"

"I did a traffic stop on a man who was driving your Jeep, and I wanted to be sure he had your permission to use it," I said.

"Someone stole my *Jeep*?" His voice rose higher with each word.

"It's not gone; it's in your garage. But someone was using it."

"No one asked to use it. Who in the hell was it?"

"A man named Ross Warren. He said he was helping you with some chores."

"What? What chores? I got nobody helping me. Ross Warren, you say? Never heard of him. Wait a minute. When I bought my place from the Grants, I remember meeting their grandson, and I'm pretty sure his name was Ross. But if it's the same guy, I don't know what he'd be doing there now after all these years. And how'd he get a hold of my Jeep anyway?" Woody said.

"Do you keep your garage door locked?"

"Well, sure."

"It wasn't locked when we checked it earlier."

"What in the hell?"

"And I noticed the key was in the ignition," I said.

"You got me there. But I keep the garage locked up."

"Have you changed the locks on the garage since you moved there?"

"Well, no, I guess I haven't. I'm leaving here now, on my way home."

"Okay, we'll see you later."

The MEs and investigators waited until the call ended then I recounted Woody's side of the conversation.

"We need to do some digging on Ross Warren," Smoke said.

"He'd be the first person to check on, see where he's at, or if he's our victim here," Chapman said and nodded at the body. "Are we ready to move him?"

"Yes," the doctors said in unison. They were, but I could put off turning him over and viewing the condition of the rest of his body indefinitely.

Patrick, Helsing, Smoke, and I got into position with our hands underneath the body to lift and roll it away from us. I had his calf and knee area, Patrick was next with the thighs, Smoke had the pelvic area and middle torso, and Helsing had the shoulder and head. I felt muscle and flesh on the underside of his legs.

Patrick gave the direction, "On the count of three. One, two, three." We lifted and rolled. I was taken aback by the contrast between the charred black backside of him and the mostly unburned white front. There was a collection of audible reactions from all five of us. I think mine was a sucked-in breath, like a wheeze, and I couldn't say what came out of the others' mouths.

The victim's eyes and mouth were open and his expression was much like the subject in Edvard Munch's painting, "The Scream." Even his hands were melded to the sides of his head in a similar way. An involuntary reaction to fear in the one, and what looked like a protective act in the other. The expression on his face captured the horror he must have felt and seeing it, I felt it too. I was fairly confident I knew who he was, but he had changed dramatically since last we'd met.

By unspoken agreement we paused to give our victim a moment of silent respect. I sent up a prayer, and maybe the others did too. The clothes on the back and sides of his body had been burned into his skin, and the hair on his head was gone. The fire had extinguished when it reached the dirt floor of the barn, but there wasn't a neat line of where it had stopped burning on the various parts of his body by any means. His lower legs were more impacted than his thighs, no doubt from his movement and ending position.

"I think this is Ross Warren," I said.

Smoke shook his head. "If it is and Woody Nevins doesn't know who Ross Warren is for sure, then we've got a helluva puzzle to put together."

"Starting with the fact that Warren, a man Woody didn't know, was driving his Jeep without his knowledge or permission," I said.

"That's true enough."

"We can get fingerprints and DNA from the Jeep and compare them to his." I indicated the victim.

"You think we can get fingerprints from him, Doc?" Smoke asked Bridey Patrick.

Her eyes zeroed in on the victim's hands. "It's possible. We'll find out soon enough."

Smoke turned back to me. "What'd Warren give as his address?"

"It's in Chaska." A city in neighboring Carver County.

He nodded. "Good to have a place to start, see if he lived with someone we can talk to. Or neighbors who can give us names of next of kin to verify his ID."

"A loved one should not see him in this condition," Dr. Patrick said.

"I agree. I've never seen anything like this," Smoke said.

Agreed.

Chapman sucked in a small breath. "Unfortunately, I have."

Dr. Helsing, Chapman, and Smoke snapped photos. I kept my eyes on what they were doing instead of on the victim. I'd carry his image with me until I took my dying breath. The whole scene was distressing and unreal at the same time. The unkempt man whose story I'd wondered about two days ago had left this earth in a horrific way. Who was he, really? Why had he told me Woody Nevins was his friend? And why was he helping himself to Woody's Jeep and likely sleeping in his barn when Woody was away?

The doctors concentrated on the victim's body and the task ahead of them.

"His organs will largely be intact and will tell us about any medical conditions, if there are drugs or alcohol in his system, and the cause of death. The manner of death? At this point we can't rule out suicide, accidental, or homicide," Dr. Patrick said.

"Evidence of trauma, a knife or gunshot wound, blow to the head, or poison in his system would give us reason to investigate it as a homicide," Smoke said, verbalizing the obvious.

"Yes," Dr. Helsing said.

"Keep us in the loop, and we'll see where the investigation goes from here," Chapman said.

Dr. Patrick nodded then stepped back, and the rest of us lifted the victim-laden sheet and placed it in the body bag on the gurney. Helsing took care of the tucking in and the zipping up. The finality of that got me every time no matter how many times I'd witnessed it.

Chapman stayed behind, looking for more clues and evidence while Smoke and I helped the doctors put the gurney in the back of their van.

The crowds of curiosity seekers dwindled after the ME was gone, but Paul Moore, lead reporter for the *Oak Lea Daily News*, waited patiently on the sidelines for a statement. No metro television station or newspaper reporters had gotten wind of it yet. Old barns burning down didn't capture much beyond regional attention unless livestock perished. So we'd been able to keep the first two fires relatively quiet while we conducted our investigations. But I'd overheard a deputy telling another that people had posted videos of both fires on YouTube. People loved capturing curiosities on their cell phone video cameras.

Smoke and I went over to have a chat with Paul. "Afternoon, Officers. How much can you tell us?" Paul cut to the chase.

"Not much at this point, Paul. We got one deceased, but no identification yet," Smoke said.

"Man, woman?"

"The unidentified victim has been taken to the Midwest Medical Examiner's Office. That's all I can tell you at this point. The investigation has barely begun."

"Are you drawing a connection to the other two fires here this week?" Paul said.

"Not at this point, no. We'll continue to look into it and hopefully will be able to answer all your questions in the not-too-distant future. But now it's time for us to get back to work."

"Okay, well thanks for that much anyhow." Paul closed his notepad, but held onto his pen. I don't think I'd ever seen him without one in his hand.

Weber walked over after Paul Moore and a few other onlookers drove away. "The gawkers have dwindled, Detective. Do you want Mandy and me to hang around a while yet?" Zubinski was standing guard by the driveway.

"No. We're covered here. The fire investigator will be here as long as it takes, and I'll stay to assist him. And then we'll put our crime scene team to work," Smoke said.

"I want to talk to Woody Nevins when he gets home, and that should be soon." I looked at my watch: 2:52 p.m. Weber looked at me, squinted, and then nodded.

That made Smoke focus first on Weber then on me. "You two have a hot date, or what?"

Weber jerked his head back and lifted his eyebrows. "The sergeant and me? Hot date? Nah."

"You look like you're up to something," Smoke said.

I shrugged. "We're always up to something."

Smoke shot us a dubious look. "No doubt. Well, I'll be in the barn if you need me."

"You usually have a better poker face than that, Vince," I said.

"What do you want me to say? The detective's got a way of peering at you that makes you think you should spill your guts whether you want to or not."

I chuckled. "Yes he does. Anyway, I should clear here in an hour or so. That'll give me plenty of time to make it to River's Edge by five forty-five."

"Where you'll be hanging out in the parking lot, spying on Darcie, and watching to see how she walks?"

"That's where. I won't tell you what I'll be driving and we'll see if you can spot me."

"Ha!" Weber tapped my arm then smiled as he walked away.

22

Belle and Birdie

Belle climbed up the boards that were nailed as steps on their favorite tree and sat down next to Birdie who was looking up at the clouds moving in the sky. It was one of the activities she seemed to love the most.

Belle moved in closer to Birdie and nudged her arm. "Birdie, we did it. We accomplished another one of our goals. I can't believe the way it worked out. How it all just fell into our hands. We'll keep working on the other things along the way until we're done. How does that sound?"

Birdie moved her head in a small nod, and Belle noticed her lips curve up slightly. It warmed her heart knowing her sister was pleased with all she was doing to make things better for her. So she'd be happy again.

"You will be relieved and free when this is all over, won't you, Birdie?"

Birdie laid her head on Belle's shoulder and Belle imagined she heard the word, "Yes," coming from Birdie's mouth. If only that were true.

Nothing would bring Belle greater joy than hearing Birdie's sweet voice again.

23

Woody Nevins' vehicle came to an abrupt stop in front of the crime scene tape crossing the front of the driveway. He and a middle-aged woman got out and stood by the side of the truck looking at the burned remains of the barn. Woody was a huge man, inches over six feet and carried plenty of girth. The top of his companion's head didn't quite touch his shoulders. She was on the chubby side with dark brown, shoulder-length hair held behind her ears by a headband.

Woody's mouth dropped open, and he shook his head back and forth, again and again. The woman reached an arm around his waist and leaned into him. They stared for a bit longer until Woody noticed me, and I waved him over. He surprised me when he pushed his hefty body into a lumbering jog around the tape and met me by his garage. The woman followed behind him at a walking pace.

"This is unreal. I can't get my brain to register any of it," Woody said.

I had removed the protective clothing I'd worn in the barn and felt comfortable giving him a little hug. "No, that'll take some time. I'm so sorry this happened to you."

He nodded. "Thanks, Corky." When the woman stepped in beside him he turned his upper body toward her, like she'd surprised him. "Oh. Corky, this is my girlfriend, Delia. Delia, Corky Aleckson. She's a sergeant with the sheriff's department here."

We shook hands, and I got the impression she was a rock-solid person, the kind Woody would need going forward. The kind I hoped Sybil had by her side. Why did my thoughts keep returning to Sybil and her well-being? "It's good to meet you, Delia."

She managed a little smile. "Likewise, except that it was because of this."

"So what do I do now?" Woody asked.

I pointed at Smoke who was picking up the clipboard from the hood of his unmarked squad. "The detective has the release forms for you to sign. What you agreed to verbally, giving us permission to search."

Smoke joined us. After meeting Delia, he gave Woody his sympathies and then got his signature on the fire marshal consent form. "You probably want to have a look around, huh?" Smoke said.

"I guess I do, and I don't." Tears formed in Woody's eyes. "We had horses when my son was young. But after he graduated college and moved away, we haven't had any animals in the barn. But I was sort of attached to it anyhow. Lots of great memories from those days."

Delia slid her hand into his and gave his arm a gentle pull. He looked down at her and nodded. They acted like a couple that had been married for years, like they were a team that knew what the other one needed. "Let's do it," Woody said.

Smoke led the pack, and I brought up the rear. Chapman was finishing his tasks and packing up his tools. Smoke introduced them then said, "Woody here is going to take a look-see then we can have a chat with him."

"Sounds good," Chapman said.

Smoke pointed out the areas Chapman had marked where the fire started and where the body of the yet-to-be-identified man had been found. Woody was in a state of total disbelief, trying to comprehend how someone had gained access to his property without his knowledge or tipping off his neighbors. "Why me, and who is this Ross Warren anyway? Did he think because I was gone so much it was okay to use my property? Don't get me wrong, I wouldn't have wished the guy any harm, especially nothing like this. But I'm thinking he could've been the one that started the fire in the first place."

That was true. He may have, and it might turn out he'd set the other barns on fire as well. Could he have been the one on my back property who lost the lighter? He had a slight build, like that person had. But given his age, he could not have served in the Navy during either of the wars in question. He wasn't Buzz.

My cell phone dinged, and it was the message I'd been waiting for from Communications. I'd asked for Ross Warren's driver's license photo, and it had come through. The photo was several years old showing a younger, longer-haired

Warren than I'd met two days prior. The burn victim had no hair, and that wasn't the only component that had altered his appearance dramatically. "Excuse me, Detective Dawes and Investigator Chapman. I have something to show you," I said. We stepped off to the side and I handed my phone to Smoke. "It's Ross Warren's DL photo, five years ago."

Smoke enlarged the image and studied it before passing it to Chapman. "Could be," Chapman said.

"Yep, could be," Smoke said. "Have Communications print some copies for us to show folks when we pay them a visit later on."

"Will do." We, as in Smoke and me? Maybe I wouldn't be spying on Darcie after all. Weber would understand and give me a pass. I called Robin in Communications and passed on the request, and she said she'd have them ready for us.

We returned to where Woody and Delia were standing. "I noticed you have a table on the patio by the house. Why don't we go sit over there so we can talk," Smoke said.

We once again followed the detective and took our places on the padded chairs surrounding the glass-top table.

Smoke, Chapman, and I all produced memo pads and pens from various pockets, ready for recording action. We noted the other barn fires in Blackwood Township and asked Woody if he believed there was any connection between the three. He didn't. Was his barn locked? No. Then Chapman asked him if he had any idea why his barn would have burned down. No idea. There were no chemicals stored in it that could have ignited. Smoke asked if he knew why Ross Warren was on his property, helping himself to his vehicle and who knew what else. He had no clue about that either. "I know my garage was locked. I checked it before I left Monday morning."

I brought up the photo of Warren on my phone and passed it across to him. Woody squinted and angled his head one way then the next while he fixed his attention on the image. "It could be the Ross I told you about, Corky. The grandson of the folks I bought this farm from twenty-some-odd years ago." He bent his head and pinched the area between his eyes. "When you work with a realtor, they take care of everything, and you don't have a lot of contact with the owners. But we had a second look at the place before we made an offer, and the Grants were home. That's when we met them. Their grandson was here. I think he was staying with them, and if memory serves me right, he had just graduated from high school."

"Do you remember anything about him? Anything that sticks out in your mind?" I said.

"Yeah, as a matter of fact, I got the impression there had been some kind of disagreement between him and his grandparents. You could sense the tension, but Ross kind of hung in the background. To tell you the truth, I didn't think all that much of it at the time, which is why I pretty much forgot about it until now. Teenagers aren't always on their best behavior." Woody lifted his broad shoulders in a shrug.

"Woody, you said you keep your garage door locked," Chapman reiterated.

"I do."

"And you left on this last tour Monday?"

"Yes, early in the morning."

Chapman's eyebrows came together. "And you're sure the service door in the garage was locked before you left?"

"Yes. I always keep it locked and don't use that door much anyway. I got my garage door opener for the overhead when I need one of my vehicles."

"I see you have a security system for your house." Chapman pointed at the notice posted on Woody's back door.

"Yes I do."

"Have you changed the locks on either your house or the garage since you've lived here?"

"I got new doors and locks on the house, but not the garage."

"There was no sign the lock had been tampered with, so that indicates Warren had a key," I said.

Woody shook his head. "But if he did, why would he use it to get into my garage after all these years?"

Smoke looked up from his memo pad. "There are many crimes of opportunity, committed on a regular basis, for a variety of reasons. Maybe Warren came back to relive some childhood memories and instead of knocking on your door and asking to have a look-see around your place, he helped himself to it instead. Why he took your Jeep is anyone's guess."

"And if Corky hadn't stopped him, I wonder if I would have even found out?" Woody said.

"Along with diligence and hard work, there's still a lot of what some might call lucky breaks in this business," Chapman said.

"We'll need to process your Jeep, Woody. Check for fingerprints and DNA. We know it was Ross Warren who was driving it two days ago. We don't yet have proof positive he was the one in your barn, and the test results will tell us yea or nay," Smoke said.

Woody kept shaking his head. "Sure. I still can't believe any of it. How can a guy think it's okay to break into another guy's garage and use his vehicle? It's got me wondering if he's done it before."

"If we find Ross Warren out there somewhere we'll arrest him for trespassing and the unauthorized use of a motor vehicle and ask him those very questions," Smoke said.

"And I want to talk to him about it, too," Woody said.

"Right." Smoke held the clipboard with a number of forms on it. He fingered through until he found the one he needed then slid it over to Woody. "Our crime scene team has been waiting for your permission to search your vehicle, if you'll sign this for them." He handed him a pen.

Woody briefly scanned the document, scribbled out his signature, then gave it back to Smoke.

"Good deal. We'll get right on it," Smoke said.

I stood up. "I'll go let them know."

Before I walked away, I heard Smoke say, "A word of caution, Woody. The media will no doubt start pressing you for information, but you need to keep what we've discussed private for now. We don't have an identity on the victim, and we can't have any false statements or rumors floating around out there."

"I understand."

Deputies Brian Carlson and Todd Mason were in the Winnebago County Sheriff's Mobile Crime Unit. The door was open, and I climbed the steps and poked my head in. "What are you guys doing?"

"Killing time, so we're taking inventory of our supplies. We've been extra busy this week and have used up a lot," Mason said. He pulled a big hankie out of his back pocket and ran it around his head and the back of his neck.

"I'm here to deliver the good news that your wait is over. The owner gave us permission to process his Jeep."

"Sweet," Carlson said.

"Good deal," Mason said.

"Let's get our gear on and the collection kits together," Carlson said.

Smoke helped Chapman load the last of his equipment into his van then Chapman hopped in and away he went. Woody and Delia had gone into the house. I thought about Weber and the day, time, and place he'd set to meet with Darcie and checked my watch: 3:48. I could still get ready, borrow Gramps' car, and be in position by 5:45. Unless Smoke needed me to accompany him to Chaska to help with interviews.

"Mason and Carlson will be at it for a while. You up for some more OT?" Smoke asked me. That answered my question.

"Sure. But if we're going to Chaska, I need to shower first. I can barely stand myself, even in the great outdoors."

"Yeah, I know I stink to high heaven. You head on home. I'm going to check in with Mason and Carlson, and then talk to Woody again. I'll meet you at the office in forty minutes? You can lose the uniform, dress like a detective."

"Good. That'll be about a gazillion degrees cooler."

"Ya think?"

The inside of my squad car was hotter than a pistol. I started it up, cranked on the air conditioner, and then got out again to let it cool for a few minutes. I needed to touch base with Weber and dialed his number. "Hey, Sarge, what's up?"

"Sorry to have to bail on you, Vince, but I need to help Smoke with the investigation, see if we can get an ID on the victim."

"Ah, geez. Well, you know what? That's okay. Now I just gotta decide whether I should meet Darcie after all."

"I think you should. You need to cut the ties with her. She needs to understand that she can't keep bugging you."

"I know, I know. Since I didn't find anything with her DNA on it at my place, I'll see if I can snatch her wine glass or something."

"That'll work, unless it doesn't. What about telling her about the dead rabbit and the blood, see how she reacts."

"I thought about that too. Maybe I will. But I was sort of waiting to see what the DNA test tells us."

"Either way. If it turns out she's the one who left the rabbits all we could charge her with is trespassing. The veterinarian didn't find an obvious cause of death for the one left at my place. No poison, no injuries. The blood drop, on the other hand, could constitute harassment. And the phone calls and messages fit the definition of stalking in the statute."

"I know. She's gotta stop that shit."

"Vince, how about you conduct a covert operation of your own? Take a short video for me with your cell phone. Your personal cell."

"Ah, geez. I don't think that'll work, but I'll see what I can do."

"Good luck tonight. I'll hold good thoughts for you." And say a prayer.

"Thanks, Sarge. I'll catch you later and hopefully give you some good news."

We hung up, and I climbed back into my much cooler vehicle, headed home, showered, dressed in a light blue button-down shirt and navy pants, took care of Queenie, and was back at the office ahead of Smoke.

I went straight to Communications for the printouts. Robin had gone off-duty, but Jody knew where they were. In the out-going tray by the fax machine on the front desk. "Thanks," I called out and carried the stack to the squad room.

I sat down at the table and studied Ross Warren's photo for the umpteenth time. He had aged substantially from his early to late thirties, an indication he'd had a hard life, or a chemical addiction, or serious physical or mental-health problems. Or all of the above. People with mental health issues often self-medicated, and that led to a multitude of complications, like problems with family and friends, job retention, and money for food and housing. We'd see what the MEs uncovered at autopsy.

Smoke sent me a text asking where I was then found me a minute later. "Feeling better?" he said.

"You know it."

"I do too." When he stepped in beside my chair our clean-soap aromas told me we smelled better too. "The enlarged photos of Warren?" He picked up one of the printouts and looked it over. "And this is his current address?"

"That's what he said."

"Let's see if we can either track him down, or find someone who knows him."

But our efforts proved to be exercises in futility.

24

Belle and Birdie

"Birdie, the officers have finished up at the farm. Everyone's gone home," Belle said.

Birdie turned to her with a blank look on her face.

"I was there and saw them. That detective who didn't help us, the sergeant who likes snooping around but didn't figure out what we needed, and the other deputies, including the one who called us that name that hurt us so bad. They were all there."

Birdie nodded, and her frown left small creases on her forehead.

"I don't know, Birdie. Now that we've taken care of one of our true enemies, I don't feel the same need to go after the ones who were more incompetent than anything else."

Birdie nudged Belle with her shoulder.

"You think we should? Well, I guess we have a good enough supply in the freezer. I'll see what I can do. Some are easier to get to than others, you know."

Birdie looked up at the cloudless sky, and it sounded to Belle like she sighed.

25

We had no problem locating the four-plex listed on Ross Warren's driver's license. The problem was the man who opened the door told us he had lived there for three years and had no idea who the man in the photo was. Nor had he ever met anyone named Ross Warren.

"Do you happen to know if any of your neighbors have lived here longer than you have?" Smoke said.

"The couple just below me was here when I moved in. The other two have changed renters, one of them at least twice that I know of," he said.

"We'll check with them. And what's your name and date of birth, sir?"

Smoke thanked him after he got the information, and we went back down the stairs. He knocked on the steel door of a first-floor apartment, and a woman about my age opened the door. Her eyes widened when Smoke held up his badge and gave our names and department. "What is it?" she said.

"We have a couple of questions about a former neighbor of yours. Ross Warren. Lived upstairs?" Smoke said.

Her look changed from alarm to apathy. "What do you want to know?"

"Maybe we could step inside for a minute," Smoke said.

"Okay." She moved aside, and we went in. The apartment was decorated with too many Precious Moments figurines for my taste, but to each their own. She stood by the kitchen counter, so we did too. Smoke got her name and date of birth then asked her about Ross Warren and if she knew when he'd moved away, or knew of any family members. She said he'd moved out right before the current tenant moved in, and didn't know much about him at all.

"To tell you the truth, I kind of avoided him. He struck me as a little creepy."

"In what way?" Smoke said.

"The way he'd stare at me made me uncomfortable," she said.

"Did he ever say anything offensive?"

"No, nothing like that. But my husband and I agreed to keep our distance. Not very neighborly, I know."

"It's good to follow your instincts, because you don't always know about people," Smoke said, and I nodded.

"Yes. So why are you looking for him, if I can ask?"

"We're working on an investigation, and his name came up," he said.

"Oh. So that's what you meant when you said it was good I followed my instincts."

Smoke smiled. "Ah, not specifically, but I guess you get the point."

"**W**ell this is a fine kettle of fish," Smoke muttered when we were back in his car.

"I had a feeling Warren wasn't being truthful when I asked him if the address on his DL was current. He said the address was right. Not exactly a straight answer."

Smoke started his car and headed toward home. "Not to mention that he out-and-out lied about helping Woody and having permission to use his car."

"I know. But I couldn't reach Woody, and the Jeep wasn't in the system as stolen, so I had no reason to detain him. I just wish I had followed up, stopped by Woody's place yesterday, or even this morning."

"Twenty-twenty hindsight, as they say. But Woody wouldn't have been there anyhow, and chances are slim to none you'd have found Ross Warren. He must have kept a very low profile to not have stirred the neighbors' suspicions."

"It makes you wonder where the guy has been the last three years, and when he showed up at Woody's place in the first place. How long did he fly under the radar?" I said.

"Could be he's been homeless. Moving around. That camper's pack Chapman found indicates as much."

"And no vehicles registered to him."

"Maybe he has a regular circuit, and Woody's place is one of his stops. He's got a key to his garage, helps himself to the Jeep when he figures it's safe. Crashes in the barn. Woody doesn't use it, so what the hell?" Smoke said.

"The irony in all this is, if Woody had gotten my message Warren would still be alive."

"Hey, we're talking like the body in the barn in fact belongs to him. And we don't have confirmation of that yet."

"And if it isn't, then we've got an even bigger kettle of fish."

"No doubt." Smoke's phone rang. "It's the ME's office," he relayed as he pushed Talk. "Detective Dawes. . . . You have? That's good. . . . Tomorrow at nine? We haven't been able to track down Warren, or his next-of kin yet, but we'll keep looking. I may do a media release of his photo, ask the public's help locating him, or someone in his family. . . . All right, well hang tight. . . . Thanks." He disconnected. "They're getting restless and would like to autopsy our barn body tomorrow."

"In the morning, huh?"

"Yep, so we'll see if we can find his family before then. They've done an external exam. The good news is they were able to get a couple of usable fingerprints and a DNA sample. They talked a tech into going in to clean up the prints so he can enter them into the database. We'll get the latent prints we collected from Woody's steering wheel to the lab for comparison. But that won't happen until Monday, and it'll take a while to sort through them, weed out the partials. And separate Woody's from any others. They'll get rolling on the DNA test Monday too."

"Wow, I'm amazed they got readable prints," I said.

"Yeah, and they also got a key, probably to Woody's garage, and what little was left of the wallet from his back pocket. The DL had melted, so there was nothing on it to read."

"Figures. But the key didn't melt?"

"No, it's older, made of brass, and they tell me the fire would've had to be two thousand degrees to melt it. As hot as it must've been, I guess it didn't reach that point."

"Really? We can find out if it fits in Woody's garage door lock."

"Yes. We'll get Warren's photo in the papers and on the department's Facebook page. We've gotten a bunch of hits when we've been looking for leads, like the time when we found that man with Alzheimer's in about an hour."

"That was fast. Someone out there must know Ross Warren."

"Let's hope. And we'll keep digging."

My personal cell phone buzzed, alerting me I had a text message. I fished it out of my back pocket. It was from Vince Weber's personal cell phone with the single word, "Her," and had an attached video. I clicked on it and watched the side view of a dark-haired woman standing tall, walking with deliberate strides toward the supper club. I played it again. With her purposeful gait, I couldn't imagine her as either the beekeeper creeper or the tree-to-tree creeper.

"What are you looking at?" Smoke said.

"Oh, just a little experiment Weber did for me."

"Is that what the two of you were talking about earlier?"

"Pretty much."

"You're going to keep me in suspense?" he said.

"You'll think it's stupid."

"Is it?"

"Maybe. All right, well, you know Weber's sister-in-law has been after him, and he suspected that she's the one who left the rabbits and blood drop. With the video of the one at my doorstep and seeing the person on my back property, I asked him to take a video of Darcie walking, to compare them."

"And?"

"After watching his video, I doubt it was Darcie on my property either time."

"That'll be a relief for Weber," he said.

"For sure. And he'll be even more relieved when she finds someone else to fall in love with and is finally out of his hair. If he had any, that is."

Smoke cracked a grin then frowned. "He may have to file a restraining order."

"He doesn't want to do that on a few different levels. His in-laws aren't that crazy about him in the first place, she's his wife's sister, and he thinks he should be able to figure out the best way to break up with her—convince her that their rendezvous was not the start of something bigger. He's talking to her tonight, so I'm praying it goes well."

"No doubt."

I watched the landscape change as we climbed out of the river valley to higher ground. "Thinking about Ross Warren, I can ask Gramps if he knows anything else about the Grants or any others in the family," I said.

"Sure, go ahead and do that. When we get back to the office, I'll get rolling on the media blitz."

As it turned out, Smoke had success with Facebook before I had a chance to talk to Gramps. It was 7:23 p.m. when I pulled into my driveway and let Communications know I was 10-7, off duty. Queenie needed attention, so I released her from her kennel, and she pranced around, happy as could be. I filled her water bowl and carried it to the back deck then sat down and watched her antics until she had spent her pent-up energy and ran up the steps to join me.

"Have a drink, girl. I need to send Vince a message. I can't stand the suspense wondering how things are going between him and Darcie." I typed a text asking him to call me when he was free. "Vince's deal is one big deal, and then we've got John Carl and Sara out on a dinner date for another. What is our little world coming to?"

Smoke phoned a moment later. "Not twenty minutes after I put up the post on Facebook I got a call. And you'll never guess who it was."

"Someone I know?"

"Someone you very recently met. Earlier today, in fact. Angela Simmonds."

I jumped up so fast it startled Queenie. "Angela Simmonds. Are you kidding me? She follows the Winnebago County Sheriff's Facebook page?"

"Should that surprise us? Thousands of people do. Over ten thousand, in fact."

"I should check it out myself sometime. See what the chief deputy posts. So what did Angela say?"

"Brace yourself for this one. She thinks the photo is that of her cousin, the one and only Ross Warren. She hadn't seen him since her family moved away all those years ago, but she said he always stuck in her memory for some reason. So she showed her mother the post. Her mother agreed it looked a lot like him, but she shouldn't upset her father by asking him," Smoke said.

I sunk back down on my chair. "Angela's cousin is Ross Warren? Does that mean he's Sybil's cousin too?"

"I didn't specifically ask her that, but yes, that would be the case. Angela said her grandmother and Ross's grandmother were sisters."

"And so was Sybil's. Unbelievable," I said.

"I was blown away trying to put it together—the ramifications of three fires on properties owned by sisters. Formerly owned, that is, in two of the cases."

"Going back to the issue of the families 'breaking up.' I wonder if whatever it was that caused the rift way back when is finally coming back to haunt them?"

"Like someone in the family seeking revenge? That'd be more likely if they all still owned the properties, but the Hardings are the only ones who still do," he said.

"I know. It's a big jumbled mess. What did Angela say about Ross's family?"

"She remembered that his parents died when he was a teenager, and he went to live with his grandparents."

"Any siblings?"

"No. And since the families are estranged she doesn't know if anyone else—like the Hardings—have been in contact with him."

"Hmm. Sybil would've been very young when the Grants moved off the farm. But they stayed in Oak Lea until they died. Maybe she'd know where Ross went after he graduated," I said.

"See if you can get a hold of her and ask her that."

"Will do."

"I'm going to pay a visit to the Simmonds' and have a heart to heart with Angela's father about their feud. You got his name?"

It seemed like days ago when I'd been at their house for the domestic. Another report to write up tomorrow. "It's Damon Backstrom. But his wife mentioned getting a hotel room for the night to let things calm down between them."

"When I talked to Angela, her mother was there. I can't pussyfoot around with Backstrom and whatever big family secret they got going on. Not if it interferes with our investigation. I'll swing by their house, see if he's there."

"Good luck."

"Thanks. And Doc Patrick called about the victim's fingerprints. They're not in the system," he said.

"Huh. We'll see if they match any the crime scene team got from Woody's steering wheel."

"Right. Oh, and in case you didn't see it, the chief deputy sent out a blast email that the metro newscasters are chasing the story about the barn fire fatality, and we all need to keep a lid on it until we ID the victim and figure out what we've got going on here. It was on the five o'clock and six o'clock reports."

"So the world knows by now. No, I didn't see his email, but figured as much, per policy."

Queenie watched me like she was waiting for the other shoe to drop as I put my phone away. She knew when I was troubled and trying to figure out the right thing to do, the best course of action. I stood up, and she wagged her tail. "Let's go see Gramps before he gets ready for bed. He might have the answers we're looking for."

I drove the GTO over, and when I spotted my mother's car in his driveway it made me consider the option of talking to Gramps another time. We hadn't talked for a couple of days, and it dawned on me that Mother hadn't called me about the fatal barn fire. I guessed John Carl staying with her had helped divert her attention.

Gramps and Mother were sitting in the kitchen eating a bowl of ice cream. Maple nut, a favorite for both of them. "Hello, dear," Mother said with a tiny smile. "And you too, Queenie."

"There's my girls," Gramps said, and a little maple nut escaped out of the side of his mouth when his smile broadened. He used the back of his hand to catch it. I grinned when Gramps referred to Queenie and me as 'his girls.' Now I was lumped in with my dog.

"Help yourself to some ice cream, Corky," Gramps said. And that's when my stomach let out a growling protest.

I'd had yogurt and a granola bar for breakfast, but apparently the traumatic events of the day had banished any thoughts of eating from my mind. I rubbed my middle. "As much as I love ice cream, I'm going to need some real food first."

My mother was out of her chair in a flash. "You haven't had dinner?"

Or lunch. "Not yet."

"I brought over a pot roast for Gramps, and there is plenty left. It's in the fridge. Let me get it for you."

I didn't object, and when Mother set the pan and a plate on the counter, I dished up a good-sized helping of beef, potatoes, and carrots. I sat down at the table with Gramps and dug in. The pot roast was still warm and I was in comfort-food lover's heaven with every forkful.

"Corinne, is it any wonder why I worry about you? Besides having one of the most dangerous jobs on earth, you don't have very good eating habits." She hadn't said much about my job or my eating habits for a long time, so her little nag gave me hope she was recovering, healing from her emotional wounds.

"I know, Mother. You're right." Agreeing was easy when I was feeling downright grateful to be chowing down the best meal I'd had in a long time. I took the last bite and set my fork on the plate. "Thanks, Mom. That was really good." Not to mention, it was one of my top five favorite meals.

Gramps pointed his spoon my way. "I heard all those fire truck sirens blaring close by today, and when Leroy stopped in, he said we'd another barn fire in our township. The old Grant place."

I should have told them about it first thing. "Yes we did, sad to say. It's one of the ones your father helped build, Gramps. So it's strange we had just talked about it."

Mother clicked her tongue. "Oh my, that is sad. I was at the shop and one of my customers told me about it. Woody Nevins' barn this time." My mother was interested in neighborhood happenings, but was not a fire-chaser.

"So neither of you caught the five o'clock or six o'clock news tonight?" Tragic news traveled the world at lightning speed, but didn't always reach the locals until later.

Gramps shook his head and Mother said, "No. I left the shop at six and picked up the meal I had ready in the crock pot at home then came right here."

"Someone was in Woody's barn and perished in the fire." Mother's hand flew to her heart. "Not Woody?"

"Not Woody. But we're not sure who it is yet," I said.

"I can't believe I didn't hear about that. But I guess the few customers I had later in the afternoon were weekend lake people, not from here, and must not have heard that either. Oh my, that's just awful."

"It sure is," Gramps said.

I leaned closer to them. "Maybe you two can help us with the investigation."

"How?" The look on Mother's face would best be described as pained.

"We're trying to find someone who knows the Grants' grandson, Ross Warren."

"Ross, you say?" Mother said. She shook her head. "I remember hearing that he lived with his grandparents after his parents were killed, but I don't know what became of him."

Gramps shook his head too. "No. As I recall, the Grants kept to themselves."

"Did you know they were related to the Hardings and the Backstroms?"

"No, I didn't know that," Mother said.

"The three women—Mrs. Grant and Mrs. Harding and Mrs. Backstrom—were sisters," I said.

"You learn something new every day," Gramps said.

Mother had sent a bowl of ice cream home with me "for later." I was eating it slowly, savoring every bite, when the phone calls started.

The first was from Vince Weber. "I'm free," he said.

"You broke it off with Darcie?"

"You said to call you when I was free. As far as being free of Darcie, let's hope she got the message loud and clear."

"Tell me about it, what you said, what she said."

"First, you gotta tell me what you thought when you watched the video," he said.

"I don't think it was Darcie who was on my property. Either time."

He blew out a breath loud enough to rattle my eardrum. "Okay, well that's good news. Anyhow, I decided to take kind of a congenial approach, asked her to forgive me for leading her on, and told her it would never work between us. She argued about it for a while, said she thinks it would, on and on. Finally I got tougher and said, 'If you're doing weird shit like leaving blood and dead things on my steps then it's time to stop.' Her eyes got as big as two moons, and her mouth dropped open so far I could see her tonsils.

"And then Darcie said, 'What are you talking about?' And I said, 'Did you?' And she said, 'Why would I? That sounds kind of crazy.' And I'm thinking, well duh. But she had me mostly convinced she was telling the truth. She got a little miffed, thinking I was thinking she was doing that stuff. It doesn't mean she didn't, but if it's her blood on my windshield, we'll find that out at least."

"You got something to test?" I said.

"Yeah, I lifted the fork and napkin she was using."

"Vincent."

"I'll return them to the club when they're done. Then I scared her, at least a little, when I said she could be arrested on stalking charges, and I had the proof on my phone with all the calls and messages she's been bombarding me with," he said.

"What'd she say?"

"Not much. I think it's gotta sink in for a while, and then we'll see what happens."

"She didn't kiss you goodnight?" I couldn't resist.

"Ha! She didn't even try."

My ice cream had melted so I picked up the bowl, drank the liquid, and was chewing on the walnuts when Sara called. "I thought you should know your brother John is really fun to be with, one on one. We made decorating decisions and had the best time at dinner. I haven't had a better date in two years. At least."

I finished crunching on the last walnut and swallowed. "Gosh, Sara, I didn't know you'd lowered your standards or expectations that much." When I laughed, she did too. "I just don't think I've ever used 'John Carl' and 'fun' in the same sentence. Serious, yes, fun, not so much."

"He has that serious and steady side, but he has a fun one too. And he seems to know something about everything," she said.

"He has been memorizing facts all of his life. I suppose some of those facts could be considered fun."

"Be nice."

"I'm just giving you grief. And it's undeserved, so I apologize. John Carl really is a great guy, but he's my big brother so don't get into any mushy stuff," I said.

"I won't, if there's ever any mushy stuff to get into. And I hope there will be."

"I quit listening."

"All right, I can take a hint. Catch you later."

My phone alerted me that I had an incoming call. "Sleep tight," I told her then I pushed the talk button to take Smoke's call. "Hello, Detective. How'd it go?"

"Best described as frustrating and irritating," he said.

"What happened?"

"I found out that Angela's folks had indeed gone into town to spend the night at a hotel, but she didn't know which one. I spent a little time with Angela, asking if she had the names of any other family members. She did not. So I asked her if she'd found out any more details about the family feud, and she said her father wouldn't talk about it. I got her father's cell phone number, but that hasn't done me any good yet because he didn't answer, nor has he returned my call."

"Did you check with the hotels?" I said.

"I called, but they wouldn't give out guest information over the phone. They'd need to see my badge to believe it was me."

"They're following their rules, protecting their guests."

"I was going to pay the Backstroms a visit, but figured it'd make them less likely to talk to me if I did. So it's back to the old waiting game. I ran a criminal history search on Ross Franklin Warren. Nothing. And did an Internet search. It showed him at that Chaska address on White Pages site, but no 'may be related to' list like most people have. Aside from the Backstrom clan, it looks like Warren's closest relatives are his great aunt and her son in Canada, Sybil's dad in New Mexico, and Sybil herself. But none of them are on speaking terms. So there you have it," he said.

"I'll find out what Sybil knows about Warren, if anything. We were supposed to meet today, but I'm seeing her tomorrow instead."

"Ah yes, the elusive Sybil and her hard-to-reach grandmother." It had been a difficult day, and he was getting crabby.

"Smoke, if you weren't on call, I'd suggest that you imbibe a good, stiff drink right about now."

"Don't tempt me," he said.

26

Sundays were quiet in the office, but calls for service ran the gamut. In the summertime, hundreds of campers and boat-laden trailers pulled behind vehicles, passed through the county after the weekend at cabins and resorts. Once in a while, we spotted one without current tabs, or that posed a safety problem.

Domestics were fairly common among couples who spent a day or two together drinking too much. Sunday mornings the calls started coming in. Many teenagers were bored, doing things they shouldn't be doing, and getting into trouble. Some of them ran away for any number of reasons and frantic parents called us for help finding them.

I spent the first hour of my shift writing reports on the fatal fire and the domestic from the day before. After filing them, I was heading for the door when Smoke walked in, looking weary but smelling fresh. "Got a minute?" he said.

I followed him to his cubicle. "Did you get any sleep?"

His shoulder lifted. "A couple hours. Then my day got off to a disturbing start. Someone left the unwelcome gift of a dead rabbit on my doorstep—"

"No way—"

"Luckily, I spotted it before I let Rex out—"

"What'd you do with it?"

"I took photos and bagged it. The vet clinic is closed today, so I threw some ice in a cooler and put it in there," he said.

"Eew. Positioned the same way as mine?"

"Yep."

"What is going on? I thought Weber had kind of a wacky theory about the rabbit and the blood drop, and why he thought Darcie would've left it. Then I got one, and we wondered if she was responsible for that. But now you got one too. What would be the connection?"

"Doesn't fit with Weber's crazy sister-in-law theory, that's for sure."

"No. He actually asked Darcie about it last night, and the way she reacted pretty much convinced him she wasn't the one who did it."

"Backed up by your observations of how she moved in the video Weber sent you," he said.

"Right. I've looked at it a few times now, and Darcie doesn't move the way the one on my back property did. That person was light on his, or her, feet. More on the graceful side. Darcie walks with heavy steps. Since the beekeeper creeper was hunched over, I can't say with a hundred percent certainty it wasn't Darcie, but I'd give it ninety-nine percent.

That one seemed more agile and had lighter steps than Darcie does."

"So if not Darcie, then who, and for what possible reason, as you said? I gotta say I'm surprised someone made it as far as my front steps between, say, ten o'clock last night and six this morning without riling Rex up."

"Unless it was during the two hours you were dead to the world and didn't hear Rex," I said.

"That's near to impossible. He's my home security system."

"Okay, so now three of us have gotten dead rabbits laid on our doorsteps."

Smoke rubbed his chin. "That we know of."

His words gave me pause. "You're saying there could be more than that, but they haven't said anything?"

"Sure."

"I guess. Weber didn't mention it until after he found the blood drop and started wondering. I might not have thought that much of it if Weber hadn't told me about his. And you?"

"Might've, depending on the circumstances, but I doubt I'd have given it a whole lot of thought. I'm going to send out a blast email, see if other deputies have gotten one too."

"Not a bad idea. It makes you wonder."

"It does. Someone's got a bone to pick with cops, and they're out to stump us? I don't know."

"Getting back to the bigger deal, any more on the autopsy?" I said.

"The ME has the statutory obligation to perform it under the circumstances, the fire fatality. So far, we know Ross Warren's closest relative is his great aunt Harding, followed by his father's cousins. Damon Backstrom is the only one of the three around here. I don't want to hold things up too long for Doc Patrick, so if Mr. Backstrom doesn't get back to me real soon, I'll give Angela Simmonds a jingle, see if she can assist me in the matter."

By 8:45 a.m. Angela had assisted him in the matter, and Smoke sent me a message saying he was on his way to visit Damon Backstrom in the lobby of the Country Inn and Suites, and I could join him. When I walked into the hotel I greeted the clerk at the desk then headed over to where Smoke and company—Mr. and Mrs. Backstrom—were seated. Damon cast his eyes downward when he spotted me. I had that affect on people I'd arrested, or come close to arresting.

Kaye Backstrom looked perplexed when I sat down in one of the armchairs in their furniture grouping. She may have thought with two officers there we'd gang up on her husband. I had the disadvantage of not knowing what was said before I got there.

"You know Sergeant Aleckson," Smoke said.

"Good morning," I said.

Kaye mumbled a quiet, "Morning." Damon said nothing. His face and neck were flushed, and if ever a person looked like he'd rather be on a space shuttle to the moon it was him.

Smoke jumped back in like he hadn't been interrupted. "I wouldn't give a rat's ass about your family feud or your buried secrets if three barns that belonged to your mother and her two sisters hadn't burned down in less than a week. Monday, Wednesday, Saturday. Three barns, six days.

"Now I'm concerned there might be another sibling with a barn in Blackwood Township—or somewhere else in Winnebago County—that's going to go up in flames, maybe tomorrow."

Backstrom's color deepened. "There were no other siblings, just the three sisters."

Smoke leaned in closer. "And why would they be targeted in this way? What's the history?"

"I don't know. If there's any connection between the fires, I'd look at Ross Warren."

"Ross Warren?" Smoke lifted his driver's license photo from the table, held it up, and rattled it back and forth. "You told me you haven't had any contact with him for twenty years."

"I haven't. But he was one of those kids who liked to stir up things. Made me wonder what path he'd take in life, the right one or the wrong one."

Smoke leaned back again. "Give me an example of how he stirred things up."

Backstrom shook his head like he didn't have one then said, "One time when he collected eggs for his grandparents he threw them all like baseballs against a tree, wasting the whole bunch and making a mess."

"Sounds like an impulse problem. And vandalism. No other suspects you can think of besides Ross?"

"No. And I don't see how the fight between my cousin and me would've had anything to do with the fires."

Smoke stood and handed Backstrom his card. "We'll let you know what the autopsy reveals, and in the meantime I want you to think long and hard about telling us what caused your feud. A man may have perished because of it."

If that was true, it would take both good police work and being in the right place at the right time to prove it.

Smoke and I walked toward our vehicles, and then he stopped at mine. "Before I got there you talked to the Backstroms about Ross Warren, that we suspect it's his body in the morgue?" I said.

"I did. And making notification to his next of kin. He said Ross had a maternal aunt, his mother's sister, and gave me her name, but doesn't know her current status. I'll run a search. Otherwise, his great-aunt, Mamie Harding, would be Ross's closest relative."

"I'll talk to Sybil, tell her we need to contact her."

"Backstrom was surprised to hear the Hardings were with their son in Canada. He didn't know his cousin lived there. But then why should he since the family doesn't speak?"

"Sometimes I just want to give people the 'life is too short' lecture."

"If it'd do any good, I would do just that." He released a long breath of air, like he was clearing out his lungs. "These fires are getting to be a thorn in my side. Were the three barns randomly chosen? I don't think so, given who they belonged to. There are no more siblings left to target, but are there others in the county our firesetter had a beef with? How in the hell do we figure out who he is and why he's doing this?"

"Without a crystal ball, or some good intelligence, or catching him in the act, I don't know. I've had my area cars beef up patrol on Blackwood Township roads, and I'll see if the sheriff will ask other area cars to swing through a few times tomorrow morning, seeing how all the fires were set in the morning," I said.

"Set by someone hiding in plain sight. I'll be there myself cruising around in one of the impound vehicles."

I smiled. "Incognito, huh?"

"Oh boy. But today I'm scheduled to witness the autopsy."

"It's set then?"

"I talked to Doc Patrick earlier and asked that she hold off until after noon, give us time to make a reasonable attempt to contact family. The family of the man we believe it to be, anyway," Smoke said.

"If Ross Warren shows up now we'll all be a little spooked."

"That we will. You want to witness it with me?"

"No thanks. You are far better at that than I am."

"You're not as grizzled as I am, but you can hold your own. You'll let me know what Sybil has to say?" he said.

"Yes, I'll phone her now."

Smoke took off, and I got into my car and dialed Sybil's number. She answered after the second ring. "Hello, Sergeant. Are you calling about a time to meet?" she said.

"Sure. What's good for you?"

"Um, I'm in Oak Lea now."

"Good. How about we meet at the sheriff's office in ten minutes? Will that work?" I said.

"Oh, okay. Ten minutes."

"The sheriff's office is on the south side of the government center. I'll wait for you on the veranda." I disconnected, pleased that she'd actually answered her phone and agreed to meet without pressing me for the reasons why. I'd delivered enough bad news over the phone of late.

Sybil was waiting by the steps at the bottom of the veranda, holding onto a bicycle, when I pulled into the parking lot. She was dressed in light gray biker shorts and a white t-shirt with a fanny pack around her waist. Her helmet was strapped to the handlebars.

I told Communications I was 10-19—at the office—then got out of the car. "Hello, Sybil. I'm glad this worked out. You rode your bike, but not all the way from Golden Valley, I hope?"

"No, I keep one at my grandparents' house."

And it was a nice one, too. Titanium frame, in the $500 range, at least. One of the deputies had spent over $3,000 for his racing bike, so Sybil's might have cost more than $500. I thought the $200 I'd paid for my mountain bike was plenty. "You want to bring it up the steps and leave it by the office entrance?"

"Okay." Before I could offer to help her, she lifted it with ease and rolled it up the steps with minimal effort. Stronger than she looked.

"I need to ask you if you're carrying a jackknife or other item that could be used as a weapon before we go in," I said.

Her eyebrows lifted and she patted her fanny pack. "Why no, I just have my wallet and sunglasses."

She parked her bike by the stone wall of the building. I swiped my access card across the reader then pulled the door open, and we went inside. I lifted my hand toward the corridor straight ahead. "This way."

Sybil hesitated a bit then walked with me to the squad room. With no one else in there, it was a good place to talk. Less intimidating than the interview rooms. She looked around at the row of mailboxes on one wall, the cubbyholes filled with forms on another, the computers and copy machine around the edges. Then she focused on the large conference table in the center when I said, "Have a seat."

I sat kitty-corner to her right and took a second to study her. She seemed more at ease, less vulnerable, a little more confident than the first time we'd met. Granted, that had been under dire circumstances. She looked over her left shoulder like something was there.

"Is everything all right, Sybil?"

She turned back to me and blinked. "Um yes, fine."

"I've got some important things to tell you and some questions to ask. All right?"

She nodded.

"You've heard about the other barn fires in Blackwood Township?"

"Yes."

"It turns out someone you're related to recently bought the one over on Ames Avenue."

She frowned. "What do you mean?"

I shared the story Angela Simmonds had told me about the fight between the families, how they had moved away, and how she and her husband had gotten the farm after her grandmother died.

She shook her head during the account. "I didn't know I had a cousin named Angela."

"You would have been young when it all happened, twenty years ago. Angela didn't remember your name either."

Sybil looked down, hugged herself, and rocked gently back and forth.

"She'd like to meet you, but her father seems to have a problem with whatever it was he and your father fought about back then."

"Okay," she said.

Okay? "So your father never told you about it, what the fight was about?"

"My father? No, he didn't."

"You might want to ask him. Angela doesn't know the reason either, and her father won't share that. It seems to me it must have been pretty serious."

"It must have been. But if Angela's father won't tell her, mine probably won't either." She didn't seem all that curious. I would surely want to know.

"Here's the other thing. The barn that burned down on Saturday? Did you know that it belonged to your grandmother's sister, before she and her husband moved into town?"

"My grandma never told me that."

"Tragically there was someone inside, and he perished in the fire," I said.

She looked down and hugged herself a little tighter.

"We think it might be another relative of yours."

She braved another look at me. "A relative? Of mine?"

I stood up and retrieved a copy of Ross Warren's driver's license from my mailbox cubby and handed it to her. She looked at it, shook her head, and handed it back.

"His name is Ross Warren, the grandson of your great aunt. So he'd be your second cousin." I felt like I'd filled in the names of the leaves on Sybil's family tree for her.

"No, my grandma never talked about him either," she said.

"Sybil, even though your family was estranged, we need to inform your grandmother. We have a body at the medical examiner's office that we believe is Ross Warren's. We haven't made a positive identification yet, but they're still working on that. The autopsy is scheduled for this afternoon."

"Okay. I can let my grandma know. But there's nothing she could do about it anyway."

"Well, tell her about it, and we'll take it from there," I said.

"Okay."

"How did your grandparents handle the news about their fire?"

"Okay, I guess. I think they'll ask me to sell their farm. I don't think they're coming back."

"Really, why's that?"

She shrugged. "I guess they like it where they are. With my uncle."

After I'd escorted Sybil out, I watched her carry her bike down the steps, strap on her helmet, and climb on her bike. Then she rode away like the wind, like she'd been born to ride. When she headed west on County 35, I jogged to my car, let Communications know I was "Clearing ten-nineteen," and headed west on 35 myself. I drove a good distance behind Sybil so she wouldn't think I was following her, but of course I was. She was a speedy rider and deftly climbed the hills and rounded the two big curves without slowing down much at all.

The more contact I had with her the more curious I got. Part of the reason was her elusiveness. Part of it was her secretive nature. It was a chore trying to pull out information about her life, her activities, and her family. Was Sybil guarding family secrets, as well? She said her grandmother hadn't told her that she had two sisters who lived on farms close by. Was that the truth?

My own family hadn't been all that forthcoming with certain bits of information over the years, but that was often to protect another's feelings, or for other good reasons. That may have been true with Sybil's family too. My brother and I had our little spats over the years, but I couldn't imagine them growing into rifts. We loved and trusted each other and wouldn't let that happen.

Sybil turned left on Collins Avenue, and I waited until she was out of sight then I turned and followed her. When she went up the hill that then dipped by her grandparents' house, I stopped, turned around, drove a ways down the road, then pulled over to call Smoke. "Greetings, Sergeant. What's up?"

"I met with Sybil Harding, and I cannot figure her out. It's like she's sitting in front of me, but she's not there."

"I agree that she is different," he said.

"She didn't have much of anything to say that helped. What it boils down to is nobody told her she had relatives here, or about the feud, and that her grandparents will probably stay in Canada with her uncle and have her sell their house."

"Well that's that then. I'll be heading over to the ME's office in Ramsey for the autopsy. Sure you don't want to come? Patrol has been pretty quiet so far today."

"No thanks. Hey, you know better than to say the "Q" word when we're on duty."

He chuckled then disconnected.

And doggone it if five minutes later I didn't get busy with one call on top of another until the end of my shift. My first week on the job I was warned never to utter the word "quiet" out loud at work, and I never had.

27

At the end of my shift, I decided to swing by the three burned-barns properties before heading home. No one had reported seeing any suspicious activity in the township, but someone had committed three acts of arson.

And then we had the odd rabbit deliveries. Was there a link between the two? But Weber lived in town, not in the township, so how might they be connected? It was a conundrum at that point. When I got home, I'd see if any of the other deputies had responded to Smoke's email about the unwanted gift.

I stopped some distance from the Hardings'. If Sybil was still there, she'd wonder why I was sitting in my car staring at the farm. Admittedly, it would be unnerving if a cop did that to me. Every case I worked, I was inevitably drawn back to the crime scene again and again. I visually perused the surrounding area. Much of the land was open fields and pasture with windbreaks of trees in the back.

I drove down Collins to Woody Nevins' place and again kept enough distance so he wouldn't see me if he looked out his window. We would learn more about the victim in the barn and the cause of his death soon. I was relieved Smoke gave me a pass on witnessing the autopsy. The image of "The Scream" had been in my head since we'd turned the victim over, and the thought of seeing it again made me slightly squeamish. Okay, immensely squeamish. Smoke understood that about me.

I scrutinized the dry earth. The lack of footprints or vehicle tracks around the crime scenes got increasingly maddening and frightening with each fire. How were we going to nail down the firesetter's identity? Was he done now, or were the fires of the three barns that once belonged to sisters, truly a happenstance after all? Would he keep going, lighting old barns on fire until we finally caught up with him?

I conducted a mental survey of barns that no longer housed animals in the township and came up with a few, but there were likely others I didn't know about. And many, many more in the whole of Winnebago County. I turned around, headed back to Ames Avenue, and drove past the Simmonds' house. A Buick with Wisconsin license plates was parked in the driveway. It gave me hope the family was reconciling. And better yet, bringing to light the dark secret that had torn them apart in the first place.

Ten minutes later, I was out of my uniform and changed into a pair of shorts and tank top. Ditching the twenty pounds of equipment weight gave me immediate relief and made me feel about twenty degrees cooler besides. I grabbed a bottle of iced tea from the refrigerator then filled a dish of fresh water for Queenie and carried it outside. She was running around, stopping to sniff the ground here and there. When she noticed me, she joined me on the deck, took a long drink, and then sat beside me begging for some attention. "You're warm, girl. You need to cool off for a while. We both do."

The temperature was in the high eighties, but the clouds helped temper the intensity of the sun. I pulled out my phone and checked the weather forecast. Possible thunderstorms tomorrow afternoon. Half the state was praying for rain. I signed into my work account and scrolled through the list of messages looking for the one from Smoke about the rabbits.

That's when I saw the Reply All response from Todd Mason. He'd found a dead rabbit on his steps about two weeks before. That was around the same time Weber had gotten his. Mason said he buried it before his kids got up and saw it because they would have felt bad for the little bunny.

Smoke hadn't yet replied, so I found Todd Mason in my phone contacts and dialed his number. I disconnected when it went to voicemail. On a Sunday afternoon, he needed family time. I'd catch him at work tomorrow.

I wondered if Vince Weber had seen the emails from Smoke and Mason, and asked him via text. He called me a second later. "What emails?"

"Sorry Vince, my bad. I meant to tell you. I ran into Smoke first thing this morning, and he'd been gifted with a rabbit during the night—"

"No shit?"

"He sent out a blast email to see if others had too, and I see Mason got one too, a couple of weeks ago."

"Geez Louise. A couple of weeks, huh?"

"You think we can officially rule out Darcie now?" I said.

"Probably. So who's leaving the rabbits?"

"Nothing about that makes sense to me."

"No. So there's four of us that we know of. So far. The only thing we all got in common is we're sworn deputies serving in the Winnebago County Sheriff's Office," he said.

"We'll have to put our heads together about that one. We've worked a lot of cases over the years. Could one of them have triggered this bizarre reaction in someone?"

"You got me there. Oh, to let you know I have not gotten a single phone call or text message from Darcie today."

"Wow, you must have put the fear of God into her last night."

"Yeah well, thanks for making me talk to her," he said.

"Sure thing. See ya."

I phoned John Carl next. "Hello, Corky," he said.

"Hey, just checking in, seeing how your moving plans are coming along. And no, I'm not trying to snoop about your date with my BFF Sara."

"Okay. Plans are coming along. Sara's helping me here at our grandparents' house . . . I guess I can start saying *my* house, huh?"

Sara was there again? "Good. I think it's kind of exciting you're sprucing up the old house. What'd did you decide to do about the floors?" I said.

"We'll start with the main level first—rip out the carpet to expose the maple hardwood floor underneath. It sounds like Grandpa and Grandma won't be taking much of their furniture, so they said if I want to start refinishing the floors I should move everything out to their shed."

"I heard that, too. About the furniture."

"They want us to divide up what they don't take."

"John Carl? I think we should bring Taylor in on that. She's as much their grandchild as we are."

"That's fine by me. I have the house, so if you and Taylor want all the furniture I'd be cool with that," he said.

"We'll see. When are you going to start on the floors?"

"I have someone coming to give me an estimate tomorrow. We're actually working on moving the furniture out now."

"Just the two of you?" I said.

"I have a dolly."

"I can come over and help."

"I don't want to make you do that."

"You'd be doing me a favor. I could really use the distraction."

"Mom and I talked about the barn fires around here. We know how obsessed you get about solving crimes," he said.

"That's part of the job. See you in a few then?"

"Sure."

"Queenie, let's head over to the Alecksons'. I'll get my running shoes."

A few minutes later, we were on Brandt Avenue gently jogging south toward my grandparents' house. They were on the same side of the road as I was, a half mile away. They had given me twenty acres of their 1,600-acre farm, and I loved living there.

I thought about John Carl. He and I were not just opposites in looks—he was tall with dark brown hair and eyes like our father's. I was average height, small-boned with blonde hair like our mother's—we also had polar opposite personalities. John Carl was sober and studious. And he'd felt more stifled in his pursuits than I had during our younger years with Mother and both sets of grandparents all living within a mile of each other.

I'd been more independent and adventuresome growing up and had learned to take our mother's hovering protectiveness more in stride than John Carl had. Most of the time, anyway. I'd rebelled against my mother more than I should have and turned to my grandparents for refuge and support from time to time. I was especially close to Grandma Aleckson. We had like personalities, and she understood me like no other. But I loved my grandfathers and my Gram Brandt equally as much, and the saddest day of my life was when Gram passed on a few years before. I missed her every day.

I was turning into the grandparents' driveway when I saw someone a distance away coming toward me on a bicycle. If I hadn't seen Sybil riding that morning, I wouldn't have known who it was. Her head was bent over like she was watching the road, a good idea on gravel. I didn't want Queenie to get excited, so we headed down the driveway without calling out to her. Sybil said she loved riding.

I knocked on the door of the house and yelled, "Hello," before barging in. "I hope it's okay that Queenie came with me."

Sara and John Carl were on opposite sides of the dining room table carrying it out of the room. I was struck by what a nice-looking couple they were.

"Set her down," Sara said, and they did. "Reinforcements are here. Hi, Cork."

"Hey. You guys should take a water break. You look hot."

Queenie ran first to Sara then to John Carl for a little head scratching.

"I suppose," John Carl said.

I followed them to the kitchen, and we helped ourselves to bottles of water. "Sara, how did John Carl rope you into this?"

She chuckled. "It was more like the other way around. I wanted to see what the hardwood floors looked like so we decided to clear out the room and pull up the carpet. I have a friend who does floors and called him. He's swinging over tomorrow."

"Sweet. It'll be nice to get rid of the carpet. They put it down because it was easier for Grandma to clean, but John Carl's so rich he'll probably hire a cleaning service." I loved giving him a hard time, except he choked on his water when I said it. I gave him a swat on the back.

"Corky, you're pretty rough on your brother," Sara scolded.

I held my hands up in surrender. "I apologize. Put me to work, tell me what to do."

"You can carry the chairs out," John Carl said.

"I know their condo won't be ready until August first, but since they spend July at that resort, I'm surprised they didn't finish sorting and packing before they left. No offense to our grandparents." I picked up a sturdy dining chair and headed toward the door.

"Mother said it was because they didn't know how much would fit in there. And they have done a lot of purging," John Carl said.

"Speaking of Mother, where is she today?"

"Home, cooking. She said you're getting too skinny."

Score one point for John Carl. "Good one, brother." And then I took a quick glance down at my midsection. I guess I had lost a little weight.

We spent the next hour carrying the most easily-moveable furniture pieces to the shed that had once served as a sheep barn. Their main barn housed milk cows back in the day. It wasn't quite as unique as the one my great grandfather had built—the one my mother had converted into a cool place to entertain—but it had the same old-world charm. I went over to the barn, slid open the door on the front side of it, and stepped in, appreciating the drop in temperature from the outdoors. Queenie followed me in a moment later. I looked at the stalls where the cows had rested and the milking stations where my grandparents worked diligently twice a day, supplying the local creamery with quality milk, and earning a good living in the process. I had fond memories of watching them, and pitching in myself as much as I could.

My phone rang as I was closing the door. Smoke. "Hello, Detective."

"Corinne. You busy?"

"I was helping John Carl and Sara move furniture, but we're about done."

"It's John Carl *and* Sara now?" he said.

"It seems like it. And it feels a little strange and natural at the same time."

"I'm back in town and thought I'd give you a verbal report on the autopsy, but it sounds like you're busy."

"Where are you?" I said.

"At the office."

"If you want to swing by my house, I'll be there in about ten minutes."

"That works. Oh, and Mason called me. He had a rabbit delivery on his doorstep, too."

"I saw his email, and I've already talked to Weber about it. We agree that likely rules Darcie out as the culprit. But who is it, and what kind of message are they trying to send us?"

"We know it's someone that dresses like a beekeeper. At least once, that is. Who was under that garb and why? I have not a single clue," he said.

"I'll get Queenie and see you in a few."

We hung up, and I found John Carl and Sara drinking another bottle of water in the kitchen. "I'm going to take off, guys."

"Thanks for helping, Corky." John Carl smiled at me with his teeth showing and everything.

It made me smile too. Sara was a having a positive effect on him. There had been a measure of sadness around him since his marriage failed, and we had all prayed he'd have joy in his life again.

When Queenie and I started for home, I had the strange feeling that someone was watching us. Little shivers danced up and down my spine and pushed me to run a little faster until Queenie started panting. I slowed down and turned my head very slightly right, then left, to see if I spotted a person or other creature. Nothing apparent. I told myself Queenie would be alerted if someone was lurking, wouldn't she?

Smoke was standing by his car in my driveway when we got there. Having him nearby made me feel better in a flash. Secure. Protected. Safe.

"Is everything okay? You've got a funny look on your face." I stuck out my tongue and crossed my eyes. "Okay, okay. Now you have a goofy look on your face."

I shrugged. "It's probably nothing, but I got that creepy I'm-being-watched feeling on the run home."

"More of your doo-doo-doo-doo, huh? Want me to take a drive, check things out?"

"No. Like we've talked about before, it could be an animal out there. Maybe a wolf." I looked down at his hand. "I see you have the envelope."

"Yeah, some pictures you probably don't want to see, but my notes you will."

I punched in the code to open the garage door, and when it lifted we headed inside. "Want something to drink?"

"Got a soda?" he said.

"You never drink sodas," I said.

"I need a pick-me-up."

"No pop, but I have some sweetened iced tea that's really good."

"Okay." I found him one and handed it over. He read the label then opened the lid and took a gulp. "That is good. Thanks."

I filled a glass with water for myself and drank the whole thing before coming up for air.

"I don't know how you do that," he said. He sat down on a stool at my island counter, and as he was pulling papers out of the envelope my mother called on my landline. "Hi, Mom."

"Hello dear, I was hoping you were home. I've been craving seafood salad lately and finally made some today. Of course I ended up with way too much, even for Gramps and John Carl and me. Can I drop a bowl off for you?"

"Sure. I'd love some." Had I eaten lunch? Ah, no.

"And lemon chicken and fresh green beans out of the garden."

"Sounds nummy. Oh, and Smoke just stopped by with a file I needed to look at."

"There'll be plenty for him too, if he wants any. I'll be by in about ten minutes," she said.

"Thanks, Mom."

"So your mother is cooking again, eh?"

"Yes. It's a huge relief that she's healing."

"No doubt." Smoke pulled his reading glasses out of his pocket and put them on. I sat on the stool next to him as he sorted through his notes and printouts of the photos he'd taken during the autopsy.

After seeing the condition of the body after the fire, it was a little less shocking looking at the photos. But I didn't feel the need to closely study any of them, either.

"Cause of death?" I said.

"Smoke inhalation. It'll take a couple of weeks for the toxicology report, but they'll run the blood alcohol test either tomorrow or the next day. That empty booze bottle at the scene makes me wonder how much he drank, how impaired he was. That may have been a contributing factor."

"For sure. I had a thought on the way home. When I stopped Ross Warren the other day, he was on his way toward Emerald Lake. We should check in with some of the business owners there, find out if they recognize him and if he's been in more than once."

"Sounds like a plan. Especially the gas stations and the grocery and liquor stores. Sheriff thought I should take tomorrow off, but I got way too many irons in the fire." I tapped his arm at the word "fire." He shrugged. "I'll find a better day to stay home."

"You are in the thick of things, that's for sure."

"Oh, and since the sheriff called, I asked if he'd tell the other area cars to take a few tours through Blackwood Township and he agreed, so that saves you a call."

"Thanks. And 'fingers crossed' we won't need them," I said.

"Fingers crossed."

Queenie barked, announcing my mother's arrival. I got up to help her. "You better put those photos away. Mother won't sleep the rest of the week if she catches a glimpse."

Smoke nodded, gathered them up, and slid them into hiding. I opened the door to the garage, and my mother was already on the mat holding a bowl. And David Fryor was behind her with a small box. *David Fryor.* She could have warned me.

"Hello," I said, trying not to look surprised.

"Look who stopped by as I was loading the car," Mother said.

I sort of smiled. "Nice to see you, David. Here let me take that." I reached out and lifted the bowl out of my mother's hands. "Come in. Smoke, say hi to David Fryor. You can set that on the counter, David."

Smoke had stood and was close behind me. "Hello, David."

"Good to see you, Elton." He slid the box onto the island's countertop then shook Smoke's hand.

"Can I get you anything to drink?" I said.

"No, Gramps' dinner is in the car. I asked David to join us," Mother said.

"Okay, well um, that's good," I stammered then turned to David. "I've been thinking about your father, wondering how he's doing."

He lifted his shoulders slightly. "He's struggling with a number of health issues to be honest. And trying to come to grips with everything my brother did. But I get up here regularly, and I've hired a home health aide to help out. Dad wasn't exactly happy with the idea at first, but now that he's gotten to know Maggie, he's more on board with it. He even admitted to me that he feels better having her there in case something happens. And they get along incredibly well, a big bonus. They play Scrabble and cards. Dad's not as lonely anymore."

"I'm glad to hear that. You've both gone through a lot this year."

"Yes, and it'll be one day at a time coming to grips with all of it. But it's getting better little by little," David said.

I nodded. I was still trying to come to grips with it myself. So was Smoke, even more so than I was.

"I guess we better get over to my dad's. If you're ready, David?" Mother said.

"Sure. Good to see you, both."

"You too," I said.

When I heard two car doors shut I turned to Smoke. "What do you think?"

"That your mother seems to be moving on. What do you think?"

"Oh my gosh, Smoke. I think David is a genuinely nice guy. He's caring. I mean look at how well he looks after his dad. But my mother is vulnerable right now, and part of me is afraid he's going to sweep her off her feet, and the next thing you know she'll be flying back and forth with him to Texas."

"And who will take care of your gramps if she does that?" he said.

"That's not what I meant."

Smoke put his hands on my shoulders and gave me a gentle shake. "I think you're jumping the gun here. Kristen has devoted her entire adult life to caring for other people and running her business. She's not going to make any rash decisions and leave your family hanging in the lurch."

I smiled and nodded. "I know that. She's been the helicopter parent poster child for over thirty years and then started caring for Gramps when Gram died. Now that I think about it, it would be good for her to have more freedom, have some fun."

"No doubt." He turned my body around to face the counter then dropped his hands. "Let's eat. It smells too good to wait one minute longer. And you could stand to put a little meat on your bones."

Smoke too? "Why do you say that? I'm not that skinny."

"I didn't say you were, but I know how you sometimes forget to eat, and we can't have you wasting away. You need to keep up your strength to fight the bad guys."

I got out plates and utensils and set them on the island while Smoke took the containers of chicken and beans out of the box. We removed the lids, dished up our plates, and then he joined me in the common table prayer. My mother's lemon herbed chicken was another one of my favorites, as was her shrimp and tuna pasta salad. And I could eat green and wax beans fresh out of the garden every day for two weeks straight before I started getting tired of them.

Aside from our "mmm" sounds, we ate in silence for a time then Smoke said, "This is a purely selfish statement, but I sure missed your mother's cooking when she was going through all that business with Denny."

"Me too. I've been spoiled forever getting the meals she leaves in my fridge or drops off, like tonight. I wish I liked cooking, because I have to admit I get tired of deli food and pizza."

"That makes two of us." He put his fork down and leaned against the back of the stool. "I'll help you clean up then I gotta shove off, take care of Rex, and get to bed early. And hopefully sleep."

I got up and shook my head. "Go ahead and take off. I'll have Queenie lick the plates and silverware clean, so I won't have to wash them."

He was still snickering when he walked out the door.

28

I woke up too early Monday morning, but couldn't go back to sleep, and I stared at the ceiling for a while. A host of things were rattling around in my brain, both personal and professional. John Carl and Sara, Mother and David. Grandma and Grandpa and their move. Gramps. And Smoke, because.

With all the craziness of the past week, it was no wonder I couldn't sleep. Queenie stirred when I did. It was 5:15 a.m. The sun would be rising in about twenty minutes, but it was light enough to go on a run. Queenie joined me in some wake-up stretches then she whined while I freshened up in the bathroom.

I looked out at the sky hoping to see a dark cloud, with the promise of rain, but no such luck. I dressed in running shorts and a t-shirt and we went downstairs. I let Queenie outside to do her business while I got my running shoes out of the front closet and my Smith and Wesson and pancake holster out of the safe. Then I called Queenie back inside.

"You get to stay home while I go on a power run." I grabbed my phone and clipped it on my waistband then adjusted my shirt so my weapon wasn't obvious. Stepping outside, I drew in a large breath through my nostrils, appreciating the relative coolness of the early morning air. I walked to the end of the driveway, turned left, and ran past my grandparents' place. When I reached the mile mark, I turned around to head back, and saw tendrils of smoke coming from the back of my grandparents' barn. Dear God. I got out my phone, dialed 911 then took off at a sprinting speed toward it. Half a mile had never seemed so far away.

"Nine—"

"Rick, it's Corky Aleckson. My grandparents' barn is on fire. 3428 Brandt Avenue, Blackwood Township. Tell Oak Lea Fire to hurry."

"Copy. Are you injured, in danger?" he said.

"No. I'm a ways away, running there. Call me back when Oak Lea is rolling. And call Detective Dawes." I didn't have my radio, but I knew Rick's partner would be getting the page out that instant. I prayed at least two of the volunteer firefighters would be up and at 'em, or there'd be a delay before they responded. I surveyed the area and didn't see a solitary soul moving about, either on foot or in a vehicle.

I reached their yard in less than four minutes and was behind the barn four seconds later. Smoke was pouring out from around the old double door, and I was momentarily paralyzed by all-encompassing panic. *Think. Rely on your training.*

I forced myself to look away from the smoke and examined the ground for footprints and vehicles tracks around the door. Nothing evident. The parched earth was doing us no favors with evidence collection lately. I felt compelled to see what was happening inside, but I knew opening the door and feeding the fire with more oxygen would be a mistake.

My grandparents had a well about twenty away. A faucet with an attached hose, once used to water the animals and gardens, jutted from the ground. I was there in a flash, turned the faucet on full bore, picked up the end of the hose, and ran as fast as possible to the barn door. Water splashed all over the ground in front of me and on my feet and legs, but my only thought was getting water into the barn through the cracks between, and around, the doors.

I'd stuck my phone in my back waistband, and when it rang I pulled it out and punched the talk button without taking my eyes off the barn. It was Rick in Communications. "Oak Lea is rolling out of their station with one rig as we speak. The second should be close behind, but I think Detective Dawes will be the first one there." A sense of relief trickled through me. Smoke's emergency-response time rivaled Speedy Gonzales's.

"Thanks." I pushed End thinking that was a particularly ominous word at the moment. The department was stepping up their efforts to locate and stop the firesetter in his tracks. And if this was another one of his criminal acts—and I had little doubt that it was—he'd fooled us once again, lighting the fire hours earlier than the others.

No flames yet reached out the cracks of the old doors, and I prayed the firefighters would get there before the barn was engaged. Random thoughts darted through my mind. Thank

God we'd put our grandparents' furniture and possessions in the shed instead of the barn, we weren't related to the Hardings or Backstroms or Grants, were my grandparents being targeted as we suspected the others were? If so, what was the connection?

I heard a car door slam and figured it had to be Smoke. When he came running toward me, I was struck by his apparel. He was wearing jogging pants and a t-shirt with his tactical holster and gun strapped across his chest. His badge and radio were clipped on his pants. "What in tarnation?" he yelled.

"I don't know. I'm trying to hold it together, but this feels like a personal attack on our family." Sirens screamed in the distance, and I mouthed the words, "thank you."

"Let's hope that's not true. Another fire? We can't say the firesetter's crimes are escalating necessarily, because he started off in that mode from the get-go." He reached over and tried to take the hose from me. "You're shaking like a leaf."

I had trouble releasing my grip on the hose, but Smoke finally peeled my fingers off. "Adrenaline dump," I said.

"Yeah. Why don't you go around to the front and direct the guys back here."

"I can't leave my post. I have to stay here."

The sirens were deafeningly, obviously close. I willed them to hurry. Seconds later, the sirens cut out abruptly and were replaced by the loud crunching of gravel. Smoke handed the hose back to me. "I'll direct 'em." He went to the south side and waved them in closer. I backed away from the door, giving them a wide berth to do their job. Water from the garden hose stopped flowing when the truck ran over it then started again when it passed. "I'll shut off the water," Smoke yelled above the loud rumbling rig, pointing at the hose.

The truck stopped and Chief Corey Evans and a young fireman named Jack jumped out. Both had their turnout pants and boots on, and Evans was also wearing his jacket, holding onto helmets and gloves. After Jack slipped on his jacket, Corey handed him a helmet and pair of gloves. In seconds, they were protected and ready to firefight. "Any animals in there that you know of?" Evans said.

I shook my head. "It's my grandparents' barn, and I know there aren't."

"Yeah, bad deal. Really sorry, Corky," he said.

Smoke peered into one of the back windows. "Lots of smoke, so it's hard to see any flames, what the fire's doing."

"There might be straw in there that hasn't been completely cleaned out," I said.

The sirens from more emergency vehicles indicated they were getting close. Then one was silenced, and I heard Sergeant Leo Roth announce he was "10-6," via Smoke's radio. Roth was the area supervisor on the overnight shift. Seconds later a second fire truck pulled into the yard. "The neighbors should be awake by now," Smoke quipped.

Roth joined Smoke and me, and the new team of firefighters rushed in to assist, pulling on their gear as they did. Chief Corey pulled off a glove and held his hand a few inches from the iron door pulls. "Not radiating much heat. Jack, grab the hose. One thing on our side is that this old barn has outside air creeping into the cracks, which cuts down on the risk of an explosion when we open the doors. Let's break the two windows first to direct any fire inward and upward. Wyman. Matty."

The three of them sprang into action. By the time the windows were shards of glass and shattered wood, the hose was in position. Wyman and Matty each slid one of the barn doors outward, and Corey stood in a ready-for-action position.

My stomach was tied up in all kinds of knots, but when the doors were open and I looked inside, the fire was surprisingly and thankfully less threatening than I'd expected. "Hold off on the water, Jack. We're gonna need to preserve the scene here," Evans yelled then dropped the hose. The fire was small, about six feet in from the back door, and surrounded by rocks. My brain struggled to make sense of what I was seeing. Someone had built a *campfire* on the dirt floor.

All of us gathered in front of the open doors, trying to grasp what the strange scene meant. Positioned on the outside of the rocks at twelve o'clock, three o'clock, six o'clock, and nine o'clock were four dead little rabbits. Jagged dark lines and specks in the dirt indicated where the water I'd squirted from the hose had gotten through.

"This is really weird," Corey said. The others added similar commentary. I was speechless.

"Those little guys are layin' there like they're sleeping by the fire." I think Matty said that.

Smoke and I were the only two on site that had seen other rabbits similarly placed the past few days. Sergeant Roth spoke up, "Detective Dawes, you sent out that email yesterday asking if any of us had a rabbit left on our doorsteps."

"That I did. Turns out four of us have. And now we got this . . ." Smoke shrugged. "I don't know what we got here."

"Some of the wood in the campfire must've been a little wet given how much smoke there is," Chief Evans said.

"I was thinking the same thing," Smoke said.

We were still standing there considering our next course of action when my mother and John Carl rounded the corner of the barn. Their outfits were casual like Smoke's, minus the official equipment. Getting rousted out of bed for an emergency gave people permission to wear what they normally wouldn't in public. Mother's mouth was open and her hands were crossed on her heart. John Carl's face was blank like he was too shocked to know what to say or do.

"What *happened*?" Mother said.

"I couldn't sleep and went on a run and then saw smoke coming out of the barn so I called nine-one-one and then everyone started showing up," I blurted out in one long breath.

Mother and John Carl moved closer and Smoke said, "Except it turns out it wasn't much of a fire after all. But you may not want to look inside, Kristen."

Mother looked at Smoke. "What is it?"

"Viewer discretion advised. There are four dead rabbits laying around a campfire in there," he said.

"Oh." That gave her pause, but John Carl wasn't deterred. He moved in closer to see what Smoke was talking about.

John Carl shook his head. "It looks like some sort of ritual. But who would be using Grandma and Grandpa's barn for that?"

Smoke put a hand on his shoulder. "The only thing we know for sure is that we don't have a clue what we got going on here. And we need to start digging to find that out, so here's the deal . . ." He turned to the firefighters. "Thank you, Oak Lea Fire, for your quick response, but you can get back to the station." Then he put one hand on my mother's shoulder and the other on my brother's. "Kristen and John Carl, if you want to go in the house, have a cup of coffee, hang out for a while, that's cool. We'll be getting Major Crimes out here, and we'll need room to work."

All of them headed off without saying much. But Corey Evans leaned in close to me as he walked by. "Let us know what you find out."

I nodded and said, "Kudos to you and your guys for getting here so fast. I really appreciate it."

"You bet. Super relieved you didn't lose the barn."

"Thanks."

Smoke phoned Communications, and asked them to page the crime scene team then turned to Roth, "Leo, will you be able to stay on duty until we get Corky's shift area covered? She'll be tied up dealing with this mess."

"Yeah, no problem. I can cover the first half of her shift," he said.

"Thanks. I'll have the chief deputy take care of the second half," Smoke said.

"I'll start a sign-in log," Roth said.

I pulled out my phone to check the time. Six twenty-four. My shift would have officially started in thirty-six minutes. "I'm going to run home and get ready."

"Literally? Roth can give you a lift," Smoke said.

"Yes, literally. It's only a five-minute run. I won't be too long."

"Wear street clothes, you'll be doing detective work."

"All right."

John Carl's car was on Brandt Avenue, so I popped into the house. Mother had brewed a pot of coffee, and they were both standing by the kitchen counter holding a cup with almost identical expressions of alarm on their faces.

"Corky, that was really freaky," John Carl said.

"Your brother told me about how those poor little creatures were laying there like that. It boggles my mind that someone would do something like that. It's sick. And why do you think they picked your grandparents' barn for such a thing?"

"The owners of the three barns that burned down were all gone at the time. We don't know if they were crimes of opportunity, or if they were picked because there were no animals inside that would die in the fires.

"The other possibility is the owners were targeted for some reason. But now we've got this campfire in Grandma and Grandpa's barn, and that just adds a layer of confusion to it all. It doesn't fit with the others."

"You know for sure someone started those fires on purpose?" John Carl said.

"No question about it. But we're struggling with a lack of evidence to prove it."

"What kind of evidence?" Mother said.

"Like the use of an accelerant. Footprints at the scene. Tire tracks at the scene."

"So what are you going to do?" John Carl said.

"We're beyond frustrated." I took a quick breath then said, "Besides the fires, there have been other strange things going on. I didn't tell you about this because your plates are already too full, but someone left a dead rabbit on my doorstep last week. It was about the same size as the ones in barn."

Mother gasped and set her cup down on the table. "That's horrible."

"Corky. Why?" John Carl said.

"That's the burning question. But I'm not the only one. Vince Weber, Todd Mason, and Smoke all got one too."

"The four of you?" Mother said.

"That we know of, but there might be more."

"Oh dear," Mother said.

"Did the sheriff shut down someone's commercial rabbit operation?" John Carl said.

Had he? "Not that I can recall. But there have been issues with farmers and animal complaints over the years. We'll do some research. But now I gotta get ready for work."

"Corinne, surely Denny will give you the day off. You have weeks and weeks of sick time coming."

"I'm not working my usual shift. I'm assisting Smoke on this case. I need to be here."

Mother sniffled. I gave her a quick, tight hug then took off before she started crying. I'd be done in by that.

It would have saved me a minute or two if I'd asked John Carl for a ride but running helped me focus and process information. Whoever left the strange rabbit campfire scene in the barn was no doubt the same person who'd left the rabbit on my doorstep. So that begged the question, was a female committing the crimes? Setting fires and making disturbing deliveries? Could she be acting alone or did she have an accomplice? Fire setting was more common among males than among females. So maybe it was a female helping a male.

When I heard Queenie barking I remembered I'd left her alone in the house, something I only did for short periods of time now and then. She licked my hand when I opened the door.

"It must have been way too loud for you with all those sirens." I rubbed her neck. "There are more weird things happening here in Blackwood Township, and I need to go to work." Queenie followed me into the kitchen and waited while I drank a glass of water and started a pot of coffee. "It's kennel time for you, my dear."

When she was situated, I got ready, filled two large travel mugs with coffee then stuck four bottles of water and two granola bars in an insulated, soft-sided lunch cooler. As I climbed into my squad car, I set the mugs in cup holders and the cooler on the seat next to my briefcase. I backed out of the garage then pushed the talk button on the sheriff's band radio. "Six oh eight to Winnebago County."

"Go ahead, Six oh eight."

"I'm ten-eight with unit four twenty."

"You're ten-eight at seven fourteen."

I pulled up in front of my grandparents' house and parked on the township road. Sara's car and another one I didn't recognize were parked behind John Carl's. I phoned in my location to Communications, gathered the coffees and treats, and got out. Sergeant Roth was in his squad car talking on the phone, and I nodded at him as I walked by. Mother, John Carl, Sara, and David Fryor were all gathered on my grandparents' back steps observing what they could from there. They had a limited view, nothing much past the southeast corner of the barn.

Seven fifteen in the morning and Mother and John Carl already had their support team by their sides. I stopped to say hello.

"Morning, Sara, David."

Sara crossed her hands on her chest. "I'm so sorry, Corky."

"That goes for me too. What a shock," David said.

"Thanks." That's all I could manage.

"Corky, you look professional today," John Carl said.

"I'm supposed to look professional every day."

"I should have said you look like a police detective."

"Oh." I was wearing an elbow-length white cotton shirt—buttoned to the second from the top button, thank you very much—and pleated gray pants. Poor guy was trying to give me a compliment, so I held back my smart comment and smiled instead. "Well, I got some detective work to do."

Mother had tears in her eyes, and I knew from her smile they were her motherly-pride tears. She regularly fought the dueling battle of being fearful *for* me and being proud *of* me. Smoke came around the corner from behind the barn, and I handed him a mug of coffee. "Thanks." He waved at Mother and company then we made our way back to the scene. "My, my, my. Should I be surprised to see Sara Speiss and David Fryor with your mother and brother so bright and early?" he said.

"It caught me a little off guard, too."

"Yeah?"

Amanda Zubinski and Vince Weber had the Major Crimes duties for the day, and they drove the mobile unit to the south side of the barn and parked. Smoke and I were standing in front of the open barn doors, and he waved them over when they got out. Roth fell in behind, and the five of us formed a semi-circle to examine the scene. Weber shot me a quick glance and raised his eyebrows in a way that signaled this officially let Darcie off the hook.

"That is one of the strangest things I've ever seen. Anyone have a clue what it means?" Zubinski said.

"I think it's safe to say that none of us do." Smoke held up his phone. "I sent photos to Emmet Chapman, our area investigator with the State Fire Marshal's office, so we'll see if he has any ideas."

"It holds some kind of meaning for the person who built it," I said.

"Yep." Smoke said.

"That's the obvious part, and you gotta wonder what crazy purpose a crazy person would have," Weber said.

"Let's hope we find him so we can ask him. Or her. I got the impression the person who delivered Corky's rabbit was a female. We may have a couple, a team, working on these antics together. We'll find out.

"In the meantime, grab some of your bright lights to illuminate the scene. Let's get our protective gear on and see if they left any evidence behind. For a change," Smoke said.

29

Belle and Birdie

"Birdie, I think we've been very clever this time. The clues are all there, so we'll see if they can figure them out."

Birdie looked at Belle, and her mouth lifted in a small winsome smile.

"Birdie, I don't know how you manage to stay so sweet and look so innocent in all this. Basic nature, or not. We've been involved in a lot of major happenings around here lately."

Birdie put her head on Belle's shoulder, and all of Belle's concerns evaporated like water on a sweltering day.

30

Word about the bizarre campfire in my grandparents' barn traveled through the sheriff's office, and a number of deputies stopped by to have a look. It was curious Sheriff Twardy wasn't one of them, given our relationship. But on second thought it shouldn't have surprised me, given our relationship.

When our team was dressed and ready, we stood at the barn's back entrance for a last look before going in. My watering efforts had done little more than dampen a limited area on the barn floor, not reaching as far as the campfire or the bunnies. The five of us moved in slowly, eyeing every inch of ground in and around the scene.

"The dirt floor has been somewhat disturbed but not enough to capture even a single good print," Smoke said.

"It's so packed down it's almost like concrete," I said.

"Yeah. So why is it some of these barns have concrete floors, some have wood, and others are dirt?" Weber said.

"It depends on their age, when they were built, and what the owners wanted or could afford. In my grandparents' case, it was this way when they bought the farm. They built the wooden walkways but didn't feel the need to do anything else," I said.

"Ah, makes sense. It's one of those dumb things I've thought about once in a while and never thought to ask," Weber said.

"The thing is, whoever set up this deal must have known the Alecksons had a dirt floor," Smoke said.

The little hairs on the back of my neck awakened and stood at attention. Of course. They'd brought in rocks and kindling and half-grown dead rabbits. It took planning, and the dirt floor would have been the first item on the list for consideration.

Sergeant Roth got called out on a report of theft and carefully made his way out of the barn to respond.

"So Sergeant, Detective, this has gotta be somehow connected to the rabbits that got left on our doorsteps," Weber said.

"Gotta be," Smoke agreed.

"Yeah, what was that all about? That email you sent out yesterday, Detective?" Zubinski said. I wondered if Vince had said anything to her about Darcie yet.

"Someone has been delivering them to our cops. We don't know why. We did get a video of someone in a beekeeper outfit dropping one off for Corky here," Smoke said.

When she frowned, I said, "Vince can tell you all about it, Mandy."

"Yeah, 'cause I got the first one. Or it could've been Mason because it was about the same time. Then Corky, then Detective Dawes," Weber said.

"So I started wondering if others got one, too. That's how we found out about Mason," Smoke said.

"Why didn't you say anything, Vince?" Zubinski said.

"No good reason I guess," he said.

"We need to figure out if the four of us were on a case together that was somehow related to rabbits. When I told my brother about it, he asked if the sheriff had shut down a commercial rabbit operation," I said.

"That's a valid theory, but I can't think of a one in my time here," Smoke said.

"My apartment manager would freak out if I got one. Maybe I would too," Zubinski said.

"Let's hope it ends here, Mandy. Then you won't have to worry about it," I said.

The crime scene team photographed the staged campfire from all sides, and Smoke did a slow walk around the inside walls of the barn and then along the wooden walkways, past the stanchions where my grandparents had once milked cows. He stopped and looked into the now-empty stalls where animals had slept.

I was off my game and watched as the others performed the investigative tasks, letting my mind go back to memories from my childhood instead: helping my grandparents on the farm, doing the many chores I loved. At that moment in time it seemed like my memories were all dreams. The whole world was atilt, and it felt like I'd fall off if I didn't hold on tight.

I pulled out my phone and called John Carl. "Are you and Mother still here?"

"Yeah, but we're about to take off. Mom needs to get ready for work."

"Sure. I'm checking to see if you called our grandparents."

"No, I wasn't sure what the protocol was on that," he said.

"Let's let it ride for now. They need to know, but I'll talk to them later, after we wrap up here."

"Okay, I'll let Mom know."

After we'd hung up, I examined the spent campfire again and the rocks around it. At first I thought it was my imagination, but when I squatted down and looked closer I realized three of the rocks were ones I had among the bushes by the side of my house. I'd picked them out of the rock pile at my mother's farm. The one Gramps had built up with all the rocks he'd pulled out of his fields over the years.

"Smoke, come here."

He was there in a second. "What? What do you see?"

Weber and Zubinski came over too.

"At least three of these rocks are from my place, my garden."

Weber looked at me like a third eye had sprouted between the other two. Zubinski studied the rocks like she was trying to pick out the differences.

"Say what?" Smoke said.

"I had them in with the hydrangea bushes on the south side of the house," I said.

"Ah, geez, how would you know that?" Weber said.

"I handpicked them because I thought they were cool." I pointed to each one.

Weber shrugged. "They're all right as rocks go, I suppose."

Zubinski used her elbow to give his bicep a nudge. "But the question is, how did they get here?" she said.

Smoke pushed out a loud breath. "Think you caught the culprits on your video camera?" Then he smiled. "That could break our case."

"I hate to be doubtful, but it depends on which direction they came from. If they came down the driveway, yes. If they came from the back forty, yes. If they came from the north, yes, because they'd have to walk by the front door. If they came in directly from the south then maybe not."

"Vince and Mandy, we'll need to process the rocks anyway, so I'd like you to put flags with numbers on 'em, and get a good shot of each one. In case somebody else has Corky's keen powers of observation and notices rocks from their landscaping décor are missing. We can return 'em to them."

A skeptical look briefly crossed Weber's face. "Okay, how many we got here?" He pointed as he counted. "A nice little circle of twenty-eight, huh?"

As he was counting, I noticed one on the other side looked familiar, too. "There's another one of mine." I indicated it with my finger.

"Do you want to keep looking, see if you can pick out more?" Zubinski said.

"No. They could have gotten more from my property, but it doesn't matter. I just hope we got the thieves going about their dastardly deeds on camera," I said.

"That would be sweet. And tell you what—by the time the property techs check 'em for trace evidence and finally release 'em, you'll have time to see if you're missing any others in your garden." Weber was being considerate, given the troubling circumstances and kept his wise-guy cracks to himself.

"I'm going to take a look at what Corky's cameras captured. We'll leave you two to carry on, but holler if you need me," Smoke said.

"With you being about a *stone's* throw away, hollering will probably work, too," Weber quipped.

Zubinski followed Smoke and me out and then headed to the mobile unit for more supplies. Mother and John Carl had left at some point. I found the insulated cooler with the water and treats on a bench where I'd set it earlier. I opened it and handed a granola bar to Smoke, tore one open for myself, and ate it on the way to the car. "I'll let Communications know we're clearing the scene," Smoke said as we climbed into our separate vehicles.

He pulled into the driveway behind me. "I need to look at my hydrangea garden, check if anything else is missing. See what you can pull up on my computer." I opened the garage door, and Smoke let himself into the house. I went around to the south side and visually scanned the garden. The four missing rocks were the only disturbance I observed. I'd watered the bushes on Friday and would have noticed if they were gone. I looked at the lawn around the area, but there weren't any signs that a vehicle had driven on it. The grass was browning, but intact.

Queenie was more than ready to get out of her kennel when I opened her door. "Run off your energy and come to the door when you're done," I told her.

Smoke was in the den remotely accessing the video data on the computer. "Any other rocks missing from your garden?"

"Nope."

"Queenie sounds energized," he said.

"Getting let out in the middle of my work day is a special treat."

Smoke smiled. "No doubt. Have you looked at any video since the rabbit incident?"

"No. And that would've been Monday the fourteenth. I watered the bushes on the eighteenth, and if the rocks hadn't been there, I would have seen the holes."

"Okay. And what time was that?"

"Right around six p.m."

"Let's see what we can find." He went back to that date and time and ran through the footage. I was the one who triggered the camera most often since then. Of course. My mother, David Fryor, and Smoke were there on Sunday. Not a suspect among them. The suspect, trespasser, and rock thief, did not appear on any video from Friday night at six p.m., through the overnight hours of Sunday into Monday.

I shook my head. "Now I need cameras on the sides of my house, too? I've been wondering how they hauled those rocks. I didn't see any evidence that they used a cart, so it would take either two people or one making two trips. At least. The rocks aren't that big but they have some weight. My guesstimate is they each weighed between three and eight pounds."

"A fair amount of weight to carry. Without a cart an individual would have needed some type of carrying case, maybe a backpack. Not to mention being very cunning, coming in from the south side to avoid getting picked up by the motion-detection camera."

A crawling sensation up my back onto my shoulders made me reach back to try to rub it away. "We figured the person who left the rabbit on my step in broad daylight knew the cameras were there and that she'd be captured on video. Is that part of the game?"

"Makes you wonder. Couldn't avoid detection going to your steps but was clever enough to pull it off the second time. Aside from that small grassy strip on the south side, you got cornfields on both the north and south sides of your house this year. Makes for good cover," Smoke said.

"Good cover for bad people." I watched the monitor as Smoke scanned through the videos then returned to review the beekeeper creeper one. "Smoke, we haven't talked about the core issues here, the whys. Why are we getting dead rabbits, why would someone steal rocks from my house and use them to build a campfire circle in my grandparents' barn? We figure it's a woman, right? Did she get the idea from the three barn fires, or is she the firesetter? Someone who delivers dead rabbits and sets barns on fire?"

"Similar questions have been jumping around in my brain all morning. I got a rabbit too, but as far as the rocks go, I wouldn't have a clue if any were stolen rocks from my property." Then he raised his eyebrows up and down a couple of times and grinned. "I haven't picked out any particular ones for my landscaping design, however."

Despite the gravity of everything we were dealing with, his smile made me feel better. "I better go check on Queenie." I found her sitting on the deck, watching the world go by. "Want to come in and cool off for a while, girl?" She yipped then ran in the house and found Smoke within seconds.

He petted her then stood up. "Queenie, you're reminding me I left my own dog when I dashed out this morning. I need to go take care of good old Rex and change into respectable clothes before I get back to work."

"I have to say, I've never seen you in jogging pants before. They suit you," I said with a smirk.

"I obviously don't use them for jogging. I call them my loungers, and they were the first thing I laid my hands on when I rolled out of bed at dawn's early light."

"Ahhh."

Smoke went home, and I returned to my grandparents' barn. Weber and Zubinski had finished photographing the rocks and were putting them in individual evidence bags. Weber was wearing a white cotton cap on his head and had a thin cloth towel around his neck, tucked into the top of his coveralls. "I started sweatin' like a horse and didn't want to contaminate the evidence," he said.

"That works," I said.

"I've collected rocks for a case before but never twenty-eight of them," Zubinski said.

I remembered something. "Vince, you've got rocks you use for a campfire in your backyard, don't you?"

"Yeah, sure."

"You should look, see if they're all still there," I said.

"Ah, geez. That fire pit was there when I bought the place, so I couldn't tell you by looking if any of those rocks," he waved his hand at the remaining group, "would be any of mine."

"Check it out, Vince. Whoever is doing this must have a reason," I said.

"With the extra challenge of being on an elevator that doesn't go up to the top floor," he said.

Zubinski shook her head at him. "There has to be a connection to an incident you were all involved with."

"We've had more than my little brain can begin to remember the last eight years. But like Dawes said, nothin' related to shutting down a commercial rabbit farm," Weber said.

We fell into silence as we wrapped things up. I helped them remove the last of the evidence then closed the door on the barn. Getting a good strong lock on it was long past due. The sheriff's office needed to remind everyone in the county, and Blackwood Township in particular, to be sure to do the same on their unsecured barns.

Weber pulled the towel from the back of his neck and wiped his face with it. "We'll swing by my place on the way back to the office. Now you got me curious about my stupid campfire rocks." He pulled open the passenger side door of the mobile crime unit then got in.

Zubinski shrugged and climbed behind the wheel.

I phoned Smoke to let him know we were done at the scene and would be reporting back to the office. "I'm heading there in a bit. I did a little search of the property around my house, and believe it or not, I found a few spots where it's clear rocks had been recently removed." Smoke lived in a log home on a small lake surrounded by woods on the other three sides.

"You got pictures?" I said.

"Sure, and I took measurements too. It's not reasonable, given the circumstances, to have a posse go over all my acres looking for more. The important thing is that we can establish someone trespassed here and took some rocks," he said.

"Yep."

My phone rang a while later. It was Weber. "What have you got, Vince?"

"It's what I haven't got. I counted four spots where some rocks used to be."

"Snap some shots of the fire pit to show that," I said.

"Already done, and we're heading back to the station."

When I got into Oak Lea, I pulled into the parking lot at the sheriff's office and phoned my mother. "Hey, Mom."

"Oh Corinne, I've been waiting for you to call. Have you figured out what's going on?"

"No, we're a ways from that. But we'll keep plugging away," I said.

"I have such an uneasy feeling about all of this."

"Me too. The good news is we've got smart people investigating. Smoke, the State Fire Marshal—"

"I know, and that's good. I know you're on duty and won't keep you. But I think you should let your grandparents know what happened as soon as possible," she said.

"I agree, and we'll take care of it. Try not to fret about it too much, Mom." When our call ended, I let Communications know I was 10-19, turned off the car, grabbed my briefcase, and went inside.

31

Belle and Birdie

"Birdie, did you notice how long they spent at that old barn?" Belle said.

Birdie looked at the sky and didn't seem to hear her.

"I think there were more people at that place than at the other ones. It seemed like it, anyway. When someone in the sheriff's office gets touched, it gets a lot of attention."

Birdie turned to Belle and raised her eyebrows.

"They carried out load after load out of the barn. They might be getting the message, after all. You think so?"

Birdie closed her eyes like she had suddenly grown weary.

"Go ahead and rest a while, Birdie," Belle said.

32

The weekday pace in the office was nothing like it was on the weekends. Fingers flew over keyboards. Command staff officials reviewed reports to be sent off to the county attorney and other agencies. I was planning to talk to the sheriff about my grandparents' fire, but Twardy wasn't in, so I found Chief Deputy Mike Kenner instead. I knocked on his doorjamb.

Kenner looked up and waved me in. "Come in, Sergeant. Well, I hear you had a heck of a deal at your grandparents' barn."

"I can't even tell you," I said.

"Dawes said the suspect stole rocks from your house and used them to build a campfire ring. And the dead rabbits? Another strange twist after four of you had them delivered to your houses."

"Weber and Smoke had rocks taken from their properties too."

"I hadn't heard that," Kenner said.

"Mason? I hope he got a pass on this one. With kids, things like this happening at his house would be scary."

"You know it. Remember that he's gone on vacation this week, so he won't be able to check things out at his place 'til he gets back. Meanwhile, we've got to track down the culprits who are wreaking all this havoc and lock them up before there's any more death and destruction."

"Mike, I have a request. Can you get a public service announcement to the media outlets asking people in the county with barns to make sure they have locks on the doors? I think there's some kind of motive behind all of the fires, that they're not just crimes of opportunity. But the firesetter has had easy access to all of them. And there may be others out there that he's got his eyes on."

He jotted notes on the pad on his desk. "Sure thing. No problem."

"Thanks. I see you're going over the reports on the fatality." I nodded at the papers on his desk.

"Yeah. I'm playing catch up after being gone up north over the weekend. It's the preliminary autopsy report Dawes left for me. I had a phone conference with him on Saturday about all the happenings, since I've been helping the sheriff with more of his duties."

"I noticed he's out again today," I said.

He nodded but didn't comment, and then changed the subject by holding up a photo of the burned body. "That's about as bad as they come."

"It *is* as bad as they come."

"Are you going to be in the office for a while?"

"Yes, I have to write my reports then I'm going to check with some businesses in Emerald Lake, see if any of them recognize Ross Warren from his DL photo."

"Sure, that'd be good. When Dawes gets in we're going to have a conference call with that state investigator, Emmet Chapman, to see what he's got to say. I think you should be here for that. Hopefully he'll give us some insights into the type of suspect we should be looking for. With the first two fires, I was thinking it might be kids doing some vandalism. But now we got a fatality, and I don't know what to think."

"Whoever set the fire might not have seen the victim if he was asleep in the animal stall."

"True, but if I was sleeping in someone else's barn, I'd wake up right quick if I heard the door creak open."

"Me too, but then I'm kind of a light sleeper. And there was an empty booze bottle near his body, so alcohol may have played a part."

"Yeah, I saw that in the report, and you might be right. We'll know more when the toxicology tests come back."

Smoke stuck his head in the chief deputy's office. "You waiting on me?"

"Come in, Detective, and we'll get this show on the road. Chapman's expecting our call."

Smoke sat down on the chair next to mine. He'd showered and smelled like a pine forest after a cleansing rain. Nice. While Kenner dialed Chapman's number, Smoke's eyes sought mine with an imploring look. He was wondering how I was holding up. As I fought to maintain control of my shaky emotions, he leaned closer and braced his shoulder against mine. I almost gave in to my waiting tears.

"Hello, Emmet? Mike Kenner here with Detective Elton Dawes and Sergeant Corinne Aleckson."

We exchanged brief greetings then Investigator Chapman jumped right into it. "After reviewing the reports from the three fires, and given the fact that the barns were owned by sisters, I'm convinced these are crimes of revenge. I'm sure you know that's the most common motive for a serial arsonist. Retaliation for some injustice they've suffered."

"Yes," Kenner said.

"It might be something real, or it could be something they perceive as real. It could have happened months or even years ago. The sister—whose barn was the scene of the fatality—hadn't lived there for two decades. That tells me whatever sparked this arsonist's need for revenge took place over twenty years ago. It germinated and kept growing through the years until they finally decided to do something about it as payback. In this case, with fires."

"Emmet, it's Dawes here. I've been thinking along those same lines. Are we talking about an older person or a younger person here? Firesetters strike me, generally speaking, as individuals who are not very mature emotionally."

"Immaturity is certainly true among juvenile firesetters in particular. They're often developmentally delayed, have impulse control problems. And some adult firesetters have the same characteristics and issues. Some are impulsive, others are thrill-seekers. Immaturity may be a good descriptor for a lot of those behaviors.

"But to answer your question, I can only guess about their age. We've been surprised too many times over the years with what our investigations have uncovered. Some firesetters are easy to identify based on early patterns of behavior or some psychological disorders. Others are a big surprise to officials and the public alike. The fire chief everyone trusted. The small town bank executive. And the sad truth is, the large majority of them are never identified, and therefore never caught. So we don't have data on them.

"Your firesetter is certainly clever and has managed to start four fires without detection. But an intriguing aspect is that three of them were set during the day when people were around, likely driving by or even out in nearby fields. Building that campfire involved a lot of prep work. I believe you have a single firesetter, but it's possible there are two. Not more than two. These arson fires were set for personal reasons, and only a very close friend or family member would go along with something like this."

"Male, female?"

"That's a good question. Females set only a fraction of fires that males do, but the numbers are increasing. Females are more likely to set fires on their own properties, or those of neighbors, relatives, and friends. Not someone you'd want for a friend, right? I read a study that was conducted at a prison on female firesetters not long ago. They found the majority— over ninety percent—had a psychiatric illness, and most had suffered early sexual abuse. They're often socially isolated, introverted, unemployed."

Smoke cleared his throat. "It's Dawes again. I've read similar data on female firesetters. Many have antisocial or borderline personality disorders. Or schizophrenia."

"Yes, that's true," Chapman said.

Smoke continued, "Getting back to the three barns that were owned by the sisters. We know that at least two of the families have been estranged for more than twenty years.

Whatever caused the feud has been festering as a dark secret ever since."

"One that prompted these revenge fires now?" Chapman said.

"It seems more like it all the time. We've talked to one of the family members involved in the dispute. Name's Damon Backstrom, son of Mrs. Peters and the father of Angela Simmonds, the current owner of barn number two. Backstrom clammed up and wouldn't say what happened—just that it's a private family matter. I'm ready to bring him in for a Come-to-Jesus meeting, and if he doesn't cough up the info, I'll charge him with obstruction."

"He may very well be holding a key piece of the puzzle."

"No doubt about that. So what's your take on the campfire in the Alecksons' barn?" Smoke said.

"It certainly adds an odd twist," Chapman said.

"Agreed, and it gets odder. I told you about the four of us getting dead rabbits on our doorsteps the last couple of weeks."

"Yes."

"Now come to find out the firesetter got rocks from at least three of our homes to build the ring around that fire."

"Hmm." Chapman was silent a moment. "It's the arsonist's way of communicating something. But is it a warning, or some other sort of message? There is the possibility that it's not directly connected to the other fires. That these are separate crimes by different individuals."

"You think so?" Kenner said.

"I'm just throwing that out there. You have the one setting barns on fire, and you've got another delivering rabbits, who in turn gets the idea for the campfire in the barn because of the other barn fires. He staged that campfire surrounded by rabbits to get your attention."

Smoke screwed up his face and rubbed his temples. "He did that all right. We're going to need to brainstorm, see if there's a case we worked together that has some sort of rabbit connection. And to find out the family secret—and whether it would've caused one of them to seek this level of revenge."

"A lot to sort through. Good luck. I understand we'll both be getting the toxicology results on the burn victim when they're in, but be sure to call if you find out anything else that'd be useful to the investigation. Or if you have any questions I can help answer," Chapman said.

"Will do, appreciate it," Kenner said.

Smoke, Chief Deputy Kenner, and I each gathered our thoughts then threw them back and forth for discussion. After ten minutes, Kenner stretched his arms then clapped his hands together. "I'll have our clerical staff search the databases for calls for service to the three residences in question over the last twenty years. Plus, we'll do a broader county-wide search to see if the four of you were on a call together that might have sparked the rabbit incidents. What key words should we search?"

"Try Feedlots. Animal Nuisance. Animal Neglect—" Smoke said.

"Cruelty to Animals," I added.

"See what those searches bring up," Smoke said.

Kenner jotted them down. "Sure thing, we'll take care of it. And I'll get word out to farmers advising them to get locks on the doors of their barns and other outbuildings if they don't have them already." Kenner pointed at me. "Per the sergeant's request."

Smoke glanced my way then nodded. "Mike, it wouldn't hurt to beef up patrol in Blackwood Township. I've mulled over the possibility that the firesetter is a neighbor, someone we know and who blends in with other folks in the township. After talking to Chapman, I'm thinking it's more a probability than a possibility. Frankly, I'm concerned about what the firesetter might have in store for us next."

"I'm with you on that one, and I'll make sure we show plenty of presence out there, let whoever is committing these crimes know that we're looking for him," Kenner said.

I nodded. "Thanks. I better call my grandparents, tell them about the fire in their barn. Then I'll stop after work and get a lock—"

"Kristen's barn is secure, isn't it?" Smoke interrupted.

His question made my heart skip a beat. If her barn burned down, it would be a devastating loss for our family. And the annual Labor Day weekend parties Mother hosted would come to a sudden, sad end for the scores of people who looked forward to the popular shindig every year.

"Yes, it is, but I'm going to double check her locks after all this," I said.

"Good idea," Smoke said.

"Anyway, back to my grandparents. I'm really conflicted about what to tell them. I have to be honest—my grandma knows me like the back of her hand—but I think whoever set that fire did it because it belongs to my grandparents, to get back at *me* for some reason. Taking the rocks from my place supports that theory. So it's a double whammy. They'll be more worried about me than about the fire."

Kenner narrowed his eyes on me. "Why do you think someone's trying to get back at you?"

"I don't know, but we do things in the line of duty that make people mad sometimes. I've had someone trespassing on my property at least three times in the last week. One left a dead rabbit and another—maybe it was the same person—left a lighter behind. Then they stole some rocks. I have the same last name and live on the same road as my grandparents. Their name is on their mailbox and they have that Welcome to the Alecksons' sign by their door."

Smoke nodded. "That makes it easier for someone looking for a particular someone. But they found Weber and Mason and me without all those guides. None of us have listed phone numbers, but in this day and age it's damn near impossible to hide."

"Unfortunate at times, isn't it?" I said.

"With staff looking into possible past incidents involving the four of you, hopefully they'll find something, point us in the right direction. We'll figure it out and put a stop to it," Kenner said.

I drew in a deep breath. "I've also made a decision I hope my mother will go along with. I want an alarm system installed in her barn."

Smoke raised his eyebrows then shrugged. "You could probably convince her of that. I know the guy that owns Rest Assured. They have wireless systems that are easy to install, and if I ask nice enough, I think Will could get it done today. If someone tried to break into her barn, not only would

Communications get notified, but she would get a text alert, too.

"How about John Carl and me? Could our numbers be added?"

"I'm sure that's not a problem. Tell you what, I'll go visit Kristen at her shop and give her our recommendations," he said.

"Thank you, Smoke. It'll be more convincing coming from you."

I used up most of my lunch break on a long conversation with my grandma. "We should pack up and come home," she said.

"I know how you feel, but there's really no need to cut your resort month short. John Carl has started his projects, and a lot of your furniture's in the shed. We're fine here. After we get locks on your barn doors and the security system installed in Mother's barn, I'll feel a hundred times better."

"Oh My Heart, there are times like this that you seem to be carrying the weight of the world on your shoulders."

My voice caught in my throat, and it took me a few seconds to free it. "Not quite the whole world, Grandma. Blackwood Township is heavy enough."

"I wholeheartedly agree, so you take good care," she said.

"I love you, Grandma."

"I love you more, My Heart." I'd decided many years before to let Grandma have the last words, and it was always those six.

I was on the road to Emerald Lake when Smoke phoned. I pulled onto the shoulder to answer. "A few things you should know. First off, your mother acquiesced after I promised we'd have the security system removed as soon as we caught the firesetter," Smoke said.

"She can be stubborn about the dumbest things sometimes. As safety minded as she is, you'd think installing an alarm system would be a no-brainer under the circumstances."

"You'd think. But at least she agreed, and Will is going to install it this afternoon. John Carl will be there to meet him."

"Nice. My computer-expert brother will be all over that."

"The other thing is, the ME's office just called to tell us one of the toxicology screens just came back on the blood alcohol level. Our victim's BAC was point-two-five," he said.

"Oh my gosh. Over three times the legal limit."

"He was blitzed, all right. The poor guy didn't have much of a chance."

"No. He was probably too impaired to escape," I said.

"Chances are he was sleeping then woke up choking from the smoke, was overcome, and went face down like we found him."

"The look on his face will haunt me to my dying day."

"I'm sure that's true for all of us. Oh, and another thing. I've got Bob Edberg calling dentists in both Oak Lea and Chaska, Ross Warren's two known cities of residence, trying to find one who treated him. I was hoping we could get an ID from dental records." Edberg was long-time deputy.

"And we're running his DNA, right?"

"That'll be next if we don't score with a dentist, or if it turns out our victim isn't Warren. If he's not in the database, getting a relative to give us a sample might be challenging. And they're working on the latents from the steering wheel to compare to his fingerprints."

"Speaking of fingerprints, anything back on the one from the Zippo?" I said.

"No. I'll make a note to check on it, see if we can speed it along."

"There are days we have way too much fun. I'm on my way to Emerald Lake to see if any of the business people recognize Warren, if they know anything about him."

"Good. And I'm about to track down Damon Backstrom," Smoke said.

"For your Come-to-Jesus meeting?"

"That's the one. I'm holding on to the belief that he'd rather give up the secret than spend the night in the Winnebago County Jail."

Getting a hold of Damon Backstrom proved more difficult than Smoke had hoped.

I hit pay dirt at the second gas station when I showed Ross Warren's photo to Harry, the clerk at the checkout counter. "Yeah, I know that guy. He drives an old green Jeep. And he looks different now than he used to. He looked rough when I saw him a few days ago, like he needed a haircut and a shave and a bath. But it could be he was doing some yard work, or other dirty work."

"So you've seen him in here before?" I said.

"Oh sure thing, Sergeant. Off and on for the last few months." *Months?* "Since around Easter, maybe. He's not the most talkative guy, but he's been coming in for gas for several years now. When I mentioned that I hadn't seen him for a while, he said he just got back from where he winters in Arizona," Harry said.

Several years? Like three years, about the time he moved away from Chaska? "Do you know his name?"

"The first time he came in he was wearing an old work shirt with the name Buzz on the pocket."

My heart started beating so fast I needed to catch my breath. I lifted my arm and coughed into my sleeve instead. "Buzz?"

"That's right. I remember things like names better when I read them."

I nodded. "Did Buzz happen to mention where he lives, when he's not in Arizona?"

"No, and I never asked him. Like I said, he's not what you'd call outgoing. I thought maybe he was lonely so I'd try to draw him out a little, you know, be nice to the guy, make him feel a little better. I always kind of wondered what his story was."

I'd thought the same thing on the traffic stop. "Everyone's got a story." And it seemed his had ended tragically. "How did he pay for his gas?"

"Always cash. That's why he paid inside instead of at the pump. Otherwise, I might not have remembered him," he said.

"Right."

Harry leaned in closer and lowered his voice. "Why are you asking about him, if you don't mind my asking?"

"It's about a case we're working on."

"Okay. Well you be sure to let me know if you need anything else." His face brightened like he was proud to be doing his part by helping me out on a case.

"Thank you, sir. I'll do that," I said.

My next stop was the liquor store. Gidget, a body double of Rosanne in her early days, was arranging wine bottles. I'd gotten to know her in my years on the job. "Greetings, Sergeant. Or did you make detective by now, seeing how you're not wearing your uniform."

"Hello, Gidget. No, I haven't made detective. But every once in a while they let me play one."

Her belly jiggled when she laughed. "Good one. So what can I do you for?"

I pulled out Ross Warren's photo and handed it to her. "Wondering if you recognize this man?"

"Oh sure. This must be an old picture, huh? He looks pretty good there." Few people made that comment about anyone's driver license photo. Mine looked like a mug shot.

"Do you know his name?" I said.

"Sure. He told me it was Ross. I think so I wouldn't call him sweetie. Don't remember if he gave me his last name."

"So he's been coming in here a while?"

"For the last two, three years now, I'd say. From spring until fall. And he comes in spurts. Like not every week, and then he might come in twice, even three times in the same week," she said.

"Did you ever ask him where he works, where he lives?"

"I tried to, believe you me. You know how nosy I am." She laughed again when I smiled. "He's one of those private guys who doesn't have much to say. All I know is that he works for a friend over the summer—but I don't know who that friend is—and then he goes south for the winter."

"What does he buy here?"

"Vodka mostly. And gin. Cheap stuff." She screwed up her face like she had taken a bitter pill. I doubted she displayed that same look when she rang up Warren's purchases.

"How did he pay, credit card, cash?"

"Always cash. Why? Is he in trouble with the law?" she said.

"We're working on something he may be involved with."

Gidget frowned and nodded. "Wouldn't surprise me one little bit if he was up to something."

33

It was after two o'clock when I pulled into the sheriff's parking lot. I sat for a moment wondering when all the balls we had up in the air were going to land. And how. It was the seventh and last day of my work stretch, and I needed to get my squad car to the night shift sergeant, per our rotation schedule. I sent him a text asking when and where he'd like to pick it up, and then headed into the office to write reports on the day's happenings. Smoke was waiting for me in the corridor.

"Edberg's had zero luck locating a dentist in Chaska, Oak Lea, or the surrounding areas. I'm sure there have been retirements in the twenty years since he lived here. And he may not have gone to the dentist in Chaska," Smoke said.

"True, maybe he had one in another city."

"I haven't been able to reach Damon Backstrom either. They checked out of the hotel and are most likely on their way back to Wisconsin. I got their address and home phone number, but he's not answering. I'd drive over if I knew he'd be there."

"Have you checked with his daughter?" I said.

"I tried her cell. I'm guessing she's at work and will call me after."

"Man, the time we can spend tracking people down. Well I had a couple of intriguing visits at businesses in Emerald Lake."

"Do tell."

"Both clerks I talked to said Ross Warren has been a seasonal customer for the last few years," I said.

"Seasonal?"

"As in a Snow Bird. One knew him as Ross and the other knew him as Buzz."

Smoke's eyes widened. "Unbelievable. No one else we checked with had a clue who Buzz was. If we'd only known who to ask in the first place."

"I know."

"What do you think? Could that person back by your trees have been Ross Warren?"

"I've been pondering that since Harry at the gas station told me he was wearing a shirt with Buzz on the pocket. And the answer? All I can say is that it's possible. Ross wasn't a very big guy, but since I only saw him sitting in the Jeep, I don't know how he moved, if he was as quick as the one back there."

"And you didn't get much of a look," he said.

"No, I didn't."

"If Warren was part of a fire-setting team, he can't tell us about it now."

"Not if he was the victim in the barn he can't." I swung the arm holding my briefcase. "I better get my reports written up and turned in."

Smoke nodded. "Catch you later."

At 3:35 I got a text message from the night sergeant asking about our shared squad car. I let him know it was in the parking lot and I'd gotten my things out of it, so he was welcome to pick it up any time. I'd find a ride home when I was ready.

By the time I distributed my reports my brain was fried. Smoke was stepping out of the chief deputy's office as I dropped the last of my reports in the plastic box holder outside his door. "I wondered if you were still here. I saw Hughes drive off with your squad car a while ago," he said.

"I'm done, and I'm done in."

"Long day."

"Longer week," I said.

"No doubt. You need a ride home?"

"If you're going my way."

"I am."

"I'll get my briefcase and meet you outside." When I turned around I caught several administrative assistants eyeing us with interest. I knew the question raised by staff from time to time around the water cooler was, "Are they or aren't they?" Involved or not? I smiled at the group and said, "See you Friday." Several of them smiled back.

Smoke was in his vehicle when I climbed into the passenger seat. "Is it still Monday?" I said.

He snickered. "The good thing about the long stretch you've had is you can look forward to three days off."

"Unless something else happens in Blackwood Township," I said.

"Let's try for some optimism."

"Whatever."

He reached over and patted my arm. "You want to stop at Kristen's house, see how they're coming along on the alarm system?"

"I would, thanks."

When we pulled into my mother's driveway, John Carl was helping Will load equipment into his van. They acted like a team. A team of techies.

"All set, Will?" Smoke asked when we were out of the car.

He nodded. "It was a dream job. Went off without a hitch," Will said and then zeroed in on me. "Are you Corky?"

"I am."

"Okay then. Your number is programmed in, and you'll get an alert if someone tries to enter the barn without the code," he said.

"Good deal."

Will raised a hand as a wave. "I'm off to finish a job I started earlier, but I wanted to be sure I got this one done."

"We appreciate you taking care of this so fast," I said.

"Not a problem. Old Elton here has helped me out a time or two." Will gave Smoke a pat on the back.

Smoke's eyebrows lifted. "Old? That's the pot calling the kettle black."

Will laughed, and it sounded like he was wearing a body mic the way it reverberated. Maybe he was. "Catch you all next time." He jumped in his van and off he went.

"He's on the jolly side," I said.

"Yep, always the same. Accommodating. Easy to work with."

"Someone you'd like to have a beer with, Corky," John Carl said.

"Me?" I crossed my eyes, stuck my tongue between my teeth, and wiggled my head a little. A face we'd all learned to make in kindergarten. He shook his head back at me.

"How are you and Mother doing after the shocker this morning?" I said.

"Okay, I guess. I'm thinking of staying at the grandparents' tonight."

"And leave Mom alone? Maybe that's not such a good idea."

"She's lived alone for ten years," he said.

"I meant because of all the weird stuff going on."

"I suppose."

Smoke lifted his hand. "I talked to Chief Deputy Kenner, and he's posting a deputy at the Alecksons' house tonight. Actually, there'll be five deputies doing two-hour shifts."

"Why didn't you tell me before?" I said.

"I was focused on Kristen's alarm system, and it slipped my mind." Smoke hadn't gotten nearly enough sleep for a number of nights.

I pulled out my phone. "I'll send him a thank-you text before *I* forget."

"Touche´. Let's take a look at the system before we leave."

John Carl walked us through it, pointing out technical details I didn't need to know because he did. "It looks good. We can all sleep a little easier now, huh?" Smoke said.

Smoke dropped me off at home, and tired though I was, I was more restless than anything. A cloud cover cooled the later afternoon air, and with Queenie having more kennel time than usual, I thought a longer, slower run was in order for both her and me. We'd go to County Road 35 then stop at Gramps' on the way back. After I'd changed and was ready, we were off. When we reached the county road, I saw a familiar figure heading east, toward us. I stopped, slipped Queenie's leash on her collar, and told her to sit.

We were all but blocking Sybil Harding's way, so she came to a stop on her bike and planted her feet on the ground, but kept her butt on the seat. Queenie tugged on her leash trying to reach Sybil, but I held her back. Barely. Sybil jerked back a bit. "Hi Sybil, sorry if she scared you. My dog loves people."

"Oh, okay."

Queenie kept tugging and stretching her nose as far as possible, sniffing at Sybil. "Queenie, be polite." But she ignored me and let out a persistent-sounding bark that startled both Sybil and me.

"Well, I better go," she said.

I stepped back pulling Queenie with me. "I apologize again for my dog's behavior."

"It's all right." She pedaled away before I had a chance to find out how things were going and if there was any special reason that brought her to her grandparents' house on a Monday.

"Queenie, what in the world is the matter?" She looked at me and whined then moved her head back and forth. "What? Do you sense something's off with her, too?"

Queenie barked again, and I read it as, "Yes." We turned around and ran to Gramps' house.

Mother was there as well, and the three of us commiserated far too long about the strange fire in my grandparents' barn. I'd decided not to tell my mother that some of the rocks used for the fire ring had come from my yard. Based on my years of experience as her daughter, I knew that when big things happened, or were in the works, it was best to give her the information in smaller doses over time to ease their digestion.

"Your brother was happy with the work the security man did. Thank Elton for arranging it," Mother said.

"Sure. Yes, it seems like a great system. And isn't it nice to know that if someone ever tries to break into your barn the sheriff's office will know about it right away?" I said.

"I suppose it is."

Later that evening I needed to do some investigative exploring, so Queenie and I hiked to the tree line on my back property then headed toward my grandparents' house. The sun was low in the sky and the floor bottom among the trees was darkening minute by minute. Queenie busied herself sniffing the ground and following trails along the way. It was a prime area for deer and smaller creatures to seek shelter and safety, so it shouldn't have surprised me when a deer darted out for her evening meal of field corn. I smiled at the graceful creature and chided myself for being jumpy. Other evening feeders and nocturnal critters would be emerging from their hiding places at any time.

I gave Queenie free rein, and she was hot on something's trail. I had to jog to keep up with her as she moved faster and faster, and led me straight to Grandma's and Grandpa's barn. She stopped, turned to me, and barked. "You've got a good nose, girl." But whose scent had she picked up? Animal or human?

There were sheets of wood nailed across the broken windows, and crime scene tape spanned the width of the barn doors. John Carl had added a steel padlock that secured the door pulls together. A burglar would need a heavy-duty bolt cutter to break through it. I wandered for the last moments before the sun disappeared below the horizon, looking around and hoping to find some piece of evidence we had missed earlier in the day. But there was nothing there. Our crime scene team had done their job well.

After making sure my grandparents' house and shed were locked, Queenie and I took what had suddenly become the long road home. At a slow walking pace. In fact, by the time we got home it was more of a dragging pace. But I had to make a final pass by the other three barn fire sites. I punched in the numbers on my garage door keypad.

Queenie was as excited for the final adventure of the day as she had been for the first. I opened the driver's side door, moved the seat forward, and she jumped into the back. I pushed the seat back then climbed in and picked up the copy of Ross Warren's DL photo lying on the passenger seat. "What is your story?" I said to it for the hundredth time.

I backed out and pulled the light button toward me. The disappearing headlight covers opened, and two circles of light appeared on the garage door as it closed. Twilight was fading but a bright moon kept the black of night at bay. I drove to the Simmonds' place first. There were lights on in the house. I drove by slowly looking at the barn's base, wondering if they would rebuild. Were the fires lit because of what happened in their family all those years ago? If Angela learned what it was, would she want to stay in Blackwood Township in her grandparents' home?

I turned around in the next driveway and crept along watching for anyone who might be sneaking around on the road or around the farms. When I reached County 35, I drove west to Collins Avenue and turned south. As I approached the Hardings' farm, I noticed a dim light shining from the attic window. There were no other lights on in the house from what I could see. I thought back to a few nights before when I'd imagined someone moving in the attic. Strange.

I pulled over, turned off my headlights, and waited. Sybil? I'd seen her earlier in the day, and it was possible she was still at her grandparents' house. But what would she be doing in the attic? Unless they had a great ventilation system it would feel like the inside of a hot oven up there. I waited, wondering if someone might pass by the window. But when Queenie whined, I took it as my signal to leave. Tempted though I was to phone Sybil, it could wait until morning.

Woody Nevins' barn was another mile down the road. His house was completely dark inside, and I figured he was on another truck run. I stopped and picked up Ross Warren's photo. Woody's yard light and the moon's beams added an eerie hue to his image.

"Seriously, how were you able to squat in Woody's barn? And use his Jeep without him noticing? How many times had you been here the last three years?" Queenie whined again. I reached back and scratched her head. "I'm not scolding you."

I turned around in Woody's driveway and went home. As I climbed the stairs on the way to my bedroom, all I could think about was my comfortable bed beckoning me. I had never been happier getting under the covers. I stretched to loosen my muscles then smiled, thinking that with the next day off work I would sleep as late as I wanted to.

At least that was my hope.

34

When the security alarm from my mother's barn rang on my cell phone, I jumped out of bed wishing I'd laid out some clothes, just in case. As I pulled on a pair of black jogging pants and a black hoodie, I uttered, "Thank the good Lord we got it in when we did."

I grabbed a pancake holster from the bed stand, clipped in on my waistband, secured my Glock into it, clipped my phone case on the other side of my pants then ran down the steps. Queenie was so close on my heels I nearly tripped. "You need to stay here, girl." I picked my radio out of its charger on my way through the kitchen, slipped it in its case, attached it to the back of my pants, and was in the GTO and flying to Mother's in less than three minutes.

I turned the interior lights switch off so they wouldn't come on when I opened the door, then killed the headlights before I pulled onto the side of the road, south of her driveway. I slid out, drew my weapon, eased the car door shut as quietly as possible, and visually searched for signs of the intruder. Seeing no one, I cautiously jogged down the row of lilac bushes toward the barn.

I'd warned John Carl not to play hero in case of an event, but he was standing outside by the back of the house anyway. And to make matters worse, so was my mother. At least they were in the shadows. I got their attention then lifted my left hand with my thumb sticking up and indicated they needed to get back in the house.

Sirens in the distance gave me hope a deputy was coming our way, and I prayed he'd silence them before he got much closer. The intruder didn't deserve a warning. I crept to the barn then backed up against it and made my way down the length of the front, around the side corner, down to the back, and stopped. Then I covertly peered around the corner. The door wasn't standing open and the lock appeared intact. But the alarm had not activated without reason. Someone must have attempted access.

No one was running away—or moving at all—as far as I could see by the light of the moon. Then my eyes landed on a little object on the ground in front of the door. It was gray with a white belly and had a white cotton ball tail. I'd been pulled out of REM sleep for another rabbit delivery. That revelation filled me with both anger and angst. The emotions set my hands to shaking, so I secured the Glock in its holster before I dropped it. A vehicle's tires crunching on the driveway shifted my focus, and I crept back to see who it was. Sergeant Brad Hughes, in our shared squad car, sans the emergency lights and sirens. Thank you, Brad.

I moved over to the lilac bushes and waved him over once he was out of the vehicle. He leaned in close to me and whispered, "Did you check the area in back?"

"I did, and didn't spot a living soul."

"Gone before you got here?"

"I guess. But they left a gift." I gave him the rundown on the rabbit deliveries, past and present.

"All the craziness out here the last week has got us all scratching our heads," he said.

"I know, and now that my grandparents' and my mother's properties were tagged, I'm ready for battle. The last thing I feel like doing is to 'keep calm and carry on,'" I said.

"I'm with you on that one. Do we need the crime scene team out here?"

"No, that's not necessary," I pulled out my phone and checked the time, "at nearly four in the morning. You can interview my mother and brother, and then I'll help you process the scene. It shouldn't take long."

Hughes got a bright spotlight from his trunk and handed it to me. "So you haven't talked to your family yet?"

"No."

"All right, I'll go see if they heard or saw anything."

My phone gave a single buzz indicating a text message. It was from John Carl. "Can we come out now?"

I phoned him back instead. "Not yet. Sergeant Hughes is on his way in to visit with the two of you, so you can let him in."

I used the spotlight to illuminate the ground and around the door of the barn as I checked for evidence. Hughes joined me a few minutes later. "They got nothin'."

"I figured as much or I would have heard about it first thing."

We searched the area to the best of our abilities. "It needs to rain for about three days. The farmers are crying, and so are we," Hughes said.

"We've been moaning about that since the first fire last week. We can't get a readable footprint. Or vehicle tracks," I said.

"It's supposed to rain tomorrow, so let's hope the weather gurus are right this time."

Hughes left with the photos and the rabbit at 5:12 a.m. There was no other evidence to collect. My mother and brother were anxiously waiting for me in the kitchen. "Would you like a cup of coffee, dear?" Mother looked beyond weary.

"No thanks. I'm crawling back in bed as soon as I get home. Brad said you saw nothing and heard nothing."

They both shook their heads. "Just the warning alert on our phones," John Carl said.

"Okay. This is my warning, and I mean it. Do not go running out to get a look at the bad guys, or try to catch them if this ever happens again. We have no idea if they're armed or what. The way they're racking up a growing list of felony charges, they may be dangerous if cornered. You get the alerts to be alerted *not* to respond."

John Carl's face colored. One of his pet peeves was getting lectured by his younger sister. I didn't blame him, but it was critical that it was driven into his thick skull. He finally nodded. Reluctantly.

"Corinne, you don't have to be so harsh with your brother," Mother said.

"Sorry, but apparently I do. I don't want anything to happen to either one of you."

After attending to Queenie, I fell into bed exhausted beyond words, and even with all the turmoil in my life I fell into a deep, dreamless sleep. About the same place I'd left off a couple of hours before.

Queenie nudged my arm with her nose and startled me awake. I realized my phone was ringing and snatched it from my bed stand. "H'lo?"

"Sorry I woke you, sleepyhead. I thought you'd be up by now." It was Smoke.

"What time is it?"

"Ten fifteen," he said.

I rubbed my eyes and sat up. "Really? What's up?"

"First off, I read Brad Hughes's report about the alarm at your mother's house at three forty-three this morning. Why didn't you call me?"

"We had it covered, and you needed an uninterrupted night's sleep," I said.

"Which I got, so thank you. But another rabbit? What is going on?"

"It is getting freakier and freakier. I wonder if they knew we had an alarm, and rattled the door to set it off. Or if he—she—was surprised by it and laid the bunny down then got the heck out of Dodge."

"Suffice it to say that it's good to know the system worked. How is Kristen doing?" he said.

"I'm not sure, but John Carl was with her, and she should be at the shop by now."

"That should help keep her mind off things. The admin staff finished running the reports, looking for a case that Mason, Weber, you, and I worked together that might've prompted this mess. First they ran ones that had any reference to animals. And when that came up dry they checked all of our mutual cases. Ones we'd written reports for. We may have been at other scenes together that didn't require reports from all of us."

"How many are there?" I said.

"Two hundred and three."

"I would've guessed that."

"No, not the kind of thing you keep track of."

"But none related to fires or rabbits?"

"No. So I scanned through the reports and one in particular jumped out at me. It was at the Hardings', years back. Coincidentally, the first barn fire was at their place. We referenced that nine-one-one call when we were out there."

"Sure, from the young girl," I said.

"That's the one."

"You think there could be a connection between that and what's happening now?"

"I don't know. Nothing I can put my finger on. Truth be told, I had a strange feeling about that report at the time and whenever I've thought of it since. Is there anything you remember from back then that could have triggered all this?"

"Oh man, let me think. All of us got to the Hardings within minutes of each other. We knocked on the door and got no answer so we entered the house, announced ourselves, walked through every room, main level, basement, upstairs. I remember the basement was more of a cellar: stone walls, dirt floor, musty smelling. Not much down there except for a small freezer and some canning jars on a shelving unit.

"The rooms in the main levels of the house were tidy, no signs of a struggle, no blood anywhere, no unusual odors. Nothing to indicate anyone had been killed. We left and then later on, after you talked to the Hardings, we determined it was unfounded."

"That's right on with my recollection and what the reports state. But there was something about the way Mr. Harding reacted to the incident that didn't sit right with me. Nothing I could put my finger on, more of a gut feeling. Obviously, if kids really had gone into your house to make a prank call you'd be upset, but my impression was there was more to the story, something Harding wasn't telling me," he said.

"Like his granddaughter. It'd be easier to pull wisdom teeth than information out of Sybil."

"Speaking of Sybil, did you find out if she lived here as a kid?"

"No, she grew up in southern Minnesota. St. Peter."

"And she lives in Golden Valley now?"

"Correct."

"And her parents are in New Mexico?"

"Yes. Why are you asking?"

"Just trying to put some family background together. First and foremost, what was it that Sybil's father said or did that caused the rift? And why did the grandparents give power of attorney to Sybil instead of one of their sons? I'd like to get their contact info so we can talk to them, get answers to those questions."

"I'll ask Sybil. She didn't know anything about the family feud. As far as why the grandparents chose her, I'd guess it's because she's close by. The sons are far away—Canada and New Mexico."

"No brothers or sisters?"

"She said she's an only child."

"All right. Well, I did a little more digging and found out Damon Backstrom, the one who has wholeheartedly embraced the code of silence relating to family matters, works in St. Paul, commutes from western Wisconsin. I'm going to surprise him on his lunch break."

No one liked those kinds of surprises. "What time are you leaving?"

"Ten fifty. His break's right at noon, so I figured I'd give him time for lunch before I show my ugly mug." Smoke's mug was far from ugly.

"I'd like to tag along," I said.

"You should take the day off. Do something recreational."

"Like you? You've worked how many days in a row now?"

"I'll be catching up on days off soon enough."

"Captain, may I?"

It took him a few seconds to answer. "If you're at the office in forty minutes."

"I'll be waiting for you in the parking lot."

Damon Backstrom was a machinist for a reputable company and, as predicted, was not the least bit happy to see Smoke and me when we walked into the lunchroom. He was sitting at a table facing the door, eating with another man about his age. I hung in the background when Smoke walked over to him. "Good afternoon, Damon. Go ahead and finish your lunch. We'll be over there when you're done." He acted like Backstrom was expecting us.

Backstrom didn't say yea or nay, or nod or shake his head. Mr. Stoic. A guy I would not want to play poker with. Smoke and I sat down at an empty table. We didn't talk. We listened and casually looked around. Backstrom's tablemate moved his head toward us, and must have asked him who we were or why we were there, because Backstrom shook his head and waved his hand like it was nothing, or he'd tell him later. He spoke too low to hear, and I couldn't read his lips from that angle.

Backstrom stuffed the paper remains from his lunch into his metal pail then closed it, stood up, and walked over to our table like he was dragging a fifty-pound weight on each leg. "What are you doing here?" he said.

"Have a seat," Smoke said and pulled out a chair. "This can be a brief conversation, or it can get long and ugly. It's all up to you."

Backstrom sank down onto the chair and looked at me. I gave him my best, "I'm so sorry," face. And I was. A family had been torn apart.

"I'm not comfortable talking to you about private matters here at work. Can we meet somewhere later?" Backstrom said.

"How much longer is your break?" Smoke said.

Backstrom looked at his watch. "Sixteen minutes."

"Is there a better place to talk than the lunchroom?"

"The parking lot, maybe."

"We'll follow you," Smoke said.

The three of us trekked outside and went over to a bench by a large bush. Backstrom sat down on one end, Smoke sat on the other. Smoke turned to face him but Backstrom looked straight ahead. I backed up to a nearby tree and pulled a memo pad and pen from my back pants pocket. My main job was to listen and observe.

"Damon, I know you've been protecting a family secret for all these years. And I respect that. But here's the deal, things are escalating in Blackwood Township, and you've got a daughter and grandchildren living there. I know you must appreciate our concern. I sure would."

"They should move," was his response.

"Whether they do or don't is up to them. But what is up to you—right here, right now—is whether you're going to cooperate with us, tell us what happened all those years ago so we can figure out who's committing these crimes, and why."

Backstrom shifted his body toward Smoke. "I don't see how they can be related."

"Why's that?"

"You asked about Sybil, my cousin's daughter? If you're wondering about her being involved, she wasn't even born when it happened." Little zings ran through me.

"You said it was twenty years ago. Sybil's older than that."

Backstrom shrugged and shook his head. "I don't know. They just had the one daughter, Roberta. The one that . . . that the bad things happened to." He lifted his hands and dropped his face into them.

Smoke shot me a side look, and gave Backstrom a moment before he said, "Roberta. How old was Roberta at the time?"

"Six."

"What bad things?"

Backstrom didn't lift his head when he sniffled and said, "The worst things."

"Sexual things?" Smoke said.

"Yes." And then he cried.

"And your cousin accused you of doing those things?"

He sniffled some more. "No. It was my son."

"Okay. When you're ready, I need you to tell me what led to that accusation."

Backstrom used his shirt sleeve to dry his eyes. "We were at my aunt and uncle's place. The Hardings. It was my cousin Buzz's birth—"

Smoke jerked slightly and interrupted with, "Buzz?"

My cousin's name is Melvin, but he always went by Buzz." More little zings set my heart a pounding.

Smoke stopped, and he jotted that down. I knew his thoughts were racing, and he needed a few seconds. "Melvin Harding, and he went by Buzz. I interrupted you, sorry. Go on."

"Anyway, it was his birthday, July fourteenth."

The same date as the first fire. Smoke managed to keep his expression noncommittal.

Backstrom went on. "Buzz had just gotten out of the service, and his parents decided to have a little celebration since it coincided with his birthday and all. I can tell you we would never have gone if we'd known what was going to happen."

"We've all had twenty-twenty hindsight experiences. Please go on," Smoke said.

"Buzz had taken Roberta, my son, Dustin, and Ross Warren, my other cousin's son, to the barn. The rest of us hadn't noticed, or paid much attention. Everyone else was in the house, except for Perry and me."

"Perry?"

"My cousin, Roberta's dad and Buzz's brother."

Smoke nodded. "Go on."

"We didn't know anything was wrong until we heard Roberta scream. We found the four of them in the barn. My cousin Buzz had molested little Roberta, but Perry saw red and thought they'd all taken part. Ross's pants were unzipped. Dustin had a pained look on his face. He told me later that Buzz had told Ross to get ready because he was next in line to be with her."

I swallowed slowly to calm my churning stomach.

Smoke lowered his voice. "How old were Dustin and Ross?"

"Dustin was fourteen, Ross was seventeen, I think. It was chaotic after that. First Perry hit Buzz so hard it knocked him out. Then he gave Ross a kick in the pants that sent him to the ground. Perry yelled at Ross to get up and get the hell off his property, that he'd take it up with his grandparents. Ross's parents were dead, and he lived with them. Then he picked up his daughter. She was bleeding."

Damon stopped and wiped his eyes again. It was a while before he spoke again. "Perry looked at me with what I'd call pure hatred and told me if my son ever had any contact with anyone in his family again he would make sure he was sent to juvenile detention for a long time. My son was just a kid. He should have run for help when Buzz was doing that to Roberta, but Buzz had him so scared that he didn't."

"What happened to Buzz after that?"

Backstrom shrugged. "He was still unconscious when we left the barn."

"So you packed up your family and that was the last time any of you had contact with anyone in the Harding or Grant families?"

"Yes, that's true. We never talked to either family and they never got a hold of us. Like I told you yesterday, I didn't know Buzz was in Canada. I figured he would spend a long time in prison for what he did. Life, even. I never really cared for him, but I had no idea he'd do anything like that to a little girl. And his own niece. I get the sickest feeling whenever I think of it."

As it turned out, Buzz might have preferred time in prison to what he actually got.

35

Belle and Birdie

"Things are shaping up, Birdie. And the authorities haven't figured out what's going on," Belle told her.

Birdie looked up at the sky, maybe to pick out shapes in the clouds.

"And that's just as well. We're getting closer to the big event, and the longer they stay in the dark, the easier it will be for us."

Birdie put her hand on Belle's arm, giving her the strength to carry on.

"It'll make us both happier when it's all said and done, right?" Belle took Birdie's hand in hers and kissed it.

36

Smoke and I were cruising down I-94 on our way out of St. Paul, each of us respecting the other's need for some quiet time to reflect. A multitude of thoughts were vying for my consideration, and needed processing. As we passed the Minneapolis city limits sign, Smoke hit the steering wheel. "I don't have to tell you that's the worst for me. I've had to walk out of an interview with a suspect so I didn't reach across the table and ring his neck. Or worse."

Crimes against children were despicable on every level. "They are the worst. No question."

"We need to pull the records on Melvin Harding, find out about his disposition, how much time he served," he said.

"We also need to find out where Roberta is. According to Backstrom, she'd be twenty-six now, and that doesn't make sense. Sybil said she didn't have any siblings, and her license says she's twenty-six."

"It makes no sense, unless she changed her name from Roberta to Sybil."

"That might be the case, and it's yet another question to ask. What an awful thing she went through, if it was her. It could explain a lot of things," I said.

"Not to mention that sexual abuse is a top reason females set fires."

"We've got to track her down. Like right now."

"Not *we*. Me. It's your day off," he said.

"Last night I drove by her grandparents' house, and there was a light on in the attic. I planned to talk to her about it today, so I'll give her a call, and you can follow up with her later. Is that all right?"

"You drive a hard bargain."

But Sybil did not answer my call, as per usual. When it went to voicemail, I said, "Hi Sybil, Sergeant Aleckson calling. I drove by your grandparents' house last night, and I noticed there was a light on in the attic. It's been so hot, and I was concerned with no one living there that it may pose a hazard. Please give me a call. Thank you." I disconnected. "Smoke, how about we stop by her place in Golden Valley? She might be home. And to be frank, I think I should be there when you talk to her. Girls who have been abused would rather talk to another girl."

"You got that right. What's the address?" he said.

I found it in my memo book then punched it into the map app on my phone. "Head west on Highway Fifty-five, then turn north on Winnetka." Smoke followed my directions, but it led to a dead end. The address was not a home or an apartment building. It was a restaurant.

"You don't say." Smoke pulled over to the side of the street and pulled the mobile data terminal in closer. "Do you have her full name and DOB?" He accessed the state motor vehicle records. I read the information I'd recorded on Sybil, and he typed it in. A few seconds later it came back with the same information. "Her mailing address is a restaurant?" Smoke opened his door. "I'll be right back." He got out, jogged into the store, and was out again in minutes shaking his head. "They have no idea who she is. And she does not get her mail there," he said as he climbed behind the wheel.

"I don't get it. I know it's easy enough to get a fake license, but the state issued this one. It's in the system."

"Looks like she got a bad address past them, and that tells me she doesn't want the authorities to know where she really lives. Unless the state screwed up the address, and she didn't correct it. Either way, it's on her," he said.

"Is Sybil really Roberta? If she's the firesetter, it's scary to think what she'll do next, what she's capable of. My impression is she got lost in the shuffle of life, that she could use some help. I didn't peg her as a cunning conniving criminal."

He chuckled. "That was a mouthful. And you're right about her needing help. If she is the firesetter she needs big-time help."

"Our next step?"

"For starters, I'll let the DMV know about the bad address. Then it's tracking down Melvin Harding and his criminal history. And Perry Harding to verify Backstrom's story and tell us where his daughter Roberta is. Sybil said she's an only child but that might be a lie too," he said.

"I agree. We need to set up surveillance on the Hardings' house. Sybil is bound to show up there sooner or later."

"True. But you gotta be more creative hiding out in the country when there aren't houses and other buildings around to conceal you."

"Our firesetter's been successfully doing that for over a week," I said.

"You got me on that one."

37

Smoke pulled up next to my car in the sheriff's lot and parked.

"No sheriff again today," I said noticing his empty spot.

"Some folks at the office are getting kinda frustrated. He's been going through his office, packing up stuff, but he won't say whether he's hanging it up, or not."

"Elections aren't until next year."

"It's not a good situation, all the way around." We got out of the car then he said, "Your job—for what's left of today—is to try to forget about your job."

Like that was possible. "Can I make a request?"

"What's that?"

"That you'll call me if we get any lab results back," I said.

He sucked in a breath. "All right, will do." He headed to the office, and I climbed into the GTO. As I started the engine, I noticed a silver Honda Civic drive slowly down the street in front of me. The woman in the driver's seat turned her head my way as she passed by. Her sunglasses covered half her face, but I had little doubt it was Darcie. Vince Weber lived three or four blocks away. I pulled out my phone and called him. "Yo, Sergeant, what's up?" he said.

"Are you home?"

"No, I'm actually grocery shopping."

I got straight to the point. "I think I just saw Darcie."

"Ah, geez. Where are you?"

"Sheriff's parking lot. She was heading south on First then turned left on Thirty-five toward downtown. I didn't get her plate."

"Yeah well, she stopped by my house yesterday when I was gone. I alerted a couple of my neighbors about her, asked them to let me know if they ever saw her. And one of 'em told me he saw her knocking on my door," he said.

"Did she call, send a text?"

"No. But if she's trying to catch me at home to surprise me or something, that makes my skin crawl. I'll call her, see if there's something specific she's itching to tell me. I was hopin' our last meeting was going to be our *last* meeting."

"After your warning, she's probably afraid to call or text, realizing you'll have a record of it."

"I'll give her this one last chance to tell me whatever it is. After that, I'll tell her to have her parents relay any messages," he said.

"If you end up filing a no-contact order, she won't even be able to do that."

"Yeah, so we'll see where the discussion—ahem—leads."

"Take care," I said.

"You, too."

I pushed the end button and considered whether to swing by Weber's house in case Darcie showed up again. But owning the only 1967 red GTO in Oak Lea put me at a disadvantage for blending in, surveillance-wise. That's where Gramps' old Buick came in handy. But on a different day. Today I needed to spend my investigative scouting time on the lookout for someone else. Someone who had lied about her address.

Smoke's heart-to-heart with Damon Backstrom had raised questions we needed answers for. Smoke would be running checks on Melvin, Perry, and Roberta at the office, where he'd have computer access to criminal histories. I'd leave him to Melvin, but I was too curious to wait on Perry and Roberta. When I got home, I let Queenie out and then headed to my office den for a little Internet browsing.

I logged in then searched for Perry Harding in Minnesota and New Mexico. I found his past and current addresses plus his phone number in minutes. But after typing in Roberta's name, the wind was knocked out of my sails. The first thing that popped up was her obituary. Eight years earlier. I clicked to open it and read the frustratingly few words about her. She was born to Perry and Vienne Harding. She was survived by her parents and sister, Sybil. The dates of birth and death were listed, but not where she was born, nor where she had died. Or the cause of her untimely death at age eighteen. Natural, accidental, unexpected, what? The service was private: family only. Roberta's date of birth jumped out at me. I fished my memo book from my back pocket and paged back to the date of birth Sybil had given me. Yep, it was exactly the same.

I sat for another minute re-reading the obituary and wondering if my eyes were playing tricks on me, if the eight was really a three. Or maybe there was a typographical error.

If Sybil and Roberta were twins, Damon Backstrom would have known that. So would Angela. She remembered having a cousin, she'd certainly know if there had been two. Plus the obituary would read Roberta was survived by her twin sister, Sybil. Twins always got that recognition.

The Backstroms didn't know Sybil, yet Sybil shared Roberta's birthday. She'd told me she was an only child. Her driver's license said she was twenty-six. Then again, her address was incorrectly listed on it. So what was true? It seemed that all roads of unanswered questions led back to Sybil.

I was trying to decide what to do next when Smoke phoned. "I heard back from forensics on your beekeeper creeper," he said.

"What'd they find out?"

"Not enough, sorry to say. All they could do was give an estimate of the person's height and weight. They think she is around five five, and weighs one fifteen to one thirty. They couldn't pull out any kind of image of the face, even a partial."

"You said 'she.'"

"Forensics isn't positive about that, but given their experience looking at tons of videos over the years, they're basing that on the person's size and how she moved," he said.

"Backs up what we thought."

"It does. And I reported Sybil's incorrect address to DMV, and they said they'd look into it."

"Good."

"Well, that's all for now."

"Actually, I have something, too," I said.

"Do tell."

"Roberta Harding died eight years ago when she was just eighteen."

"Ah, that's sad to hear. I've been thinking about her and that incident with her uncle and cousins. Something was seriously wrong with Melvin—Buzz. To abuse his little niece while his cousins watched—not to mention that the rest of the family was nearby—tells me two things: he was either mentally ill, or evil, and it wasn't the first time he'd done it. I'm about to search the records on him," Smoke said.

"Ross Warren was wearing his uncle's shirt, or at least one with his uncle's nickname on it. Does it make sense that he'd have his lighter, too? And was it Ross who lost it on my property last week?"

"Could very well be."

"According to the obituary, Roberta has the exact same DOB as Sybil," I said.

"That makes zero sense."

I filled him in on the few details given in the tribute then said, "Backstrom said she wasn't even born when the family broke up. Sybil's gotta be using her sister's birthday, but why? Everything keeps circling back to her, yet she claims to know virtually nothing about her family. I did find her parents' address in New Mexico, though."

"So that part is true anyway. What is it?" After I gave him the contact info, Smoke said, "When we get more sorted out, I'm going to talk to Marcella, see what her take on the family is based on what we know. Psychologically-speaking."

Marcella. The woman who interrupted my dinner plans with Smoke. Technically, I guess it was the other way around. I was curious about what she wanted to talk to him about, but it wasn't the time to ask. "She's been a good resource the last few years," I said.

"That she has. All right, I'll get back on track here and run down the leads."

After we disconnected, I sat for a minute longer contemplating my next course of action, knowing I had to find Sybil and talk to her in person. It was mid-afternoon when I drove over to Gramps' house with Queenie. He graciously lent me the use of his car, and said he'd watch Queenie for the time I was away. The Hardings' place was just over a mile west of my house, as the crow flies. Part of my Gramps' acres spanned almost the whole distance, minus the two township roads. I lived on the east side of mine and the Hardings were on the west side of theirs.

Leroy also rented those fields from Gramps, and had half the acres in corn and half in soybeans. There was a vehicle path that ran between them. I drove south on Brandt Avenue to where the path started then turned into the right of way. After traveling eight feet or so, I was in the fields with crops on either side of me. They were rolling hills, and I parked in a lower area not visible from Collins Avenue. I put on a sunhat, not as a disguise, but as shade from the heat of the sun. Then I collected the small backpack I'd filled with water, binoculars, and a book to read. I got out of the car and stepped to the south side of the cornfield, using the crops as cover as I made my way toward Collins.

There was a small clump of trees on the west side of the field, and I figured it was a good place to hunker down and keep watch. I'd planned to sit on the ground among the trees, but when I got there another opportunity presented itself instead. There were two-foot-long boards nailed to the backside of an old oak that provided steps up to its massive branches. It looked like they'd been there for years, but they seemed sturdy enough. I cautiously checked each one as I climbed up. Two branches that grew in opposite directions at the same height provided an ideal crook to sit in.

I set my pack on the branch beside me, made sure my phone was on silent, and commenced my watch on the Hardings' farmstead, perhaps two hundred feet away. Sybil supposedly lived in Golden Valley but she'd been in Oak Lea on a regular basis the past week, and I was determined to figure out what was going on with her.

Damon Backstrom's words kept repeating themselves over and over in my brain, and gave me the same ill feeling every time. Melvin was living as a free man in Canada. And his parents apparently trusted him with their care. I was counting on Smoke to get helpful answers about Roberta, Sybil, and the rest of the family from Sybil's parents. I also wondered if they'd discussed the heinous crimes Melvin had committed.

I had no idea what the traffic count on Collins Avenue was on any given weekday, but it was a low number. Over the course of my first two hours in the tree, I counted twenty-three vehicles, mostly pickups. There was no activity around the Harding house at all. It was past suppertime when I finally sent Smoke a text message asking what he'd found out.

He responded with a phone call. "Sorry, I was going to stop by your house on my way home but saw your car at your gramps' house. Are you home now?"

"Not yet," I said.

"What I found out is par for the course on this case. No records on Melvin after his discharge from the Navy. No arrest report, and I haven't been able to locate him in the U.S. or Canada."

"No."

"I'd say his brother gave him the same, 'I never want to see you again' speech, and Melvin took off for parts unknown. Could've taken on a new identity. The statute of limitations has run out on the sex offense, or I would happily travel to wherever he is and drag his sorry ass back here."

"He deserves it," I said.

"Yes, he does. And to top things off, I've gotten no response from Perry."

"I wonder what he thinks of his parents living with his sick brother."

"Family dynamics can be a funny thing. I've been wondering why an elderly couple would choose winter in Canada over New Mexico," Smoke said.

"So many aspects of this case are off-kilter."

"I even tried getting a hold of Sybil, so we'll see if she returns my call. I'm hoping the extra patrol we got scheduled the next couple of days will bring in something."

"Me too," I said.

I was about to climb down from my perch when a familiar bicyclist slowed down by the Hardings' driveway and pulled in. I didn't have a good view of the garage and couldn't see what she did with the bike. I called Smoke back.

"Corinne again?" he said.

"I wanted to let you know I happened to see Sybil ride her bike into her grandparents' yard a minute ago."

He lowered his voice. "Where are you?"

"Across the road from there."

"I'm going to pay Sybil a visit. You need to go home, and remind yourself there are very good reasons why you get days off. No argument."

"All right, but tell me how it goes." I hung up, knowing it was best to make a quick getaway when the getting was good. I slid around to the back of the tree and climbed down the steps. I wondered what kids had done the work and sent up a "thank you" for the perfect secret spying spot. I didn't think Sybil would be able to see me from the house, but I bent down low as I made my way back to Gramps' car. In case. I climbed behind the wheel, turned around, and drove to his house.

As I pulled into his garage, something on the windshield of my GTO caught my eye. *A red blob.* I couldn't get the car parked fast enough. I grabbed the keys, hopped out in a flash, shut the overhead door behind me, and moved to my car, keeping my eyes on the deposit.

Dear Lord! I pulled out my phone, snapped a picture of it, and sent it to Weber. He'd know how I felt. A few seconds later he wrote, "You home?" I replied, "Gramps'. Heading home."

Queenie was barking as I ran to Gramps' door. I was relieved when I opened the door and saw him sitting in his chair. A vandal had been in his driveway, and his house was unlocked. Queenie greeted me, so I gave her a quick scratching.

Gramps lifted a hand when he saw me. "Hi there, Corky."

I willed myself to sound calm. "Hi, Gramps. I was wondering if Queenie was barking earlier, like someone was outside."

"As a matter of fact, she was. Maybe an hour ago. She ran over to the door and barked away. I was about to get up to check it out when she stopped. Why would you ask that?" he said.

"Um, someone left something on my car."

His brows knitted together, and he shook his head. "They didn't come to the door."

"And that brings up a good point. I really need you to keep your doors locked when you're here alone. Even if Queenie's with you. Will you do that?"

He lifted his hand like he was going to argue then set it down again. "If it makes you feel better, Dearie, then I will."

"It does, so thank you. Can Queenie stay a while longer? I need to take care of something."

"Of course," he said.

I put Gramps' car keys in their designated dish and retrieved mine from the same spot. "See you later." I dashed off, fueled by adrenaline.

I wasn't home a minute before Vince Weber pulled into my driveway. "This is becoming a bad, bad habit," he said as he joined me in the garage and looked at the deposit. "It's gotta be blood, right?"

"Looks like it to me."

"And nothin' back from the lab on Darcie's DNA yet?"

Another vehicle on my driveway caught our attention, and when we saw it was Darcie, I don't know which of us was caught more off guard.

We went out to meet her as she stepped out of her car. "What are you doing here, Darcie?" Weber said.

She pointed at me. "She's the reason you broke up with me. You two are always together."

"We work together," I said.

"It's more than that. You're not working now. So what were you doing in the garage together?"

"It's none of your beeswax," Weber said. "But what *is* my business is: you followed me. You've been spying on me," Weber said.

Darcie stuck her chin up. "I was on my way to your house when I saw you leave, that's all."

Weber was red from the top of his head on down. He took a step closer to Darcie and pointed at her car. "Get back in there, drive yourself home, and we'll call it a day."

"Vincent—"

"No." He opened her car door. "Go."

The hateful look Darcie sent me as she reluctantly complied mentally prepared me for whatever she might pull next. I casually slid my hand to my side, ready to draw my weapon if she did anything stupid, and then moved for a better view of her.

"Vince," I said to redirect his anger—his tunnel vision—to alert him he should back away. It took a second to register. He walked around Darcie's car and then to the other side of his truck.

Darcie gave me one last look of disgust before she backed out onto Brandt, and slowly drove away.

"That woman is frickin' nuts," Weber said.

"You need a restraining order. Now that I've seen Darcie in action, I agree that her beauty really is only skin deep."

"Told ya." Vince rolled his shoulders a few times. "I'm gonna talk to the county attorney tomorrow, give him all I have on Darcie so I can file that order. Now let's focus on your deal."

I phoned Communications and requested a deputy to report to my house to collect some evidence. While we waited, I filled Weber in on all that had transpired that day. "So you think Sybil is wrapped up in all this, the fires and the other shenanigans?" he said.

"She's gotta be. The trouble is, all we've got on her so far is false info on her DL. At least that gives us a foot in the door."

"Why do you think she'd be pulling this crap?"

"If she's the firesetter, a common reason females set fires is because they've been sexually abused. Her sister was. Maybe she was too," I said.

"So her sister died eight years ago, right? And she lived in St. Peter. We should see if there was a rash of fires down there before she died."

I elbowed Weber. "Sometimes you're worth your weight in gold."

When his brows drew together, his eyes squinted. "Have you weighed me lately?"

I shook my head and laughed.

Deputy Holman arrived and collected the evidence and the information he needed for the report. After Holman and Weber left, I leaned back against the trunk of my car, baffled and riled-up. On top of everything else that was going on,

Darcie had to show up and throw some more drama at Weber and me.

Smoke stopped by while I was still fuming. He walked over with a frown on his face. "What is it?" he said.

I told him about Darcie's visit and what Weber was planning to do.

"So she didn't accept his 'no way in hell' speech?" he said.

I shook my head. "He realized how serious it was when she followed him here and accused us of being together."

"Better late than never. If she contacts you again, I think you should get an order too."

"I hope it doesn't come to that," I said.

Then I told Smoke about the blood drop, and he punched a fist into his open hand. "No cameras at your gramps' place, of course. Why has nobody—besides you, that is—seen anyone suspicious in the neighborhood?"

I shrugged. "It's gotta be a combination of good planning and better luck."

"I'd say. Well my visit to the Harding household was fruitless. Sybil won't answer the door or her phone. But we got nothing really to bring her in on."

"No word from her parents yet?"

"Nope," he said.

"Funny how no one in that family wants to talk to you."

"You think?"

"Weber gave me an idea of something to check out. We talked about how sexual abuse sometimes triggers fire setting, and he suggested checking out suspicious fires in St. Peter, where Sybil's family lived. He was thinking before Roberta died, since we know what happened to her, but I say check any in the last ten years, at least."

"I'll get on that in the morning. I made a plea to Kenner before I got here, asked if I can assign a deputy on each shift to keep tabs on Sybil, see where she goes. He okayed the OT, starting tonight at twenty-three hundred."

I sucked in a deep breath, looked heavenward, and said, "Thank you."

38

Belle and Birdie

Belle climbed up the tree and joined Birdie on the branch. "Well, what do you think, Birdie? I saw that sergeant sneaking around here earlier. What was she doing?"

Birdie searched Belle's face and raised her eyebrows.

Belle shook her head. "Maybe we should find another place to meet."

Birdie shrugged.

"No, you don't think so? I understand. This has always been our favorite place, our special place. You've been here every time I've asked you. Maybe that's why I feel closest to you here, like nothing will ever really separate us."

Birdie leaned her head on Belle's shoulder, cajoling Belle to feel more relaxed than she had for a long, long time. "Yes, I forgive you, Birdie. But I don't have to tell you how happy I was when you came back."

She felt Birdie's gentle nod.

39

Vince Weber sent me a text at 10:18 on Wednesday morning. "Paperwork done."

I called him back. "It was the right thing to do, Vince."

"I guess."

"Even though your relationship with your in-laws is strained, you need to talk to them about Darcie's behavior. She needs to be evaluated," I said.

"Yeah, I plan to do that. Oh, and I volunteered to take an extra shift this afternoon, keeping a watch out for Sybil Harding."

"Good. Don't tell Dawes, but I will unofficially be doing the same thing."

"Ah, geez. Well, if you come across a guy who's worth his weight in gold sitting somewhere in an older tan Chevy Cruze, don't be surprised."

I laughed. "Thanks for the warning. Take care." I hung up feeling relieved that our deputies would be watching for Sybil around the clock.

Smoke phoned while I was throwing a load of uniforms into the washer. "Are you ready for this? Roberta Harding died in a house fire she set herself. The State Fire Marshal determined it was intentionally lit. She used an accelerant. A helluva way to take your own life," he said.

I backed up to the wall then slid to the floor in a sitting position. "Dear Lord. Was it their family home?"

"Yes. She was home alone when it happened. I talked to the sheriff down there, and he provided a wealth of information. He knew the family, and I'll get to Roberta and the parents. But first off, he said Sybil was much younger than Roberta. He thought about six years."

"So she's twenty, not twenty-six."

"Yep. The sheriff said Roberta had struggled with depression, some drug use. The parents—both of them—were in denial about how serious it was. After they lost their daughter and their home, they left their old life behind, started a new one in New Mexico."

"What about Sybil?" I said.

"She went with them."

"I wonder when she came back to Minnesota. It's strange she didn't mention living in New Mexico, if she'd spent half her life there. She gave me the impression her parents had more recently moved."

"Sybil is not forthcoming with information. She tends to dole out bits and pieces when she's forced to," he said.

"No kidding. Have you had a chance to talk to Marcella about the Harding and Backstrom families, now that we know what caused their split?"

"I haven't. But with this latest shocker, I'd like her to focus specifically on Sybil. She's gotta have unresolved issues after what her sister did and how her parents ran away."

"If she's twenty now, she would've been twelve when her sister died. That's a bad age to go through something so awful."

"Yes it is. And we're on the lookout for Sybil. I understand the overnight cars and the day car—so far—haven't seen her leave the grandparents' house," he said.

"Who's out there now?"

"Zubinski."

"Good. So where have you got them positioned?" I said.

"About a football field's distance south of the house, on the other side of that cornfield there."

"Hmm. It seems both the good guys and the bad guys are using the corn to hide in lately."

"It's coming in mighty handy this year, that's for sure. See ya."

"Bye."

Thinking about Roberta, and how tortured she'd been, left me feeling like a wet rag. Our office dealt with people suffering from a variety of mental health issues, and it pained me when people fell through the cracks and didn't get the help they so desperately needed. I gradually managed to push myself up from the floor, but it took me another moment to muster the energy to leave the laundry room.

I wanted to learn more about Roberta, about Sybil, and their parents. I headed to my computer in the office den and signed on. After I had found Roberta's obituary the day before, I'd quit looking. But there were other articles.

CHRISTINE HUSOM 327

The newspaper piece about the Hardings' house fire was a few searches down the page. I opened the story and felt squeamish all over again. I understood more clearly why Roberta's obituary had been so terse. It was probably all the family could manage.

My next search was on Sybil. But the only things I found on her were as Roberta's survivor, and in her father's White Pages listing as a possible relative. How was it some people were able to fly under the radar without getting caught somewhere along the way? No references to being on a sports team or other organization in school. No social media sites. No employee of the month at wherever she worked. Nothing.

Smoke said he'd check on other fires in St. Peter in the morning, and that was fine with me. I had something else to attend to. With Queenie tucked away in her kennel, I loaded some supplies in my pack, then clipped the holster and weapon and phone case on the waist of my jogging pants, and set off on my journey.

I hiked over to the tree I'd spied from the evening before. If the Hardings' house was at twelve o'clock, the tree was at six o'clock, and the surveilling deputy would be sitting at nine o'clock. From my vantage point, I might see something he or she couldn't.

It still hadn't rained in Winnebago County despite the predictions. We had drought-like conditions, and the farmers were crying for as many inches as it'd take to save their crops. The path was a bit rough for walking in places, but I managed a good pace and was at the clump of trees in about twenty minutes. Something new had been nailed to the tree, in between two of the steps.

I crept over for a closer look. It was a heart cut out of tin with the words, BIRDIE AND BELLE LOVED SITTING IN THIS TREE. The letters had likely been formed by hammering in nails, then removing them to create the holes. We'd done a similar project in junior high art class. Flowers adorned the outer edges made by the same technique. Someone had attached the plaque after I'd left. Clearly, the climbing boards had been nailed to the tree sometime ago. But who'd put the plaque there now? Belle and Birdie? They *loved* sitting in the tree. Past tense.

Things like that stirred my curiosity pot and had me imagining all kinds of different scenarios. I pulled out my phone and snapped a picture of it. Someone had just been there to reminisce, and I didn't feel right sitting in their tree.

I turned, dropped to my hands and knees, and crawled back several feet into the cornfield. Then I stood and made my way south to a single, mammoth oak about twenty feet away. I sat down in two-foot tall weeds behind a large root that stuck out of the ground. From my vantage point, I had a decent view of the Hardings' house and half of their garage, and felt well-hidden. I scanned the area and spotted an old beater car across the road parked out of view from the house. Amanda Zubinski was somewhere in the cornfield, but I couldn't see her. *Nice job, Mandy.*

One long hour later, after not a single Sybil sighting, a tan Chevy drove up from the south, turned west into the field then pulled around behind the beater. Seconds later, Zubinski emerged from the crop cover, looked briefly at Weber as he climbed out of his car, then got into her own vehicle, and drove away. Weber disappeared before my very eyes. I sent him a text telling him I was there. He sent me a thumbs' up symbol in return.

Another two hours dragged by before I spotted Sybil and rose for a better view. I'd almost given up hope she'd ever emerge. She was holding a container in both hands and was splashing liquid from it onto the garage walls. A gasoline can.

Gasoline.

I tried to take off in a run, but the knee-high grassy weeds tangled around my feet making me stumble and fall. I got up, ripped the weeds from my shoes, and had to high step my way out of them until I reached the mowed right-of-way area. I tore across the road.

Sybil had disappeared behind the garage, scaring the bejeebers out of me.

Had Weber seen her? When he came sprinting across the hayfield, I was never more relieved to see anyone. He may have had further to run but he got to the garage first. I was there seconds later, in time to see Sybil crouched down by the side of the garage holding a fiery rag.

Weber and I both yelled at her to stop, but she was too wrapped up in her intent to hear us. Before we could reach her, Sybil set the rag at the base of the building. It ignited, sending flames in all directions. I screamed her name three more times before I got her attention. She turned to me and smiled, making my panic level soar.

As the flames spread and climbed to the top of the building, Sybil took off running with Weber and me in hot pursuit. She stopped at the service door on the other side of the garage, and was reaching for the knob when Weber rushed in and scooped her up, one arm around her waist, like she was a football. "Let me go, I want to be with Birdie!" she demanded.

Birdie? The dots were starting to connect.

"Other side of the house before she blows," Weber hollered above the roar of the fire.

Sybil was fighting like gangbusters so Weber tried to wrap his other arm around her, but she wiggled free. I caught up to her, threw my body on top of hers, and heard the wind rush from her lungs. As Sybil struggled to catch her breath, I rolled away. Weber lifted her from the ground, and threw her over his shoulder in a fireman's carry. All three of us were coughing from the black smoke billowing around us.

We ran to the front of the house. Weber lowered Sybil to the ground, but held her body against his with her hands pulled behind her back. "Grab my cuffs," he said. I plucked them out of his case and secured them on Sybil's small wrists. Weber turned her around, pulled his cuff key from his pocket, and locked them in place. Sybil's shoulders sank then she bent her head and closed her eyes.

Weber depressed the button on his radio. "Seven fourteen to Winnebago County responders. Use extreme caution. Garage is engaged, and there is a vehicle inside. Unknown if there are other accelerants." Sirens blared in the distance, telling me Weber had alerted Communications earlier.

"We need to get down low and close to the house," I said and guided Sybil into position. Weber dropped down too. Seconds later there was a loud whoooomp that sucked in the air around us, followed by a deafening explosion.

My body jerked involuntarily, and I'm sure my heart missed some beats. Objects slammed into the other side of the house, and splinters of burning wood blew past us on either side. Ashes rained down on us from above. It was like being in the middle of a searing hot tornado.

"Geez Louise!" Weber got on the radio. "Seven fourteen to Winnebago County."

"Go ahead, Seven fourteen."

"The garage exploded in the fire. Six oh eight and occupant of the home are with me, out of harm's way."

"Copy that. ETA on Fire is three minutes. Deputies sooner. Rescue also responding."

"Ten-four."

Sybil started trembling. "You shouldn't have stopped me." Her voice was small, weak.

I snaked my arm behind her shoulders. She didn't shake it off. "Why'd you do it, Belle? Because of Birdie, what she did?"

She turned to me with a tortured expression. Her face was contorted into a grimace, and her eyes were shiny with unshed tears. "They killed her, and no one was there to stop it."

Weber leaned in a little closer with a "Huh?" look on his face.

"Your uncle, your parents, who?" I said.

She nodded and looked down at her hands. Then her body got rigid as she lifted her head and turned to me. "And you."

Then she focused on Weber. "And you, and the other deputies, the police, doctors, our grandparents, but mostly Uncle Buzz, the evil one who started it. He even poisoned my cousin, Ross." *Poisoned?* "I wanted you to investigate, to find out what happened. Instead, you made fun of me, called me a scared little rabbit."

"*I* did? When was that?" Weber frowned and shook his head slightly like he was trying to remember.

"I called you for help because nobody else would do anything. You deputies were here, talking in the yard. I wanted to tell you everything, but after you said that, I didn't think you'd believe me." The 911 call. Sybil had been at her grandparents' farm that day.

"Ah, sorry. Where were you when you heard me say that?" Weber said

"In the house. I went up to the attic before you came in," she said.

The conversation ended when Detective Smoke Dawes drove up and screeched to a stop on Collins, thirty or so feet south of the house. As he came running full speed toward us, a fire truck pulled into the driveway. I'd seen that look on Smoke's face before. His mouth was set, his skin was pulled tight and had colored to a deep red tone. He was frightened to the max.

Weber and I stood, and I helped Sybil get to her feet. By the time Smoke reached us, he had a smattering of ashes and particles clinging to his clothes. We all did. He looked us over, noting Sybil's hands were cuffed. "Any injuries?" he said, keeping his head low.

I shook my head. "Sybil's going to need to get checked out at the hospital."

He studied her face a second. "Yes."

Chief Corey Evans and another firefighter were already out of their rig a safe distance from the garage, pulling the hose into position. In seconds, water was blasting at the ruins of the garage and the west side of the house. A rig from Emerald Lake arrived and assisted, further ensuring no flames penetrated the house or spread to the surrounding area. By the time the second Oak Lea rig got there most of the fire had been doused.

When it was safe, Smoke walked a few feet away from the house and pulled the sheriff's radio from his belt. "Three forty, Winnebago County."

"Go ahead." It was Robin's voice.

"I'm at the fire scene on Collins Avenue, and we need to set up barricades on the north side at County Thirty-five, and the south side at the crossroad, Twentieth Street. Only emergency responders get through."

"Ten-four. Seven eighteen and Seven twenty-three, do you copy?" Robin asked of Deputies Levasseur and Carlson.

"Seven eighteen copies," Levasseur said. "I'll take north. ETA less than a minute."

"Seven twenty-three's got the south. On my way."

The Hardings' yard had again become an active scene with swarms of emergency responders. Smoke told the ambulance folks there was no need to transport anyone. We'd be taking the arrestee to the hospital in a squad car.

Weber found a lawn chair for Sybil to sit on and the two of us stood nearby on the north side of the house. I watched as Smoke checked in with the fire crews and other deputies at the scene. When he started toward us, I met him halfway, and relayed what Sybil had said about us responding to her grandparents' house and hearing Weber call her a "scared little rabbit."

"You think that would have triggered her to sacrifice rabbits to prove a point?" he said.

"It's something to ask her about," I said.

He nodded. "That we will." Smoke led the way back to Sybil and Weber. "Sybil, I'm going to need to talk to your grandparents, and I can't locate your uncle in Canada under the name of Melvin Harding. Did he change his name?" Smoke said.

She shook her head. "He's not there."

"Then where are your grandparents?"

"They're with my uncle. Buried in the cellar," she said.

You could have pushed me over with a feather. Weber drew in an audible breath, and Smoke swayed slightly. It was a "when you think you've heard it all" moment—information that sent shockwaves to your very core.

Smoke cleared his throat and pointed at the house. "Your grandparents' cellar?"

"Uh huh." Sybil looked down at her hands.

Smoke blinked a few times. "Tell me how that came to be."

"My dad killed my uncle, before I was born. He punched him, and Buzz hit his head and died."

"Who told you that?" Smoke said.

"Birdie, my sister. She was there."

"Is that Roberta?"

"Yes," she said.

"Why didn't they call the police, tell them what happened?"

"My grandma didn't want my dad to go to prison over an accident. She didn't trust the police. She made the decision, and everyone went along with it. Birdie hated being in the same house as Buzz. When we were there, she'd go to the attic, as far away from him as she could get. So did I." It had been Sybil in the attic those times, after all.

"What about your grandparents, why are they there? In the cellar?" Smoke said.

"My grandma wanted to be buried by Buzz. I thought it was disgusting because he was a bad, bad man."

"I don't blame you. Go on."

"My grandpa died first, last summer. Grandma made me help her bury him," she said.

"Do you remember the date?" Smoke said.

"June eleventh."

"Thanks. Go on."

"Then when she died this spring, I buried her there too," Sybil said.

"When was that, what date?"

"April sixth. Birdie was here, and her spirit guided me."

"How so?" Smoke said.

"She's always with me. We're twin souls." *Twin souls?*

Smoke left it at that. The legal implications of what Sybil had cited and the formal interview questions would be put on hold until she was officially arrested, and charged.

Chief Deputy Kenner came walking toward us, his normal upbeat demeanor on the downbeat side as he zeroed in on Sybil. "You're Sybil Harding?" he said.

"Yes," she said then looked slightly up and to the left. *At her twin soul?*

"Mike?" Smoke started walking and signaled at Kenner to join him. They walked out of our earshot and conversed for a while. I noticed Kenner shaking his head, then nodding, then shaking his head some more. He pulled out his phone and made some calls. Smoke did the same before they returned to us.

"Sybil, we're going to do what we can to help you through all this, starting with taking you to see a doctor at the hospital," Kenner said.

She shrugged.

"I have a deputy and her partner on the way to take you there," he said.

Deputies Holman and Zubinski arrived a short time later. Amanda had been called back on duty and was in street clothes. Holman was her backup. Sybil didn't protest or put up a fight as they led her to the waiting squad car. I followed and helped tuck her into the back seat.

"We'll touch base later, Sybil. And Chief Deputy Kenner is right. We'll do what we can to help you," I said. She was staring straight ahead as I shut the door.

Kenner, Weber, and Smoke were in a huddle and Smoke stepped back to give me a place in their circle. "I had a lengthy phone conversation with Dr. Marcella Fischer today," Smoke said. "I filled her in on the tragedies in the Harding family, and our suspicions about Sybil's involvement in setting the fires. I wanted to get her take.

"Marcella warned me if Sybil was the firesetter, she was in a downward spiral and the sooner we intervened, the better. Marcella feared she would take her life like her sister had. I'd barely gotten off the phone when Weber's call came in. All this happened before I had a chance do anything with the info." He waved his arm in the direction of the garage.

"Dawes, you did good asking that we keep eyes on the place. It saved that girl's life, and she otherwise would have taken all those secrets to the grave with her." Kenner gave Smoke a slap on the back then turned to Weber and me, and shook our hands. "You're both getting a commendation for saving the day."

"Thank you, sir," I said.

"Yeah, thank you," Weber said.

"I got Captain Randolph writing a search warrant, and it shouldn't take long to get a judge to sign it this time of day. I also called the Bureau of Criminal Apprehension and requested help processing the scene. We've never had to recover bodies from someone's cellar before. What a deal," Kenner said.

I cringed thinking that four of us had been down in the cellar walking on Melvin's grave all those years ago.

"I haven't been able to reach Sybil's parents. Assuming that game-changing info we got from Sybil is correct, I asked Edberg to write an arrest warrant for Perry Harding. We'll get it to the sheriff in New Mexico so they can bring him in for the disappearance of Melvin Harding. If we recover his body, we'll add the manslaughter charges," Smoke said.

"Look at the domino effect—all the criminal and tragic things—caused because of one man's sickness, and the repulsive things he did to a little girl," I said.

"He's gotta be rotting in hell," Weber said.

We were silent for a time then Kenner said, "It's not the best time to tell you, but I guess it's as good a time as any. The sheriff dropped a bomb on me this morning. He handed me a letter to give to the county board announcing his retirement—

effective immediately—and asking that they appoint me as interim sheriff until the next election."

Expected, but still a surprise. We offered Kenner our congratulations.

"Before I forget, Corky, I got a box in my office that Denny left for your mother," Kenner said.

Was he too embarrassed to drop it off at her shop? I nodded. "I'll pick it up later."

The crime scene team arrived shortly before the fire departments took off. They were ready to photograph the scene and look for evidence. Then they'd process the garage. I'd seen Sybil drop a lighter and showed them where it was. It was the first piece of evidence collected. Everyone was solemn, no doubt thinking of the daunting task the investigators had before them in the cellar.

Weber and I hung around, and Smoke managed to not remind me I wasn't supposed to be working. Technically, I was just observing. Randolph drove out with the search warrant, and Kenner made the call to wait for the BCA agents before entering the house.

Smoke sidled over to me. "It's going to be a while, so you and Weber should go write your reports. I called Marcella back and told her she was right about Sybil. She's going to meet with Sybil at the hospital before they take her to jail."

"Sybil is the most complicated person I ever remember dealing with. Do you think she knew her cousin was in Woody Nevins' barn when she lit it on fire?" I said.

"You think we can get her to confess to the fires and the rabbits?" Smoke said.

"You can draw confessions out of the best of us." I winked then told him about the lookout spot I'd found in the tree across the street and the tin plaque nailed to it. "Discovering Sybil's nickname helped me get her to admit to some things as well."

"Some people call it luck when they stumble over clues like that. Others call it a gift from above," he said.

40

After I retrieved my backpack from the hideout by the massive oak, I rode with Weber to the sheriff's office. Amanda Zubinski called him as we were wrapping up our reports, asking if we'd like to meet her for a beer.

I hesitated with, "I don't know."

"Hey, Mandy heard that and says we need to unwind a while. Debrief," Weber said.

I lifted my eyebrows. "All right, you talked me into it, grimy though I be." I called John Carl and asked if he'd pick up Queenie and watch her until I got home.

When we'd filed the reports, Weber phoned Zubinski and we decided to meet at the Mill Stream Inn west of town, a couple of miles from my house. "If you don't mind giving me a ride," I said.

"Ah sure, no problem," he said.

Weber deposited the keys to the borrowed Chevy in the drop box then we hopped into his truck and headed to the restaurant. We stuck our badges and side arms in his glove box, and he laid his radio on the seat. As we got out we spotted Mandy, who was standing outside on the patio waving us over.

Then three things happened at once. I sensed something behind us, I heard the roar of an engine, and I saw Mandy throw her arms out to the sides, pointing her fingers in opposite directions shouting, "Out of the way!"

Weber leapt to the right, and I jumped to the left. Thanks partly to our training, and partly to our instincts. A silver blur rushed between the cars we were standing in front of and crashed into the brick wall of the building. Fortunately, none of the patrons on the patio were hit. Mandy raced down and was at the driver's side door before either Weber or I moved. I sat down on the bumper of the car behind me, dazed. I looked over at Weber. He was frozen in place.

Zubinski looked in the driver's window then opened the door. "Call nine-one-one. We need an ambulance," she yelled.

"Already did," someone called back.

I went over to Weber and hooked my hand on his arm. "Are you okay?"

"No. Are you?"

"No. But I will be and so will you." I led him over to the Honda.

Zubinski was bent over the driver, checking for a carotid pulse. She glanced our way. "That was close. I wonder if she had a medical issue. She wasn't wearing her seatbelt and hit her head on the windshield. She's unconscious."

Weber braved a look at the driver and quietly said, "She has a mental issue. It's Darcie. My sister-in-law."

The lights went on for Zubinski. "Damn," she said. I guess Weber had finally told her about Darcie.

Oak Lea Police Officer Casey Dey was first on the scene. Weber told him who Darcie was and about her attempted assault. "She's in your custody, Casey," he said.

Emergency medical services pulled in and attended to Darcie. She was slowly regaining consciousness, but was confused about time and place. They checked her vitals then put a support brace on her neck, carefully lifted her out of the car onto a stretcher, and then into the back of the ambulance.

Officer Dey phoned his chief requesting that an officer meet Darcie at the hospital. Then he took our statements and questioned the other witnesses for his report. Weber gave him Darcie's parents' names and contact information so they could get the official version of the incident from him. We were excused after the tow truck arrived to impound the Honda.

Weber, Zubinski, and I walked over to his truck. "I don't know what to say except 'sorry.' I almost got you killed," Weber said.

"No you didn't. You are not responsible for Darcie's actions," I said.

"Corky's right, and you know it. Victims shouldn't feel guilty," Zubinski said.

"Victims. Right." Weber shook his head like he couldn't believe that's what he was.

I gave Mandy a bear hug. "You saved our lives. Thank you."

"Thanks for knowing what to do when I yelled at you guys," she said.

Then Weber gave her a daddy bear hug. "I owe you everything. Anything you want—any time—you got it."

She began to tear up and nodded.

"Mandy, I wanted to ask you about Sybil. Is she still at the hospital?"

"No. The psychologist met with her for quite a while then Holman took her to the jail for booking. They're keeping her in Holding on a suicide watch."

"Man. Well, I'm going to be the party pooper and go home," I said.

"Yeah, so much for relaxing with friends, huh?" Weber said.

"We'll do it another time," Zubinski said then looked around the lot. "Where's your car, Corky?"

"At home."

"I'll run you there." She turned to Weber. "You want to come over to my place, hang out there instead?"

"Thanks. Ah, maybe I'll ride along to Corky's. I don't think I should be driving yet," Weber said.

Mandy slid her arm around his waist. "Sure thing."

I took the back seat, and as we drove away Weber said, "It's like she came out of nowhere. She had to have followed us. I can't believe I didn't see her back there."

"You know what? It was a super intense afternoon. The worst. We made it through a critical incident, and by the time we turned in our reports we were exhausted—more than ready to forget about work for a while. You were thinking about Sybil, not Darcie," I said.

"And I never thought she'd pull something like that, trying to mow us down," he said.

"The big legal question is, did she plan it? Or was it a spur of the moment deal? She saw us and flipped out," I said.

"Yeah," he said.

Zubinski stopped in front of my garage, then she and Weber got out with me. Weber wrapped his arms around me and pulled me into a warm hug. "We'll talk. Group therapy, maybe," he said.

"Sounds good." When we eased apart and he'd turned around, I whispered to Mandy, "Take care of him." She nodded then they got back in the car and left.

My house was quiet with Queenie gone, and I wandered around a bit still too shocked by what Darcie had done to believe it. I got into the shower and let the water beat down on me for a long time while I shampooed and soaped up. When I finally felt clean I got out, dressed, and then called John Carl.

"Would you mind bringing Queenie home, and maybe staying with me a while?"

It took him a few seconds to answer. "Ah, sure. Sara's here too. What's going on?"

"Bring Sara along, and I'll tell you."

I couldn't grasp all that had gone down since Weber and I first spotted Sybil pouring gas on her grandparents' garage. The day's events felt surreal, and my brain wasn't ready to deal with them by myself.

I needed to be with people I loved and people who loved me. When John Carl and Sara arrived with Queenie a short time later, I gave them all hugs then we sat in the living room, and I took them through it all, providing more details when they asked. Verbalizing what we'd gone through helped me begin the healing process.

John Carl and Sara both seemed more distressed about Darcie, and more jolted about Sybil, than I was. And they offered words of comfort and support with their hugs, making me believe the sun really would come up tomorrow.

"You have a lot of Grandma Aleckson in you," John Carl said.

I nodded. "Good thing, right?"

"Corky, I can't believe what Sybil's been through and how badly it messed her up. Bodies buried in the cellar?" Sara winced.

"I know. The BCA is helping our guys process the scene at their house. I was thinking of heading over there, see if they've uncovered anything yet," I said.

"Is that a good idea?" Sara said.

I shrugged. "That was my plan before the Darcie incident sidelined me. I'm not part of the crime scene team, but I've been in the thick of things since the fires started."

The sun was setting as the investigators carried the last of the remains from the house and loaded them into the Midwest Medical Examiner's van. I leaned against the hood of my car with Sergeant Roth, watching, but keeping our comments to a minimum. Smoke came out of the house and spoke with the death investigator assigned to the case before the investigator drove away with the remains.

Roth looked at his watch. "Well, I better get back to work," he said then left.

Smoke walked over but stopped before he got too close. "You couldn't stay away?"

"Nope. How's it going?" I said.

"We'll be at it into the night, making sure we've done it right. The graves were just a few feet underground, and they were buried in a row. The surface was smooth and had likely been raked and tamped down. The bodies must've stunk to high heaven for some time while they were decomposing. Mrs. Harding still has a ways to go yet." He scrunched up his face.

"Eew."

"And we found out where Sybil kept her rabbit supply—small freezer in the cellar," he said.

"Poor little guys. It's scary how Weber's comment got that kind of reaction from her."

"Another nail in the coffin, I guess. We also discovered bolt cutters and a cut lock in the freezer. We're presuming it was from the Simmonds', but we'll need to verify. And bank statements showing Social Security checks were still being issued for both Mr. and Mrs. Harding to the present time. So we can surmise who was using the money," he said.

"You never know what people have stored in their freezers, do you? But that combination, wow."

"You got that right."

"Mandy told me a psychologist—I'm guessing Marcella—met with Sybil before she was taken to jail."

"Good to hear." He pulled off the protective gloves he was wearing, put them in a pocket of his coveralls then got out a clean pair. "Well, a dark and smelly cellar is calling me back. See ya."

"See ya," I said and watched him walk away. I selfishly wished he had already wrapped things up so I could tell him what happened with Darcie, and how torn up I was inside.

Darcie was under guard at the hospital. Sybil was under guard at the jail. But I felt vulnerable nonetheless. I sent Weber a text, checking to see how he was holding up. He sent me one back saying he was staying at Mandy's. Vince had Mandy, I had Queenie.

When I got home, I didn't feel like going upstairs to my bed. I felt safer sleeping on the main level in my office den. I'd be able to respond faster if something happened, whatever that might be. I got out the afghan Gram had made for me years before and snuggled under it on the couch, imagining the times she had tucked me in bed when I was young. I fell into a deep, deep sleep and woke up in the morning feeling a little more optimistic.

I heard my garage door opening and jumped up. Queenie ran on ahead, and when she let out her happy whimper I knew it was one of a handful of people. It turned out to be my mother, carrying a basket. She set it on the counter when she saw me. "I had to make sure you were all right." Tears were streaming down her cheeks, and when she drew me into her arms, we stood there for a long time and wept.

"I brought you breakfast," she said as she stepped back. She took my hand, led me to the island counter, and helped me onto a stool. Then she pulled out containers of French toast, blueberry syrup, scrambled eggs, bacon, and quartered oranges.

"It's a feast, thank you, enough for six people."

Queenie barked, so I got up to let her out. "Sit. Eat. I'll do it," Mother said and opened the door for her.

I dished up a big plateful, and it hardly made a dent in what she'd brought. Mother brewed a pot of coffee then sat down with me. "Every day I put you and your safety in God's hands. That's what I can do. And to be here if you need me," she said.

"Thank you." And that was the end of the discussion. She didn't want more details of the near miss, our narrow escape. John Carl's version was enough for now.

I was sipping a cup of coffee when I got a text from Smoke. "You up?' I wrote back I was. He responded with, "Chief Deputy and I on our way to your house." I showed Mother the message. "You should get some clothes on," she said.

I went upstairs, freshened up, dressed in shorts and a t-shirt, and was back in the kitchen in short order. I met Kenner and Smoke at the door, and after they hugged me, we went to the dining room where Mother served coffee. Kenner gushed over me, saying how relieved he was Weber and I hadn't been injured. We were two of his finest. Smoke's intense stare didn't ease up much the whole time.

Then Kenner shared the news. "Perry Harding was arrested early this morning and is sitting in a New Mexico jail. Like father, like daughter. He'll make his court appearance today and already said he won't fight extradition. I'll be sending Deputy Edberg down to bring him back."

"It worked out just as well that he never called me back. He might've fled if I'd started asking pointed questions," Smoke said.

"Probably right. Well, I better get back to the office. Oh Kristen, I brought this for Corky to give you, but since you're here . . ." Kenner stood and pulled a small box from his pants pocket, then an envelope from his shirt pocket, and handed them to my mother.

She raised her eyebrows in surprise as she accepted them. Mother stared at the box for a while then lifted the top. She gasped and held it up. The ring Denny had asked her to return. Smoke and I exchanged a quick "what next?" glance. Kenner shrugged then made his way out the door.

Mother opened the envelope. Her hands were shaking as she pulled out the letter. She read it out loud. "Dear Kristen, You brought me back to life. Thank you. I've decided to retire, and it'll be easier to do that if I move back to Iowa. I was wrong to ask you to give the ring back. It's yours. Forever, Denny." She slid it onto her right-hand ring finger. "Isn't it stunning?" she said.

Even Smoke's eyes were misty after that. And as far as I was concerned, my mother would never need to know who'd had it before she did.

Mother looked at her watch. "Almost time to open the shop. If you're okay, dear?"

I nodded. "Thanks for being here, and for breakfast."

She picked up the letter and the box then gave me a kiss. "I love you."

"I love you, too."

"Put the leftover food in your fridge, for later," she called on her way out the door.

Smoke followed me into the kitchen then stepped in front of me, swooped me up, and kissed me until I was gasping for breath. Before I had a chance to join him he lowered me to the floor. I backed up to the counter to support my shaky legs.

"Hold that thought until tonight," he said.

Are you kidding? I'd hold that thought for the rest of my life.

I drove over to Collins Avenue, drawn again to the Hardings' place. There were barricades across the driveway and crime tape around the house. I sat in my car, staring and contemplating how Melvin "Buzz" Harding's despicable crimes had led others in his family to commit many more. His brother and niece were in jail, facing prison time. His cousin's son had died in a fire. His victim had taken her own life, and her sister had come close to doing the same.

I got out and hiked over to the tree I'd found two days earlier, still adorned with the plaque. I stared at the words, BIRDIE AND BELLE LOVED SITTING IN THIS TREE. It seemed it was Belle's sad way of saying goodbye. I snapped another photo of it to show to the powers-that-be. It'd be up to them to decide what to do with it.

41

Smoke invited me to sit in on Sybil Harding's interview. I was waiting outside the room when he appeared with her. My stomach got a tickle in it thinking of his delicious kiss that morning. I switched my focus to Sybil and her ordeals. She looked at me in a way that was difficult to describe. Defiant, certainly, yet resigned that she had been caught. A measure of anger. And surprisingly, I sensed she respected me, and what I had done to stop her.

We settled at the table in the room, Sybil on one side, Smoke and me across from her on the other. Smoke told Sybil he'd be taping the interview then read her the Miranda Warning, advising her of her rights, and asked if she understood. She said she did. He asked if she was ready to talk and she was.

Smoke asked her for her story, and it was a long one, starting when Sybil was ten and Roberta was sixteen. That's when Roberta first told her how her Uncle Melvin—Buzz—and her cousin Ross had molested her. The abuse went on for some time until the horrific day when Melvin raped her—that fateful last day when Melvin died at the hands of her father, and was buried in the cellar to cover it up. And the three families parted ways. Sybil had finally understood why Roberta hated to go to her grandparents' farm for weekend visits. They'd escape to a tree away from the farmstead to sit and talk.

"My sister said I was the one who kept her alive. I tried to help her, and I thought she'd get better, but she didn't." Sybil covered her face with her hands and sobbed.

I pulled some tissues from the box on the table and handed them to her.

"Go on when you're ready," Smoke said.

"After Birdie died, her spirit stayed with me. She'd lost her body, her voice. She couldn't take care of things herself, so I had to. Our parents took us away to New Mexico, and we came back here when I was eighteen. Birdie hated being at the farm and spent a lot of time in the tree when we were there." Sybil relayed it like she was reading a textbook.

"Sybil, did you live at the farm?"

"Mostly. I know people in Minneapolis and stayed there too," she said.

"Why is there a Golden Valley address on your license?"

"Birdie thought it sounded like a peaceful place to live." *Golden Valley.*

"Why did you use Birdie's date of birth to get your license?"

"She thought it'd be easier for me. I'd be old enough to have power of attorney. We were like twins, so it worked out to put my name on her birth certificate," she said.

Smoke didn't ask for details of how she got the license. Instead he said, "Tell me about the barn fires."

"After our grandma died, I needed to get rid of the three barns Birdie said were bad places. Buzz had hurt her in two of them. Ross had hurt her in one of them."

"You knowingly set the barns on fire?" he said.

"Uh huh."

"Is that yes?"

"Yes," she said.

"You mentioned your cousin. Is that Ross Warren?" Smoke said.

"Yes."

"Did Birdie ever tell your parents about Ross?"

She shook her head. "She was afraid he'd kill her."

"Did you know Ross was in the barn when you set it on fire?" Smoke said.

She shrugged. "I knew he slept in Mr. Nevins' barn sometimes. I've seen him a few times the last two summers."

"Did you ever speak to Ross?"

"No. We've never met, but Birdie pointed out who he was in a family photo, and I never forgot what he looked like," Sybil said.

"Why didn't you tell Mr. Nevins that Ross was sleeping in his barn?"

"I thought he knew. And I've never talked to Mr. Nevins."

"Tell me what happened when you started Mr. Nevins' barn on fire. Did you know Ross Warren was in there?" Smoke asked again.

This time Sybil nodded. "I saw him asleep in there. I didn't want to go near him, wake him up, but I thought he'd smell the smoke and get out. Only he didn't." Sybil looked up at Smoke. "He deserved to die for what he did to Birdie. Like Buzz died."

Smoke asked Sybil about the rabbits, and she repeated what she'd told Weber and me when the garage was burning. She was sending us messages, trying to solicit our help. It made sense to her.

"Sybil, where did you get the rabbits, and how did they die?" Smoke said.

"There was a pair that lived in the barn. When their babies got bigger, I caught them and put them in a box by the exhaust pipe of the car and started the engine. They died peacefully. And the pair kept having more anyway."

"All right. Well I think that's all we need for today. How about you, do you need anything?" Smoke asked her.

Sybil shrugged then shook her head.

"Detective, I have a question, if I may?" I said.

"Go ahead, Sergeant."

"Sybil, last summer I responded to a call at your grandparents' house. It was about a sick-looking dog. I didn't find the dog, but there was an awful stench by the house. Do you know anything about that?"

She nodded. "It was my grandpa. I hated burying him in the cellar. I thought deputies would check out where that awful smell was coming from."

"If I'd had any idea, I would have. But why didn't you report what happened, ask for our help?" I said.

"My grandma would have found out and then what?"

Then what?

I waited in Smoke's cubicle for him to get back from the jail. "Well Sybil certainly turned out to be more forthcoming than I expected," he said.

"No kidding."

"Now that we've got her fingerprints, we'll see if they match the one on the lighter. There's a lot more I want to ask her about, but we got plenty for the complaint. We'll get her statement typed up and signed."

I shook my head. "Sybil seems to know right from wrong, but she messed up on the two wrongs don't make a right part."

"Yep. I'm interested in her diagnosis. The trauma of Roberta's death must've caused her to have a psychotic break. She talks like her sister is right there with her, that she can see her, hear her. My understanding is visual hallucinations are very rare."

"Sybil lives in a different reality. I mean, to call nine-one-one and report a loose dog, hoping the deputy would catch wind of the stench, and investigate it. And then figure out her grandfather was buried in the cellar? It's not rational. Like when she was twelve and wanted us to investigate, what? That her sister had been abused and killed herself, that her father had killed her uncle? Another cry for help, but she couldn't bring herself to come right out and ask us. It breaks my heart."

"Mine too."

I showed him the photo of the plaque Sybil had nailed to "their" tree, and he shook his head. "I'll check with Kenner about that. Maybe Sybil's mother should have it."

"Maybe she should."

"Oh, and I talked to Marcella. She's going to spend some time with Sybil, but she'll be shutting down her practice soon, joining a group in Minneapolis. That's what she'd planned to tell me the other night."

"Really, why?"

"It seems she's met someone who counsels there. They've been dating and are talking marriage," he said.

"That's a surprise. I never did apologize for my behavior."

"I don't think she expected you to. Marcella and I were never romantically involved, but we've been good friends and she wanted to tell me in person, and have one last supper together."

"She is a good person and a great psychologist. We'll miss her," I said.

"That we will. So it's okay if I bring you dinner tonight? Or would you rather grill at my house?"

"Either one sounds good." My phone buzzed, and when I saw it was Weber, I nodded at Smoke before I answered it. "Hey Vince. How are you doing?"

"I'm doin'. Say, I heard from the crime lab about the DNA test. And guess what? It was Darcie's blood on my windshield. And I'm guessin' on yours too, but they haven't run that one yet."

I almost dropped the phone. Weber had been half right—Darcie had left the blood, but not the rabbits. "I'm stunned. I'm with Detective Dawes and will let him know."

"Sure, and thank him again for checking in with me earlier, seeing if I was okay."

It was the first I'd heard of it. "Will do."

"And I got a miracle call from my in-laws. First my mother-in-law talked to me, apologizing for Darcie, what she did. And then my father-in-law got on the phone and did the same. Then they invited themselves over to my place for a visit later on. They said they shoulda treated me better over the years, that they knew how happy Stacie was with me," Weber said.

"That's great, Vince. They're finally doing the right thing."

"Yeah, it only took a near-death experience, but whatever."

We hung up and I relayed Weber's news and thanks to Smoke.

"You just never know. Getting back to tonight, should we plan for six thirty, and I'll figure out where before then?" he said.

I stopped by my grandparents' house when I saw John Carl's vehicle in the driveway. "I used to think Mom was exaggerating about the things you get into, but now that I'm here I understand why she worries."

"I'm glad you're here to help calm her. Most of the time my job is pretty routine, but once in a while big stuff happens."

"If you say so. I didn't get to tell you this last night, but grandma called and we talked about what you said about including Taylor in dividing up the things they want to give us. She liked it. Said it was a thoughtful thing to do."

"Good. John Carl, did you tell Grandma about Darcie trying to hit Weber and me?"

"No, we talked before that happened. And I know how you are, that you'd want to be the one to tell them," he said.

"I do, and I'll take care of it tomorrow, give myself another day to let it sink in. Oh, and Mother got a surprise this morning."

"The ring, Denny moving? She told me."

"I'm pretty sure David Fryor has been waiting in the wings for her," I said.

"No, he's been closer than that," he said and smiled.

I got ready for the evening with butterflies flittering around in my belly, anticipating my first real date with Smoke. He'd ordered a meal from a local caterer and pulled into the driveway promptly at 6:30. I went out to help him carry in the food. There were two boxes and two bottles of wine. *Two bottles of wine?*

"Gosh, I never thought of ordering dinner from a caterer before," I said and grabbed the smaller box.

"Except Kristen, you mean." He picked up the other box, laid the bottles on top of it, and followed me inside.

"Except."

"Where's Queenie?"

"Staying overnight at Gramps'. They both love it. So what have we got here?" I said as we set the boxes on the counter.

"First things first." Smoke swung me around and pulled me in for a kiss that held promise and drove sensations of longing to my core.

Then he rested his lips on my forehead and massaged my shoulders and the back of my neck.

My voice was hoarse, barely a whisper. "What changed?"

He took a step back, moved his hands to my arms, and studied me. "Nothing. And everything. I've wanted you—all of you—for a long time. But you know the reasons I didn't let myself go there. I worried it wasn't the best thing for you. And then this morning when I found out I'd almost lost you, I knew we couldn't keep going through life in this limbo. I've loved you a long, long time, and I've been in love with you almost as long."

Tears blinded me for a second before they rolled down my cheeks. "I feel like I've loved you my whole life. And I've wanted to make love with you for forever."

Smoke used his thumbs to wipe my tears then took my hand. "Corinne, will you marry me, be my wife?"

"Of course I will, to have and to hold."

We kissed again and again and when we needed more, he turned and put his arm around my waist. "I think dinner can wait," he said, and we climbed the stairs to my bedroom.

Smoke had more patience than I did as he unzipped the back of my sundress, slid it off my shoulders, and let it fall to the ground. I stepped out of it then stripped off my underwear. I reached over to help him with his clothes, but he pulled his polo shirt over his head, unbuttoned his shorts, and was out of them before I could.

We stood facing each other, appreciating our nakedness, and one another's bodies. "My God, you're perfect," he said. Before I responded, he wrapped his arms around me and kissed me with such intensity that every nerve in my body jumped for joy. He backed me up to the bed, tore back the covers, got in, and pulled me on top of him. It turned into a free for all after that. Smoke's lips on me, my lips on him, him nibbling, me nibbling, me on top, him on top. And when neither of us could wait another second, he took me on the most exquisite ride of my life. Then his body collapsed against mine for a moment before he rolled onto his side, still clinging to me.

I turned and kissed his lips, and when I saw tears roll down his cheeks, I kissed them too. "We have a lot to make up for," he said.

We couldn't get enough of each other for the rest of the night. In the shower, for dessert after dinner, in the middle of the night, hungry for the other's touch.

The sound of rain hitting the roof and pelting the windows woke us early the next morning. A welcomed relief from the drought.

We turned to each other, smiled, and embraced. "Now that's worth celebrating," he said.

Smoke was right. We had a lot to make up for.

Made in the USA
Columbia, SC
15 November 2017